The Hunger Inside

S0rceress0

ISBN-13: 978-0-692-54672-7

DEDICATION

For my patient husband Che. He cheers me on as I create characters that talk back.

and

Craft Beer! Your fond friendship has taught me and inspired me.

Ninkasi
Anderson Valley
Calapooia
Flat Tail
Mazama
Boulevard
Samuel Adams
Widmer
Gilgamesh
Lost Coast
2 Towns Cider
Nectar Creek
New Belgium
Deschutes
Sierra Nevada
Oskar Blues
Rogue Ales
.

CONTENTS

ACKNOWLEDGMENTS

Those who helped make this book happen:

Brian Rush (https://brianrushwriter.wordpress.com) - development editing, copy editing

Nancy J. Teppler - editing and teaching me to really look at humanity

Trish Jackson (http://www.youselfpublish.com/) - formatting

Beer:30 Corvallis, Oregon (http://beer30corvallis.com/) - my favorite place to write!

Bonnie Brozozowski from the Corvallis-Benton County Library (bonnie.brzozowski@corvallisoregon.gov) - for inspiring all NaNoWriMo novel authors.

Ubuntu Linux - for providing a free, secure operating system for my System76 Touchscreen laptop.

. . . and all those who do not have a voice.

.

1
Leaving

The page was written in a clean hand, indicating control, but the words on the paper described anything but control.

"My life is not as I wish it were. In some ways it's boring. You know how you spend two hours in line at a utility company just to have thirty seconds at the counter? Yeah. That's what my job is like. The difference is, after waiting for days upon days, there is more than likely violence involved in my job. Blood, terror. I can't do this anymore. Not like this.

Why can't it be like Rambo? Or Triple X? Well...I know the answer to that. Life isn't an action movie, and I have emotions. If I didn't, I'd be a psychopath. But why does my boss make me do this? At first it was targets, and...that was ok. And they tried to keep me thinking that it was all just...targets. But my targets are not cardboard. And I don't dare "tell." Bad reviews would follow. A bad review for being a human being, that's a laugh. But I'm expected to do a job, and I can't do that job anymore.

My hands are shaking when I pick up a weapon now. I feel like I breathe a little too loud when I walk quietly. I tried to shoot a target yesterday, and I mean a paper target, but the paper turned into a head. The eyes begged me not to do it, and I had to put my weapon down. I pleaded illness and fled the exercise.

I make a good show though. I can do the obstacle course with

1

complete confidence, especially if I know no one is actually going to get hurt. My hand-to-hand is still spot on. But when they ask me to get on board the ship in two months to go out, I will be faced with a terrible choice. Get on the ship or refuse. Being brought up on misconduct charges for refusal of duty is not appealing to me. I still want to do the job, but I can't.

I can't do it anymore. I can't kill. I'm no longer the person for the job.

Does that make me a bad person?"

The psychiatrist put down the sheet of paper and looked at Sam. Sam fiddled with the cap in her hand. Her uniform was immaculately pressed, her badges perfectly in place. Not an undone button or a misplaced crease on her. Her hat, however, bore the brunt of her discomfort. The soft cloth was now wrenched, and a few stitches were loose.

"Sam?"

Sam looked up at the psychiatrist briefly before looking down again. The psychiatrist tried again.

"Sam. Look at me."

Sam reluctantly lifted her eyes to the doctor's face. She could feel her spine trying to curve as she ducked her head as much as she could in emotional defense while still keeping her eyes forward. The pressure gave her a small headache. Her body wanted to retreat back against the wall. Sweat broke out under Sam's armpits. Her hands were damp and cold.

"Sam, I want you to tell me what makes a bad person. Not a bad employee—a bad person."

Sam swallowed and spoke very softly. To her own ears she sounded like a kindergartner.

"A bad person doesn't care about others. They disrupt others' lives without thinking about the consequences. They assume they are superior to anyone else. They take advantage of other people."

"Okay. What makes a bad employee?"

Sam had to stop and think. Her voice was a little stronger with this answer.

"A bad employee is one who doesn't try to improve themselves. They make life difficult for the group. They consciously decide to be lazy and not get the job done. They are disrespectful."

"And by your definition are you either a bad person or a bad employee?"

Sam shook her head. The psychiatrist waited for a verbal answer.

"No. I am not."

"Well that is settled. You asked if you were a bad person, and the answer is no. But there must be something to your concerns, or you wouldn't be here, would you?"

Sam didn't say anything. She felt as if the air was getting thicker. The psychiatrist considered.

"So let me ask another question. What makes a good leader?"

"A good leader takes care of the group. They organize and consider each member of the group carefully. They put the good of the group above the needs of any particular member. If a group doesn't work well, the leader finds a new way for the group to work."

"What happens when a member of the group can't do their job anymore? Let's say that one of them, through no fault of their own, caught a serious illness?"

"I would have to put them on medical leave and reorganize the group," Sam said.

"What if it was the leader that caught the illness?"

"I don't know."

"That's a cop-out answer."

Sam sighed uncomfortably.

"Well, the leader of the group would need to resign and allow someone else to step into her place. It might be an outsider or someone promoted from within the group, but a group can't be without a leader."

"Sam. Thinking about what you have told me, are you a good leader?"

Sam shifted in her seat trying to point her body any way but at the psychiatrist, which was hard, because it was a small room. The door seemed so far away, and the fact that it was closed was unnerving. The urge to flee was strong.

The minutes began to stack up, and Sam's eyes slid away to stare at a trash can next to the door. The wall was such a bright blue. How could she have not noticed how bright it was?

"Sam. I can't answer this question for you. You must answer it yourself."

Sam swallowed hard and felt the tingle in her nose that signalled real discomfort. She remembered that when she was a little girl it happened just before she started crying. She didn't want to cry now. It was undignified.

"No."

"No what?"

"No. I am not...at...this time a good leader."

The psychiatrist nodded.

"I can understand that, Sam. The military understands that too. Out there, you are Chief Larou Olabode. But inside, you are Sam, and Sam has a problem with the job that Chief Olabode has to do. Now we need to determine the extent of your problem and how to deal with it."

Over the next few weeks Sam went through an intense series of questionings. Some verbal, some on paper. She found herself having to admit to things that were so humiliating she found herself sitting in her car very far from the base, tucked inside her sleeping bag, crying herself to sleep in the back seat. She felt completely isolated and alone. She also felt that there was not a single person who could possibly understand her at those particular moments.

But as bad as this was, it was nothing compared to having to formally request medical dismissal from her contract. She had to present her request in person to the Colonel. This time, she wore a new hat and did not wring it between her fingers. She removed it from her head upon entering the office, smoothed it carefully into its requisite creases, and held it in her hand.

The Colonel read the request carefully. Sam had typed the personal letter on the stiff letterhead that was required of formal communications. He set the page down and looked at Sam steadily.

"Are you sure this is what you want, Chief? You don't want to try to take some time away? You have plenty of vacation saved up."

Sam had practiced this response for hours. Her voice felt steady and strong, but somehow she could tell that the Colonel could look right through her, and it was more than a little unnerving.

"Yes, Sir. This is what I want. I am certain after consulting with the doctors that I am no longer able to perform my duties—even in another capacity. Taking vacation will not solve the problem; it will only delay it. I need to move on, Sir."

"Then reluctantly I must approve the request. This interview is over."

Sam turned to go, but the Colonel stood up.

"Sam, wait."

Sam turned just as her fingertips brushed the doorknob.

"Yes, Sir?"

"Sit down. The formal interview is over, but I want to talk."

Sam looked at the chair uncertainly. Chairs did not bring comfort to her anymore. She sat, trying to shove the uncertainty away.

"I know you want...no...need...to leave, but the question is how you are going to leave. For your own sake as well as the continuity of your group, we need to make it a positive experience."

Sam stared at the Colonel in surprise.

"Yes. I know. It's not what you expected. I am not the usual superior officer. I take my job quite seriously, which means keeping all my special units functioning correctly. It means I know every single person in it. That includes you. I know your pride and your intelligence...your ability to correctly analyze a situation...and your unwillingness to be vulnerable. Your team latches onto you and trusts you. They do everything exactly as you say when you say to do it. I don't want to hurt them, and I don't want to hurt you."

"I'm not sure what to say, Colonel. I'm grateful."

"Be more than grateful, Sam. Let me provide a stage for your leaving."

Sam nodded.

"Good. Then how about this...."

Sam knew the plan by the end of an hour. She offered a few suggestions of her own. Her stomach responded by unclenching. She felt relief from the pain. Now there was a plan; she wasn't just going to run off with her tail between her legs. This would be a dignified exit.

Sam took a deep breath and stretched. Left. Right. Down. Down. Down. Crack the knuckles. Stretch the fingers. Shoulders around and around.

The ship's mechanical repair bay stretched out in front of her. It had been emptied of vehicles. Even the hazmat trailer had been painstakingly moved back to make room for the obstacles that now faced her.

"Weapon check!"

Sam heard the click of the airsoft cartridge being attached to the paint gun, and the slim weapon was slid into her hand.

"Weapon is ready, Chief."

Across the room, new transfers scattered among the ship's crew watched Sam eagerly.

"How many times has she done this?"

"Couldn't count it anymore."

"Ok, how many times successfully?"

"She's never failed."

Colonel Shaw grinned broadly at the discussion before stepping forward just slightly. The discussion stopped immediately.

"Chief Larou Olabode, are you prepared for your exit examination?"

"Yes, Sir!"

The Colonel raised his arm and everyone put on goggles. At the drop of the arm, Sam moved forward into the maze of inflated barriers. Tiny lights broken by her movements triggered spring-activated panels depicting figures and shapes. Sam dropped down but didn't fire. Staying in a crouch, Sam made three hand signals and continued on.

"I would have failed that."

"Really? You would have shot a kid?"

"I wasn't looking at the kid; I was looking at the box."

"You would have shot a box..."

"Who knows what's hiding behind it."

"What happens if you shoot the box and it explodes?"

Several pops in a row drew the transfers' attention. Sam had shot one figure in the leg and another in the arm and then tackled both. A bustle dropped from the ceiling, forcing Sam to lunge out of the way. The bustle bag exploded on the floor scattering paper pieces everywhere.

One of the spotters raised an arm, and Sam placed the paint gun on the ground and stood up, hands out to the sides. The spotter made his way over the inflatable barriers, through the paper maze, and looked at a piece of paper sticking to Sam's hip where her armored vest didn't cover her clothing.

"Winged! Minor injury."

The spotter made his way back, and Sam continued. She was forced to make several more decisions before nearing the end of the course. She was breathing hard by the time she reached the end. Her movements were smooth and quick where she was sure of herself.

The last explosion startled her into falling back. At the exit a large, bulky marine leaped from inside a paper barrel with a rubber training knife. He rushed forward slashing heavily and screaming overdramatically.

One of the transfers sucked in a breath as Sam raised the paint gun and pulled the trigger, and nothing happened. She flung the weapon into the marine's face and launched herself at his legs as he batted at the weapon. The marine didn't even budge when she hit his legs, but as he looked down and raised his arm to stab her, she tucked her feet under her and launched upward, her hands fisted together. The marine grunted at the impact, and the knife barely grazed Sam's armored jacket as it fell out of his hand, then bounced on the ground. He put his hand on his head and never noticed Sam roll past him through the exit.

The hefty marine blinked and tried to clear the stars from his eyes as Sam let her head drop to the ground to catch her breath. A whistle declared the end of the exercise, and everyone took their goggles off.

The spotters brought their clipboards to the Colonel. He spent a few moments tallying.

"Chief Olabode's final score is a ninety-seven out of one hundred, giving her the top score for any personnel attempting this exercise! Final time: seven minutes, forty-two seconds!"

The crowd burst into applause. Sam got up off the ground and removed her helmet and gloves to receive the Colonel's heartfelt handshake. She signed her name and rank for the last time.

"I relieve you, Chief."

"I stand relieved, Colonel."

Everyone chuckled at the blatant slaughter of protocol.

A week later Sam leaned back in her chair in her functional apartment. Her face registered dismay.

"Forty-two emails? Really? Forty-two."

With a heavy sigh she began to open them. Every single email was in response to her job applications. Seventeen outright dismissals of her qualifications, fifteen confusing requests for information that she had already included in her resume, and ten invitations for an interview.

She stretched and grabbed her backpack.

The separation counseling was brief. The person she spoke to offered absolutely no help in trying to figure out what the confusing emails meant.

Her medical exam was not so brief. They had insisted on x-rays of her lungs after her usual trouble with the TB prick. Then they wanted another set after the first. Each doctor insisted on going over every last place she had been. A few were angry that she wouldn't talk about certain places, but she reminded them that she wasn't allowed to talk about those places unless her direct superior with the appropriate clearance ordered her to talk about them. Nothing would do but the head physician go get the appropriate permissions.

The waiting was interminable. She was stuck in a small conference room by herself. She was surprised when another member of her team walked in and sat down.

"Henry? What are you doing here?"

Henry shrugged, "Same thing you are. Leaving."

"I'm sorry, I didn't know."

"Ah, it's okay. Separation is chaos. Compound that with the fact that we just got back from the desert, well, naturally we'd lose touch with what everyone else is doing."

They sat in silence for a while.

"So, classification trouble huh?"

Sam snorted, "Yeah. You too?"

Henry nodded, "They want to know things I'm not allowed to talk about. It's weird, isn't it? It's the last time we'll ever have to do this whole medical thing, but all I can remember is the first time I did it."

Sam nodded. More time passed. Sam could never remember

silence being this uncomfortable.

"So Chief, how did you start out on this whole adventure?"

Sam was more than happy for the distraction.

"You know, I was seventeen when my parents died in a car crash. I finished high school, but I really had no plan. I had a couple of temporary jobs, but I was just lost without my parents. Well, out of sheer boredom one day I took one of the ASVAB tests. Remember the one that recruiters give you for career testing?"

"Yeah, I think almost all of us did that one."

"To say I scored well is an understatement. I had a recruiter on my tail five minutes after they scored that puppy. I couldn't think of anything better, so I signed up under the agreement that my professional training could be transferred as complete college credits."

"Wait, you have a degree?"

"Of course. Why do you think I became your superior?"

"But why aren't you an officer?"

Sam leaned back in her chair, "Because I wanted to work for a living."

"Ha! That's a good one, Chief."

"Next thing I knew I was picked up out of technical training and offered the opportunity to go special units. You could have knocked me over with a leaf when I found I was in a group with army *and* marine personnel. I didn't think we cooperated to that extent. First thing the Colonel did was yell at us."

Sam stood up and did her best to imitate the Colonel's tall attitude down to the cigar he held.

"You little rat bastards listen to me. All that crap you got in boot about this service or that service being better than any other...get that shit out of your heads right now! You are the people who are going to keep our troops, our ships, our planes, and even our plans, safe. You got it? You'll be following intel to assess the ability to infiltrate an area. In many situations you'll be creating a technologically secure location for those who are collecting the intel. You may be asked to remove dangerous subjects from power if necessary. You are the ones. You are tactical and technological geniuses. You know how to handle weapons, and you can follow orders with flexibility. The question is, can you be flexible enough to cooperate with each other? If you can't, you better learn! If ya can't learn, get the fuck out!"

Henry was laughing so hard he was in tears by the time she finished.

"That's him! That's totally him!"

Sam sat down again, "Ahhh, well, I watched him often enough. Even if he wasn't the mean hard-ass he pretended, he told us exactly what we were going to do. And we did all of that and more, didn't we?"

"Yeah. I guess we all made a difference. To each other at least."

The space between them no longer seemed so intimidating. They chatted easily about the past, and if the subject of the future never came up, it seemed only natural that they wouldn't want to focus too hard on what wasn't set in stone.

In the end, Medical shrugged off Sam's x-rays. The dentist barely spoke to her at all after poking about in her mouth. She felt very worn out by the end of the week. Her temporary duty would be over in twenty-four hours. She took a break at a coffee shop and looked around at the people coming in and out.

Couples, business suits, and the occasional mom or dad with kid in tow. The confusing feeling of not having a "job" to do felt slightly claustrophobic. Unlike the people around her, she had no point, no direction. It was not a nice feeling.

"Hey, can I get you anything else?"

Sam looked up at the barista across the counter, "Um...I don't know."

The barista tipped her head to one side, "Are you okay? You look uncomfortable."

Sam smiled and nodded, "Yeah, I'm okay. I'm getting out of the military. The adjustment is rough."

"Oh, really? How long you been in?"

"It's been ten years. It doesn't feel like it, though."

The barista reached for Sam's cup and refilled it, tipping in a generous amount of caramel and whipped cream.

"Don't tell me, let me guess. You feel like you need something to do?"

Sam blinked, "Yes, how did you know?"

The barista laughed, "We see a lot of military come in. Some of them even take jobs with us, but we're so unstructured that they find the lack of order disturbing. It's hard to go from a completely ordered life to one in which no one tells you what to do and you don't know what to expect each day."

Sam felt thunderstruck, "You just notice that on your own?"

"Well, sure, I deal with people all day, every day."

"Can I ask you a question?"

"Can't promise an answer, but shoot."

"Ha! shoot, that's good...do you know about hiring?"

"Well, I do hiring for the shop, so yes."

Sam pulled out a hard copy of one of the confusing interview emails.

"I sent my resume to a bunch of places, but there were companies who sent me responses like these. Since all this info is in the resume, I don't know what they are asking for."

The barista looked at the sheet and laughed. "Oh, sweetie, these are automated responses. These companies have to deal with thousands of resumes a day. They have a program looking at all the applications and looking for specific terms inside the resumes, then they post questions based on those search terms. If you really want to work for any of these, then find someone alive there and talk to them; don't send in your resume to the system."

"That sounds like a lot of work."

The barista handed the copy back as a customer walked in the door, "You have no idea. By the time you find a job you want, you'll feel like you have gone through another job just to get that job."

Sam watched the barista as she greeted the customer and smoothly and efficiently filled the order. More people. Just what she didn't need in her life. She wanted equipment, she wanted invoices, she wanted computers. She didn't want to deal with people anymore. Dispirited, she shoved the email back in her bag.

Trying to find the names of hiring managers turned out to be quite simple. Even getting interviews was easy. Getting past the differences from military to civilian thought processes...that was hard. It wasn't the first time she'd been confused by the world.

As she walked back home, a memory protruded into her thoughts. It was a boy child with a seriously irritating attitude that caused her to make a serious life decision. She'd been unexpectedly locked out of the two-story apartment at ten years old and was busy trying to struggle over the fence to get to her bedroom window when he'd walked by. He was the troublemaker at school—the one everyone avoided—the bully.

"Wow. Typical!"

She dropped back down off the planks, landing hard on the concrete.

"What are you talking about?"

"You, breaking into a house."

"It's *my* house."

"Sure it is."

She stared at the boy, unsure what to say. She'd never had to justify trying to get into the place she lived. It was her home.

"You haven't figured it out yet?"

Mystified, her ten-year-old self stared at him. He curled his lip in a sneer.

"You're so dumb. I shouldn't be surprised. You're just a black girl after all."

He swaggered away, but it took her quite a bit of time to figure out what he had meant. It wasn't until dinner time that she had the guts to tell her parents what had happened. Her father had stopped, fork halfway to his mouth. Both her parents traded looks.

"Mama? Why did he say it like that?"

"Larou. He said it because of the way colored people…"

The sound of her husband clearing his throat caused Larou's mother to hesitate.

"…black people…are viewed here in America. It's not always nice."

"But I'm not black."

"Larou, I am black; your father is white. You are biracial, Larou, even if you don't look in the mirror and see a big difference between you and your friends. No matter what, some people are always going to view you as different."

This thought made Larou confused.

"But I can't change how my skin looks!"

"That's right. You can't."

"But that's not fair!"

Her father pushed his plate away and leaned on the table. His thick Brooklyn accent was gentle with his daughter.

"Life isn't fair, baby girl."

Larou shot him a nasty look.

"I'm sorry, I'm sorry. No baby-girl talk. Let me try that again. Life isn't fair, Larou. We can't spend our whole lives upset about things we can't change. We gotta   concentrate on the things we can change."

Larou thought about that very hard. She thought about it while she was brushing her teeth, she thought about it when she was watching anime, and she thought about it when she curled up with a dog-eared copy of *Green Eggs and Ham* for comfort that night. She had learned to read with it when she was four. It remained a childhood treasure. Even the closed-minded narrator of the story had been able to get past the way his eggs and ham were colored, with a little help from Sam-I-Am. When she woke up, she was done thinking.

"Mama, I want you to call me Sam from now on."

Her mother blinked in surprise.

"Sam?"

Larou swallowed carefully, unsure how her mother was going to take this turn of events.

"Are you mad, Mama?"

"Larou...Sam...oh, boy." Her mother put her hand over her face for a moment then took a deep breath to remind herself that her daughter wasn't trying to be difficult.

"No. I'm not mad. Surprised, yes. Mad, no. Maybe a little confused. You have to be the person you want to be, not who I want you to be. I gave you a name; it's up to you what to do with it. I just want you to be a good person."

Her mother never again questioned her choice or her reason. Larou didn't disappear, but Sam became a different, more confident version of Larou.

With that memory in mind, she tossed out all the emails she had and started over. When she finally found a way into a suitable job, she settled into her work chair with deep gratitude. It was a security job, designing customized systems for clients with needs beyond the normal recorded security camera footage. It wasn't more than 48 hours later she was asked to attend a conference two states away. The conference was busy. The day after she got back she found she had appointments with prospective customers hundreds of miles apart. So many people who all wanted something different made Sam's head ache. It was not what she had thought a "regular" job was going to be at all. She felt as if she had no time to think, to plan, or to do anything for herself.

She found herself back at the coffee shop after weeks of long hours and what felt like endless days of work in a business suit.

"Maybe I'm just not cut out for this," she told the woman who had become somewhat of an acquaintance.

The barista handed her a cup in consolation, "That could be true. Maybe you would be happier doing something less...official?"

"Official...I don't understand."

"Well, something not involved with an office. How about striking out on your own?"

"Start my own business? I don't know about that. What would I do? I don't have a huge range of skills. And I want a regular paycheck for regular work."

"That's becoming far less common, you know."

Sam slumped in her chair, "Yeah. I'm finding that out fast. I can't have freedom and the perfect job. It makes me want to just go anywhere but here."

"Oh really? Where?"

"Anywhere that will let me do something to feel useful. I feel like all I'm doing right now is running around like a bunny in front of a fox hunt."

The frustration didn't end. On her way back from a flight on Sunday the airline lost her garment bag with her suit. Monday she received a call from the shipping company moving all her personal belongings back from overseas. The ship had foundered, and all her items were lost. Tuesday saw her spending a whole afternoon filling out forms for compensation. Wednesday she discovered that the Veterans Administration had sent her mail she never received about her disability application. They required appointments. Her appointment was that afternoon. It meant more people asking her uncomfortable questions to which she had to be agonizingly truthful. On Thursday of that tough week she came home to discover her apartment was a smoldering, soggy mess that the firefighters had sprayed liberally. There wasn't a single apartment in the block that had been spared. She spent Thursday night at the coffee shop trying not to cry.

Friday morning found Sam in her '84 Oldsmobile. She had her briefcase, her backpack, and her laptop. In her employer's email inbox was her resignation notice. With a final, disgusted look in the mirror, she started driving.

2

Going The Distance

Coffee, then a drive-through bacon sandwich. Billboards, long lengths of highway. Stretches of empty rock-strewn ground and trees. Lots of trees. Some towns. Then finally another city.

Sam parked, fed the meter, and sat for a moment, looking around. She leaned her head back, closed her eyes, and took a deep breath. A few minutes later a sharp knock at her window startled her. Her hands went to her hip and found nothing. She turned her face to the window.

"No sleeping!" yelled a red-faced parking meter policeman.

Sam lowered the window a few inches, "Hey, do you know where the motels are here?"

"Not my job! Get moving!"

Irritably, Sam tried to remind herself that one person didn't make a city. She got out of the car. The parking policeman stepped back, his eyes frightened. Sam sighed and rolled her eyes. She locked the car, emptied a few more coins into the meter, and walked down the street. Her eyes moved from building to person to person to the rare tree to the sidewalk and again looked for people. Nobody looked at her, even when she sought their eyes. It was a middle-class area with some hotels. Apartments sat above coffee and laundry spots, various shops for food, jewelry, clothes, and tiny manufactories. Pizza places called to her, but she kept walking. Every once in a while she would pause to look. She picked up a paper from a corner stand. She walked back to the car while looking at the employment ads. Laborers, secretarial, lots of "entrepreneurial opportunities" that screamed of pyramid marketing scams. Nothing in her areas of interest. She handed the newspaper off to someone who asked for it as she was about to ditch it in a can and got back in the car. It was the only interaction she had.

More road, farmland, and the beginning of mountainous terrain. More truck stops than she could keep track of. The billboards faded away. Nobody to advertise to here. She didn't stop for lunch. The temperature dropped in the early evening. Exhausted, she pulled onto a road that her phone promised her held life. When she saw the slat-board restaurant with its glowing signage, she almost crowed in delight.

She opened the door to a small, clean, wooden paneled interior. She sat at a table and removed her sweater, pillowing her head with it. Long minutes later a soft "thunk" caused Sam to open her eyes. The steaming cup smelled heavenly, and she lifted her head just enough to take a sip.

No sugar, no milk, but the warmth hit her stomach, and the caffeine spurred her brain to begin to process her surroundings. She took a deep, appreciative sniff of the lovely earthy coffee.

"Thank you."

"You're welcome. Would you like some food?"

Sam sat up properly, gripping the sweater to her, "Sure, may I see a menu?"

The face in front of her was lined but smiling with a warm, friendly expression. The woman patted Sam's shoulder kindly. "Sorry, no menu here. You get what you get. We have chicken bean stew with bread, but the last loaf is in the oven now and only has a few minutes to go. It'll be so fresh your soul will cry."

She was right. The chicken stew was thick and hot, a little blander than she was used to, but exactly what her stomach demanded. Lots of vegetables with chunks of tender chicken meat. The steaming bread melted the butter before it could make it to her mouth. It was like biting into a tiny wheat cloud with a crunchy crust.

After eating, she began to notice the rest of the restaurant. There weren't more than seven tables and a fireplace that glowed rather than flamed. All the tables and chairs were wood. It was like a small mountain cabin. Sam settled back into her seat while the woman who served her went around the restaurant wiping off surfaces with a clean rag. It was comfortable.

"Not many customers…" Sam remarked.

The woman smiled, "Ah, it's only just after sunset. Most people don't come in till about nine in the evening. I get the type that don't really care what they eat as long as they don't have to cook it."

"Cuts down on cost."

"Yes, it does. My big expense is beer. I have to arrange for distributors to deliver the kegs. it's expensive."

"But you're off the main highway…"

"Yes, but not a whole lot of deliveries occur along that main highway. It's mainly for long-distance traffic."

"I see. Well, I better get going. What do I owe you?"

"Oh, don't worry about it. It was nice to see someone actually enjoy the bread right out of the oven."

Sam felt relief. She knew she would have to buy gas soon, and she only had a ten in cash left. It was a long way to a truck stop where she could use her debit card. The woman's kindness touched her, and she smiled.

"Thanks."

"Don't mention it. Drive safe!"

Back in the bucket seat of the Olds, Sam considered where to go next. There was a city east of her, but it wasn't supposed to be very promising. Or she could head north through the rest of the farmland. The cities north of this pass were known for being encouraging to new tech, which meant security analyst jobs would be paying. She headed north.

The farmland was long and boring with stops in motels, sleeping in the car in truck stops. She began to get lost more often than not, driving down roads that stopped being "roads" after a while and became little more than washed-out ditches. She would have to turn around, trying not to drive over too much corn, and go back. Her phone hadn't given her so much as a smudge of a bar in days. There wasn't really a reason for service out here in the miles upon miles of nothing but growing plants. She swore never to order another soy latte in her life if she could just find something that didn't have a corn ear or a flower on it.

She finally hit a town on the edge of one of the fields that had a restaurant, a worn-out motel, a tire store, gas station, and a dial public phone. She took a picture of the phone. It was about the funniest thing she'd seen in days.

After the greasiest meal she'd had since leaving the base, "Who puts chicken fat on SALAD?" she wondered, she slept and purchased a clean shirt from what could have been a gift shop. The polite waitress had pointed out the correct road on a map to get out of the hell she'd gotten herself into. If she'd stayed on the main highway she would have been in the city two days ago.

Everything after the farming town was a spiral down into hell for Sam. On one of her stops she checked on the insurance paperwork and found it had been lost. The representative's specific words were, "Yeah, good luck resubmitting." Her debit card was frozen at one point by her bank for what they thought were fraudulent charges, because she'd been traveling. Just as she glimpsed the skyline of the city, the car began to rattle. There were puddles of oil under the engine after one stop. She poured a new quart of oil into the engine and kept driving. She left the farmland and entered scattered suburbs, then back onto the highway. The last exit deposited her onto a side street with buildings that all looked the same: grubby concrete fronts with remnants of brick hanging on to them. The streets were trash scattered. The faces unfriendly. More abandoned shops than she could shake a stick at. At a corner, as she tried to decide which way to go, the Olds gave one last gasp, a shudder, and a grinding noise, and came to a complete halt. No amount of twisting the key or pumping the gas pedal produced even a wheeze. The electricity turned on the lights and radio, but that was it.

Sam pushed the car to the side of the road against the curb and leaned her forehead against the car roof while she got out her phone and called a local repair station.

While the tow truck driver who showed up was polite, his news was beyond bad.

"Sorry, sweetie, the engine is seized. The cylinders are frozen to the head. What you have is an Oldsmobile Grand paperweight. Do you want me to take it somewhere for you?"

"No..thank you, but no. I'll figure out something. Thanks again for showing up."

Sam paid him for coming and sat on the trunk of the car, trying to think. All around her, the people who lived in this part of the city walked back and forth. It was quite possibly the ugliest place she had ever seen. Everything was gray. Piles of trash bags rested next to dumpsters. Across from the car stood a small glass-fronted shop with writing she couldn't read. Everyone who passed her had hostile looks in their faces. The place next to where the car was parked was obviously abandoned. She peeked in the window through the slats, rubbing the edge of her leather jacket through the dust. The inside was a chaotic pile of chairs and tables. No help there. Maybe she should have paid the tow truck driver to take her car.

She took out her phone and searched for the nearest motel. Even without the car, she would need to find an employment center, and she'd need to buy a new suit. She had to call the insurance company...check with the bank... A motel several blocks up seemed to be closest. She'd still have to deal with the car, but that could wait for tomorrow. After food, after she had cleared her head.

The motel was fairly seedy, but it would do. She sank back onto the bed and took out her laptop. She wondered if it had been a good idea to start out on this whole precipitous journey. Normal people planned. They job hunted before moving. Maybe she just wasn't normal.

3
No Kidding

Sam woke from a sound sleep all at once. Her phone was beeping. She passed her hand over it, and it shut up.

"You're not a smart phone; you're a *stupid* phone."

She swung her legs over the edge of the bed. Would she ever get over that way of waking up? She couldn't even remember what she was dreaming about.

The shower was cold, but the coffee she found in the lobby of the motel was hot. The bored desk clerk nodded to her as she approached.

"Hey...uh, can you tell me where to get some clothing? I need a business suit, new shoes...things like that? Is there a Penney's around here?"

"Um, there's Angela's, and uh, a Macy's I think. Penney's closed, Marshall's closed, well, the whole mall closed, really. It's a ways away though. The bus runs down the street. Take the five. Transfer at the station to the seven and get off when you see the old Woolworth's sign."

Sam smiled, "Thanks!"

"No sweat."

It was very warm out. Sam shed her sweater quickly. She started out toward the bus then remembered the car. She pulled out her phone and stared at it. Reluctantly, she turned around and went back toward where she'd left her car. When she got there, a rude surprise waited for her.

All four wheels were gone, and she saw a kid prying at the license plate in the back. She walked up quietly and held out her remote.

"Snatching fuel works better when you don't destroy the cap."

The kid took a look at her and tried to bolt, but she seized him firmly by one arm. He struggled for a moment and then stopped.

"So what are you going to do now, call the cops?"

"For a runt like you? Nah. Do you know where my wheels went?"

He turned around and sneered at her, pulling himself away from her grip.

"Ain't nobody gonna give you back your shit! Nobody's gonna give a black bitch anything around here."

"Black. Do I look black to you?"

"Yeah."

It had been a long time since Sam had to consider what it meant for people to see her as different from anyone else. She lived so long as part of a group that was forced to look beyond physical differences. Anyone who had not been able to get past the way someone else looked was swiftly weeded out of the special units. She almost smiled to herself when she thought about Dr. Seuss and *Green Eggs and Ham*. It wasn't about how people viewed her. It wasn't about how they, people, looked. It was about how people viewed their own position in society. She could only change her own actions. A warm heaviness started in Sam's chest. She stared at the boy very hard.

"How old are you?"

"Go screw yourself."

Her eyes narrowed. "Stay there. I can catch you, so don't run off."

She opened the trunk of the car and pulled out her briefcase. In hindsight it was a stupid thing to do, leaving it there. It was not a "polite" area, as her mother would have termed it. She opened the case on the trunk and went through a file. She pulled out a document and held it up in front of the boy.

"Are you 16?"

His eyes looked very confused at the slip she waved in front of him printed on heavy document paper. She sighed.

"Look. It's a piece of shit. The car...the engine is seized, and it has no wheels. Get some wheels and get it the fuck out of here and it's yours. Do you want it?"

He didn't say anything. His eyes were filled with distrust.

"And I'm not black. I'm biracial."

"You're darker than anyone here. Except for Tito, but he's just a retarded Mexican shoe shiner. He doesn't count."

"So do you have a name, white boy?" she replied in a spate of heavy sarcasm.

"James. James Sutton."

"Do you have an I.D. to go with that name, James?"

"Yeah. Here."

The boy held out a driver's license hesitantly. She copied the name down onto the slip and then signed it and dated the heavy piece of paper. She handed both to him.

"You take that to the motor vehicle place, give it to them, and they'll give you a new slip with your name on it. Got it? Then get this piece of crap out of here before the city charges me for littering."

He backed up, and she noticed that he touched the paper very gently. Like it was going to fall apart on him.

"You're still black."

She unhooked the car's three keys and tossed them to him. "No kidding. You're still a pain in the ass."

"If you don't have a car, what are you gonna do? Where are you gonna stay?"

Sam blinked, then realized she was in nothing but her ratty jeans, which she'd been in for a week, and a gift shop shirt that wasn't so "gifty" as to look new. It probably looked more like something she picked up out of a bin. Her eye hit the building next to the car, its boarded up windows taunting her. Suddenly the heaviness in her chest squeezed, and she grit her teeth.

"Right here. I'm staying right the fuck here."

The boy looked at her as if she was crazy before turning around and taking off.

She took a good hard look at that building. She saw a faded sign tucked under a board and pulled on it.

"Seven's Corp. For Sale"

The tension released, and she started to laugh.

She was going to buy a building—in the crappiest part of a city that she hadn't even looked for a job in yet. She barely even knew where she was on a map!

She finally stopped laughing and wiped her eyes. She had gone from her perfectly comfortable life in the military, to having no purpose, to making a major realty purchase.

She pulled out her phone to look up Seven's Corp, "It's very amusing, Captain..." she muttered to herself.

Seven's Corp turned out to be right next to Macy's. Sam felt so grungy walking into Macy's she wondered if she was going to be turned away by security. They didn't turn her away, though she got some heavy looks.

The saleswoman behind the desk was far less accommodating when she asked where the business suits were. She actually hesitated before pointing them out. Sam wished she had looked for casual clothes in another store first. The look was so disdainful. Another woman walked up behind her as she was looking through the plain jockey shirts that suited her frame. Small, squared-off collar, clear buttons.

"Ahem. May I help you?"

Sam turned around, the shirt in hand. "Yes, please. I need this in a 12 tall or long or whatever you call it here, and I need a jacket and slacks to go with it. Nothing pinstriped or checkered. I prefer synthetics to wool. I want wash and wear."

The woman took the shirt and wrinkled her brow, "Are you sure this is what you want?"

Sam's eye twitched.

"Yes."

"Very well."

At least the suit, while cheaply made, fit. Sam blessed her easy-to-fit frame. The saleswomen couldn't seem to be rid of her fast enough. She also purchased a pair of low-rise slip-ons. There were no gray to match the suit, but she refused to wear high heels, so black would have to do. On her way out of the business-suit section, she briefly considered the red slip-ons, but she would have to purchase a different shirt, and she did NOT want to go through that again.

Her next stop was to get some casual clothes.

"I should have done this first," she muttered to herself.

She wasn't picky, though there were a few amusing shirts that tempted her almost beyond her ability to resist. "Kiss The Cook" was the lamest of them. She kept it to shirts and jeans, things she could mess up and wash quickly. With a significant amount of distaste, Sam put the shirt from the gift shop in the round file.

The closest laundromat was fairly empty, and she pushed two uncomfortable chairs together to make a less uncomfortable wait for her clothes. The spinning was hypnotizing. She ate a two-dollar sandwich from the convenience store next door and picked invisible lint off the jacket and slacks that were already acceptably pressed right off the rack. She finished up by early afternoon.

Her savings account in the phone app swiftly informed her that she had fifteen thousand in savings and a thousand left in checking. She had nothing to sell. If she wanted to be impressive, she had to do it right. She searched for a hair shop and found a tiny one stuck into a corner near Macy's. With a pang, she remembered her own mother getting her hair done in the seventies inside Penney's. The hairdressers all treated her like part of a family. She got to sit in one chair while her mother had her hair washed and styled every week. This shop reminded her of that memory: pink wallpaper, flecked linoleum flooring, the sharp smell of bleaching agents covered over by the flowery scent of sprays.

At least the woman was kind to her. She asked for a trim and something soft. The woman washed her hair thoroughly before trimming just a bit and then letting it drape down around her shoulders, curling it to settle gracefully around her collarbone.

"There you are. What beautiful hair you have."

"Thank you so much. May I use your restroom?"

"Of course, right back there, sweetie."

Sam put on the suit. She slipped into the shoes and came out. The hairdresser had just finished sweeping and seemed amazed.

"What a difference, honey! You make that suit look good! But oh, your hair is...just a moment, let me…"

She fussed around Sam's head for a moment more and produced a brand-new clip, which she used to pull the sides of Sam's hair up with. When Sam saw the clip in the mirror, she smiled. It was a red bar that looked perfect—just a touch of color that didn't conflict with her attire. She spent a moment putting on some of her lipstick and mascara that had sat ignored in her backpack for far too long.

"Oh yes," said the hairdresser, "that is perfect. Now you look like someone who could take on the world!"

Sam chuckled and held out cash to the lady, "Here you are…"

"Oh, Marge. My name is Marge. Thank you."

"Marge, it was nice to see you today. I'm Sam. You have a good day!"

"You too, Sam!"

4

Up for Grabs

Seven's Corp was a teeny, tiny office that was smaller, if possible, than the tiny hairstyle shop Sam had just come from. When she walked in, a large man behind a stainless desk was eating a sandwich. From the smell, there was plenty of onion on it. He froze when he looked at her, as if he couldn't believe she had walked in. She gave him her "business-like" smile.

He scrambled over himself to try to clear away the greedy leavings in front of him and choked on the rest of the bite as he swallowed without chewing.

"Ah...excuse me..." he stuttered and brushed bits of lettuce onto the floor. He held out his hand to her, and she looked at his hand pointedly, which had a large dab of mustard on it, and let her lips twitch in amusement.

She felt so completely in control it was almost ridiculous. She let him continue to stumble, wiping off his hands with a paper napkin and offering a handshake again before she spoke. She made sure to speak before he managed to get anything coherent out.

"Hello. My name is Larou. Larou Olabode. I am interested in purchasing a property."

His fat lip trembled, and Sam restrained herself from laughing out loud. The man reminded her of Chris Farley.

"A property of mine? Are...are you sure?"

She cleared her throat, "I assume you place signs on the properties you are selling. I found one of your signs on a property I wish to purchase. Unless that property has since changed hands, I am sure."

The man yanked out a large, slightly messy three-ring binder. "Can you tell me the address?"

Very politely she widened her eyes just a bit, and by way of a gentle etiquette reminder smiled again, "And your name?"

"Oh! I'm so sorry. I...my name is Chris."

Sam bit her tongue.

She covered her watery eyes by opening her briefcase, very professionally, and taking out her laptop.

"Here it is. Seventeen First Street."

"The old quarter! Very um...original. Part of the original city I mean."

Sam let her eyes wander over the page that he was perusing.

"You still use paper."

"Oh yeah...I have an Apple IIe; it's all I can use, and all I need computer wise."

Sam took the moment to calculate. She scanned the room, being as obvious about it as she could.

"That is apparent...Chris."

Chris glanced around himself, "Well, that's not to say I don't make good money doing this. I do! Plenty of properties going now."

Sam inhaled deeply and leaned forward toward Chris.

"Chris. Let's be truthful. This area is suffering. You don't have a modern computer system; you don't even have a phone of either the dumb or smart variety. Your car is probably repossessed, and your home is in foreclosure. This sale could give you a few months more before you have to start renting some pathetic little apartment in the "original" section of the city. I've been there; I've viewed the property; I viewed the neighborhood. It's disgusting. The rest of the city is headed that way as well. Malls closing, companies moving out. You are tucked away in the back end of beyond in an office space reserved for a janitor's closet."

Chris turned the beet red of shame and sat back down in his chair.

"I guess you're right. What's your offer?"

Sam got businesslike.

"I will pay $5,000 for the property."

"Five...that's outrageous! The fees are..."

"I pay all the fees. Another $1,000 goes to purchase you an updated computer with an operating system a lame duck with a broken wing could handle. All the software you need to run a...ah...successful...realty business will be included. I will order and set up said computer for you. It will give you access to thousands upon thousands of possible customers."

Chris looked hopeful, "How about a phone?"

"Don't push your luck. I'm sure you have some credit left. Get your lazy ass down to the Sprint store and beg."

Chris shrugged.

"And no dumb phones." Sam stared at Chris pointedly, "Well, it is good to find an honest businessman here. I'll be back tomorrow. I trust you don't have anything more pressing than completing this contract?"

Chris shook his head as she smiled toothily, like a crocodile.

"Good. It was nice meeting you, Chris. Have a good night, and I'll see you tomorrow."

She felt Chris's eyes on her all the way out.

Sam attempted not to feel smug as she sat down to dinner at a local Denny's, but she really had to struggle.

"What can I get you?" the waitress said as Sam sat at the counter.

"How about steak? I could really use something to sink my teeth into today."

"Good day?" the waitress smiled.

Sam removed her dressy jacket and stretched, "You have no idea."

"Well in that get up, it had to be something that you got, or something you gave away that you didn't want anymore!"

Sam grinned broadly and naturally, "Both, actually!"

Sam ate the steak with great enthusiasm. She imagined that it tasted just a bit better than the rest of the bland pieces of meat out there. The heavy helping of salt was satisfying just about now. As she ate, she considered the place she was buying. She could set up a security center—with its own analysis—she could do installation, programming, risk factors…

She was surprised to suddenly feel rather proprietary about the property. It surprised her how much she felt it was already *hers*.

The waitress refilled her soda.

"So whatcha buyin'?"

Sam swallowed her bite.

"Seventeen First Street."

The waitress laughed.

"That's a good joke! That place is falling down! It's too bad, too, because those people need a place to eat."

Sam looked at the waitress, "What do you mean?"

"Well, have you seen any grocery stores around here? The last one in a twenty-mile radius shut down a year ago. Those people down there on first have to get groceries from the convenience market. They don't have a whole lot past crackers and cheese."

Sam blinked, "Oh! I...didn't think about that."

"You didnt? Why were you going to buy it? Just holding onto it for better days?"

"No! Actually I was considering a security business..."

"Oh, yeah, that's one thing they don't need. Well, I mean I'm sure the big companies need security, but there are out-of-state corporations for that aren't there?"

"I...hadn't really..."

"Thought of that. Yeah. There are a dime-a-dozen businesses going up and down here all the time."

Sam drank the rest of her soda in silence and had some coffee after that. Now she was conflicted. Eventually she took the bus back to the motel and sat in her room browsing streaming shows all evening. Each time she felt comfortable with a choice, it would remind her of something she didn't want to think about, and she'd have to change the show again. Lorelei wanted to set up her own inn; Sanford's fridge had gone out, and he had to hock a car to get it fixed. Irma from the documentary *Waste Land* refused to let anyone go hungry. It was *Oliver Twist* that made her shut off the computer and lie on the bed, staring into the dark for hours.

She fell asleep to uneasy dreams and woke early. She slugged the lobby coffee while dressed in her jeans and shivered staring out the window. She looked at the temperature gauge. 52F.

She returned to her room and paced, like a caged lioness, until 10 a.m. She put on her business suit, coiled her hair into a tidy, but severe, bun, and put on the same lipstick she had on the day before. She studied herself in a mirror and smiled wickedly. She had enough force of personality not to be ignored.

She phoned the bank to make sure they knew she would be removing a significant amount of money in the next few days or weeks. With only slight discomfort, she left the motel room.

"Good morning, Scott."

Chris looked up from his desk; he was in a clean-collared shirt and tie today.

"Chris."

"Oh, yes, that's right, Chris. I'm terribly sorry."

"Well, good morning to you, Larou."

"Sam. Please."

Chris's handshake this morning was far more in control. Sam was glad she had forced him on his guard from the beginning.

"Sam."

"Yes. How about that paperwork?"

"Well, the city licensing board insists that you see the property you are purchasing. Or...your proxy. Someone has to view it. Would you like to see it now?"

Sam considered briefly, as if reviewing in her head. "Yes, please."

"We'll...have to take the bus..." Chris was hesitant. Sam lifted her head arrogantly hoping he couldn't tell she was faking.

"Are you embarrassed? I take public transport everywhere. I refuse to be responsible for the degradation of our environment."

Chris smiled uneasily, "I...guess it's a matter of perspective. Let me lock up."

Sam decided that saying "Why?" would be pushing it too far and just nodded and waited outside.

When they arrived at First Street, Chris had some trouble locating the lock of the door as it had been covered over with wooden planks. Sam was pathetically grateful that the car was gone. James Sutton obviously knew a good thing when he saw it and had leaped on his chance.

The cracking of boards caught her attention as Chris got tired of searching and just yanked. As he opened the door, Sam got her first good look at the interior.

The dust was thick, telling of a business long abandoned. Chris began reading from his three-ring binder, telling her all the pertinent details of the property itself: the square footage; the accoutrements; everything that was included, such as power hookups, water availability, gas, and any equipment that had been left behind.

Sam let Chris talk, and she walked beside the tables that were left behind. She touched the dust hesitantly. It had definitely been a restaurant. The whole place was cut in half. An eating area and a kitchen area. Double sink, fridge, a huge wide-open doorway between the two.

"Sam? Would you like to see upstairs?"

Sam blinked, "I'm sorry, I was a little lost in the moment there. Upstairs?"

Chris smiled, "Yeah, there is a living unit up there."

"Living...well I'll be!"

Chris chuckled as she ran carelessly up the stairs. Even with the dust and the ratty mattress in her view, Sam could see the potential in the upstairs studio. She put both hands to her face and closed her eyes in joy. A place to LIVE!

She turned around to see Chris at the top of the stairs giving her a sly grin.

"This is for you, isn't it?"

"It always was."

"Restaurant?"

The uncomfortable feeling in her gut melted a little and a new nervousness took its place.

"For five thousand dollars?" Sam shrugged, "Why not?"

Chris proffered a hand, and they shook on it.

The deal was done.

5
Getting it Done

There was a period of several weeks before Sam could actually get *into* the building permanently. City services never moved quickly no matter where you were, and processing paperwork, even digitally, took the pace of a snail. She took the time to study which computer she was purchasing for Seven's Corp. When the laptop arrived before the paperwork went through, she wondered if perhaps the city was still using actual paper.

She sat with Chris in his tiny office and showed him the new computer. It was a wonderful little piece with a removable touch screen that would act as a tablet to take beautiful pictures with.

"So, why the name Seven's? It's very odd for a realty company."

Chris smiled and waved a hand at a picture of another man on his desk.

"My brother Steve. He was a bit of a gambler; said realty was just like gambling. Sometimes you won, and sometimes you lost. In Craps, seven is the big number. Everything revolves around when that seven is going to show up. Steve loved the excitement."

"What about you—Oh...here, touch this and you'll go right to the menu—what did you want to name it?"

"My daughter wanted me to name it Daisy Chain Realty. I didn't really care as long as we could get some money in."

"So is your daughter happy with the name now?"

"Ah...my wife packed up about four months ago and took off. Said she couldn't be with a loser anymore. I couldn't blame her. I promised a good life, and I didn't deliver, you know? What else am I going to do? Become a welder on the buildings going up on the edge of town?"

Sometimes when life gets too much, and everything is crumbling around you, people try to hold on to what they know—tight-fisted, both hands. They don't want that one thing to change. They'll let everything else go, but not that. Sam saw the regret, the disappointment, the humiliation in Chris's face. The way he looked at the picture of his brother was with fond reminiscence. This small company was fighting an undertow but threw itself into the fight. It had incorporated and tried to take advantage of the market that was crumpling under the weight of the loss of city infrastructure. They tried to guess when that seven would hit. Chris didn't want to let that go. He didn't want to let go of the one thing that needed him.

Sam got up and swept the crumbs from lunch off her jeans.

"Well, Chris, I can't tell you how to do realty, but I can tell you that you will be able to do your job better with this computer. Play with it, take pictures, put them on the internet. When you feel comfortable, you can start a website. You need one."

"Thanks Sam. I mean, Miss Olabode."

Sam rolled her eyes in amusement. Her facade had crumbled completely after seeing the property she purchased, and she hadn't put it back on.

"You're welcome."

She walked out the door into the blazing hot afternoon and gathered her thoughts. Water, Electricity, Gas, cleaning supplies. In that order.

The water company was in the lobby of one of the big new buildings being erected. Once again Sam was in awe that this part of the city could begin to thrive while the other half was falling into ruin. Although as she took a look around, Sam's trained eye began to notice details.

The lines of people were long. Really long. The customer service reps (not many) were tired looking. Not bored, but very tired. The customers themselves shifted anxiously from one foot to another, stared at their phones, sifted through purses or backpacks. Sam frowned and looked behind her. She had noticed the metal detectors at the door, but there were no security personnel.

Sam reached the counter and placed her realty processing papers on it.

"I'd like to get the water started in this property please. I am the new owner pro tem."

The woman looked at the paperwork and typed the address into the computer. She frowned and rubbed at her temple.

"Long day?" asked Sam

"It's...getting there." replied the rep.

A silent minute passed

"Oh, here's the problem. The water has been shut off for the whole block. It was labeled abandoned by the city registrar. I will have to put in an order for the city to turn on the main. There will be a fee for that since you are the first one to request it."

Sam tried not to physically shudder. "Okay, when can the water be turned back on?"

"Well, most of the water company employees are scheduled to work on the new buildings...so...next month?"

"I'm sorry...when?"

The rep gave her an apologetic smile.

"I know, it's a long time, but the water company has been downsized several times, and there are less than half the people to do all the work. And there is more work every day."

Sam felt confused, "So...wait...are you telling me that everyone who is living in that block has no water?"

"Oh, there's no one living there. They all would have moved out."

The rep's complete confidence in that statement stunned Sam to her bones. Sam remembered the hostile looks she had gotten from the people walking by, the people she had seen hanging out windows in that block. Angry people who definitely still lived there.

"So, how much would it be to turn the water on for the entire block? Not just the main, but for all five buildings?"

"Oh, not that much extra since the water company currently takes water line price from the stated value of the property. Why, were you going to buy the whole block?"

"Um, perhaps," Sam temporized.

The rep printed out a page and handed it to her, "Here you are. All the work can be done in the same day as your building, but you will have to get each new tenant to come down and sign a new agreement for the water to be turned on for each individual building."

"Thanks.."

Sam found the electric company far more accommodating. The power could be turned on in twenty-four hours. Sam traveled across five blocks to an old building before learning from the posted sign that the gas utilities had been combined with electric, and she had to walk all the way back to talk to the same people about gas. Gas was more involved, requiring an inspection of her facility. Sam made an appointment.

The bus ride back was interminably long. She paid up the motel before she went to her room, letting them know she'd be leaving the next day. Then she settled down to make the first phone call to someone she knew since she had left the base.

"This is Colonel Shaw. How may I help you?"

"Hello Colonel, it's Sam."

"Sam! It's good to hear your voice. Please, call me Buddy now."

"That would be weird, Colonel."

"Well, I suppose so, whichever you prefer. Tell me how you're getting on."

Sam told him most of the details of her adventure. She could imagine him sitting at his desk, multitasking as always, shuffling personnel paperwork and making notes. When she got to telling him about the building she heard him drop his pen.

"You mean, you aren't local anymore? I was wondering why I hadn't seen that gas guzzling Olds around town. Didn't any of the interviews work out for you? They seemed so promising."

"Well, yes. They were. But I couldn't work for a company that insisted on my being a woman and nothing else."

"I don't understand."

"They wanted me to wear skirts, high heels..."

"Ohhhhh. Yes, I could see that wouldn't have gone over well with you. So now you are there. You own a restaurant."

Sam took a deep breath and told him the rest. She told him about James, about the people in the block she'd glimpsed, about the customer service rep who assumed no one lived there. The confused feelings she had over these people who so obviously didn't want her there. How she had paid for water to be returned to the whole block.

The Colonel chuckled on the end of the line.

"Sam. Do you remember when that idiot child recruit came in and got lost in the desert while 'taking a hike'? You didn't know him from Adam, but you made the entire squadron, even the Lieutenant Colonel, go look for him? Three days with water rationing looking for that kid. Found him fetched up against the lee side of a rock trying to avoid the wind, burned to a crisp. I don't think I've ever seen anyone so relieved in my life as you were to see that recruit alive."

There was a moment of silence on the line and then, "Sam, I'm not surprised that you are in this position. You are the epitome of no one left behind. You can't save the world, but you sure will give it a try. You were used to a very dependable life here in the military. Every day up at six, every night down at 10. Unless you were out on orders, and even then everyone knew they would always have rations; they would always have water. They knew what their job was and what you expected. So now it's just a new job in a new place, Sam. You can still get up at six; you can still go to bed at ten; you just have to do a different type of job in between. It's not what you're used to, but it's the right thing to do."

Sam felt her eyes become watery, and she nodded at the phone.

"You're nodding, aren't you?"

Sam laughed. A shaky, slightly choked laugh, "Yes, Sir."

"Well, you keep going. I have confidence in you. Even when people don't want you, keep trying and maybe they'll get used to you being there."

"I'll do that, Colonel."

6

It Is Work After All

Sam shoved her shoulder against the door while carrying several bags of cleaning supplies. The warm air drifted in and created a backwash of musty air into the doorway. The dust in the room scoffed at her pathetic pile of cleaning supplies. She would never get it done. It was here to stay.

"It was the best of times, it was the worst of times..." Sam quoted softly to the dust. The broom slipped from her hand and "whapped" against the nearest table. A puff of dust dared her to do something about it. She dropped the bags and turned to close the door, then thought differently. She wrinkled her nose. The whole place needed a good airing out. She started by going to the back of the room and just looking at everything. She removed her backpack, and then her eye for detail went to work. The whole property was supposed to be 5400 square feet on the lower level— 60 by 90—but Sam swore she could only see sixty feet of it from the door to the back, and then thirty feet for the eating area and thirty feet for the kitchen. The kitchen had a storage area that extended beyond the back wall. Where was the missing thirty feet in the eating area?

Sam went back and stood in the doorway. To her left and right were tables as well as a low wall on the right separating the kitchen from the eating area that extended for a ways. She marched off twenty feet of table space and looked to her left and right. To her right was where the short wall stopped and the entrance to the kitchen began. To her left were windows. The opening to the kitchen was about thirty feet wide. She marched that off. To her right stood a rounded eating counter ten feet long. To her left…something covered by a sheet and piles of scrap lumber and a few boxes. She'd worry about that later. She marched off the rest of the space to the back wall. It was only ten feet. Confused, she tapped on the wall. It sounded solid. Ew, flower wallpaper…pink maybe? Double ew.

Her need for organization clawed its way to the front of her brain. She would begin with the eating area. When she had that done, she would do the kitchen. The first table she tried to move fell apart, having been held together with spit and duct tape apparently. She tossed the pieces into the kitchen and attempted to move the other tables. Five more fell apart, and the rest were pretty shaky at best. A few were just folding tables that had seen better days. She swore one was from the founding of the city, itself, and decided to try to make it "antiquish." Later. When she had time. Time. *Ha!*

The whole rest of the day was spent sweeping, swabbing dust, and wiping windows. Late in the afternoon she moved the pile of scrap wood and noticed a stone column peeking out from under the sheet. She pulled gently on the sheet, and it ripped away from a nail in the wall, revealing a rather elegant fireplace. That wasn't on the asset list! It was completely not in keeping with the style of the room, and Sam wondered where it came from. When had it gone in? With the pink flowery wallpaper, it was like a sore thumb that stuck out rudely. Was it even real? She turned her phone flashlight up into the cavity, and it looked as if it had a flue and went all the way to the top.

"Well huh. Imagine that. Nice find. If it's safe, that is. Insurance rate would go up if I used it, though."

She flinched thinking about the insurance she hadn't purchased yet and shook her head to try to clear it. Later. After cleaning. After water and gas. She was grateful the electricity was on. Not that it did her much good with only two bulbs operating correctly. She coughed in the remnant dust and sat in the most sturdy chair available. Luckily there were plenty of those. She opened a bottle of water she had carried with her in her backpack. Unfortunately it was the only water around. A shadow crossed the doorway and she looked up.

"Uh...Larou...Ola...um.."

"Olabode. That's me, but you can call me Sam."

"Oh, okay, Sam. I'm an engineer from the water company. I'm just checking the lines from the main. Can I come in?"

Sam waved the shadow forward and was surprised to see it was a woman. She smiled, and the woman waved a hand in the air.

"You sure have got a lot of work to do here. Turning it over?"

Sam shook her head wearily, "I'm going to work it."

The woman's eyebrows rose up as she looked at the electronic equipment in her hand.

"In this neighborhood? Wow. Good luck."

Sam felt a bit of disappointment. No one seemed to think much of this section of the city at all. She couldn't really blame them, but still.

"Well, if the city had really wanted to fix this area they should have razed it and started over."

The woman started walking through the restaurant while her equipment beeped at her.

"Can't. City charter won't let them. So it stands and rots. When it falls down, I'm sure they'll think about replacing it."

"What about the people?"

The woman shrugged. Sam gave up on the conversation and went back to her water. Fifteen minutes later the woman was done.

"Well, I've got everything I need. Since I have pings to the gas lines as well, I'll just email those to gas and electric. It'll make the inspection a bit quicker for you. I'll try to turn the water on soon, okay? I might have to replace a hydrant at the corner outside the building before I do. To do that I have to take up part of the concrete."

"Don't tell me, there's a fee."

The woman shook her head, "Nope, no fee for that. The city will have to pay for a hydrant. Permits though—they can be a hassle."

Sam nodded and the woman left.

"I'm going to need more water." Sam said to the empty room.

The missing space really bothered Sam as she began looking at the rounded counter space. It took up a portion of the room and she didn't like it. It was so odd and out of place. After a cursory inspection she located the bolts that held it in place against the back wall.

"I'll need a wrench. Pliers...screwdrivers. Crap. I didn't think about tools."

She wasn't necessarily exhausted, but the thought of having to go out to buy more stuff was tiring. She felt like she'd barely made a dent. With no water, nothing was really clean. It was just less dusty. She leaned against the corner wall which bounced.

"What the…"

She stood up and thumped on the wall next to the counter. A hollow echo answered her whack. She moved to the left a few feet and tapped again. Hollow. Again to the left, solid. Then a light went off in her brain. that's where the extra space was. Behind the wall. It wasn't a mistake on the paperwork; the previous owners had just blocked it off! She walked out of the door and followed the building around and marched off sixty feet. A facade. It looked like the building continued as normal but obviously it didn't. She went back inside and pushed against the faux wall. It cracked just a little, but Sam didn't want it to come tumbling down on top of her so she stopped. Tools. She needed tools. The scrap lumber sitting silently in the kitchen stared at her accusingly.

Tables. Could she build tables? She remembered her dad's teaching her to use a saw. She could tear down a fifty cal machine gun and put it back together in a breeze, so she was obviously mechanically adept. How difficult would it be to cobble together tables? She'd have to cover them. Tablecloths? Oh, so pretentious and expensive with all that laundry. She didn't even have a washer and dryer. If she lacquered them, she could just wash them clean.

Basic toolset, saw, screws, lacquer, paint? Lots more cloths, disposable ones. Window cleaner, stainless steel cleaner… floor. Sam looked at the floor. Wood. Wood…cleaner? The kitchen was linoleum so Mop & Glo for that. Sponges, buckets, scrapers, a toilet brush. She hadn't even looked at the bathroom downstairs yet.

Sam leaned her head on her hands. There was so much and all of it work. Just endless drudgery. It was too late to go out now. She pulled out her laptop as her stomach rumbled angrily. She ordered a pizza and had to repeat the address three times before the guy believed her. She finally just paid with a credit card instead of with cash so they would actually make the bloody thing and bring it to her. Just before she ended the call she snapped at the person on the other end, "And you better show up!"

Forty-five minutes later, as she was typing up her plan for the rest of the week, there was a hesitant knock at the doorway.

"Uh...pizza..."

"Yeah, come on in."

"Oh, here you go; sorry, we never receive orders from this area; we thought it was a prank."

Sam was in no mood to be friendly; her stomach was complaining angrily at being ignored.

"Set that damn thing down and get out. You'll get a tip tomorrow if you guys don't give me crap about it."

The pizza guy set down the box on the nearest surface and got out quickly. Sam wolfed down half the greasy mess and another bottle of water before her stomach stopped complaining. Finally, feeling better, she closed the door to the restaurant and settled herself in the middle of the floor, her head pillowed on her backpack. It was warm enough that she didn't even need a blanket. As she drifted off, her last thought was that she'd better get a sleeping bag along with the rest of the crap she had to spend money on.

7

Running Down the Range

The next day brought tools and more cleaning supplies. She got the whole eating room done just in time to mess it up again by getting the wood off the outside of the windows and the back wall where a door was revealed. She tried to be careful around the outside of the windows, delicately unscrewing each separate piece of wood so she wouldn't have to repaint the outside. She knew she couldn't afford that.

With the windows at last freed, the light spilled into the eating area with abandon. It wasn't much of a view. She saw children get off the school bus in front of the building. After a while she shook off her lookie-loo daze and began piling wood she couldn't use next to the fireplace.

"Oh...that's right." She picked up her phone and dialed the first heating company she saw in the search list. They didn't deal in fireplaces. The second did, but not stone, only gas. No, they couldn't assess a business for a gas line. The third flat out refused to come to the area. She managed to convince the fourth to show up. An hour later, a punk walked through her door.

The hairstyle surprised her. All red and purple and green, spiked to about four inches.

"Are you...the heating guy?"

"Yeah. Haven't you ever seen a human before?"

Sam closed her eyes and shook her head a moment at her rude gaffe. She'd have to stop making assumptions.

"I apologize. That was not polite. I'm Sam; I'm glad you're here."

"That's okay. Is that the fireplace?"

"Yes. I just want to know if it's safe to toss some wood in it and start it up or if I'm going to burn the whole place down."

The boy—no, the man—he was a man...the man took a brief look around the outside and then looked at the inside, moving the grate and scraping away some dirt. Then he looked up with a flashlight and poked at the flue.

"Well, good news is that the fireplace itself seems in good shape. I'd say it's safe enough to use. Bad news is, if you put wood on this particular fireplace, it might be pretty dangerous."

Sam stared at him blankly

"What? Wait...I thought you said..."

"Oh, yes. With a good cleaning..." The man pulled out a card and handed it to her. "Here's the number of a decent sweep. With a good cleaning it's safe enough. The difference with this fireplace is that it is plumbed differently. It's meant to use a type of log that will not burn. It just spreads the heat from the gas. We have them. If you want a full inspection to show the insurance company, I can do that too."

"Oh! Gas...I hadn't even thought of that. Well, the gas won't be on for at least another day; the gas inspector will be here tomorrow."

"Tell you what, I'll show up, and after he's done, I'll do an inspection...help you turn it on. I'll even bring a log with me. Sound good?"

"I guess this answers why there weren't any ashes to clean, just dirt."

"Yes 'm"

"Well, good. I guess I'll see you tomorrow. The guy from the gas company should be here...oh...I don't know...any time from eight a.m. to...five?"

The man laughed, "No sweat, I'll just show up around two. If he isn't done, I can always come back. Trust me, I don't have very many places to be right now."

"Is work that slow?"

The man pulled out a book from his back pocket. It appeared to be some type of scutty western romance novel.

"Oh, my."

"Yeah. I find books in the bin by the book store. I don't always have a big choice though. It's not like I can just walk in and buy them."

Sam smiled to herself. He refused to take her payment until the next day. She watched him through her now almost-clean windows until he was out of sight.

Turning her attention to the kitchen, she wondered what to do with all the wood now. She walked to the doorway and considered. It was too hot to actually see anyone with their own fireplaces burning—not that anyone would use a lovely wood-burning stove here.

"The back door."

She went to the back door that she hadn't tried to open yet and turned the handle. Locked. She tried key after key, but none worked. In the end she left it alone and just hauled the wood around to the dumpster and broke it into manageable chunks so it would fit. Then it was the kitchen's turn. For the hundredth time she wished for running water. Everything looked all...smeared, even after dusting. The stainless steel cleaner did no good at all on a dusted prep table that hadn't been washed. It just smelled bad. She gave up after dusting every surface she could see and sweeping. She drank from a bottle of water and then wondered vaguely what she must smell like after a few days with no shower.

The next day was a day of wonders.

The heating guy, the gas guy, and the water company all showed up at the same time. The building was filled with workers. The gas guy declared the range a complete loss, but the deep fryer was okay. The water heater would need to be replaced. The gas lines to the fireplace were fine, so the heating guy turned it on and adjusted the spacing of not just one, but several logs. It became distinctly uncomfortable in the area of the fireplace by the time he was done and shut it off after making sure she could operate it as easily as he could.

The water company engineer came back with a crew and checked the hydrant. Sam watched them "consult" (argue) and then "decide" (throw dice) to test the line by turning on the main.

Sam thought about it. The only way to test the hydrant was to turn it on from the main. Her building's water couldn't be turned on unless the hydrant worked. That meant the hydrant hadn't been turned on. The thought that the building had been without fire protection was chilling.

For two days Sam fretted and fussed. She stared at pictures of ovens she couldn't afford. She discovered a section of floor that was loose. She paid everyone and stared painfully at her savings. She built tables. They were sturdy but not pretty. She sanded and sanded and sanded, then covered them with coat after coat of lacquer. For good measure, she covered all the wood chairs with a coat of lacquer too. She cleared everything off the walls. A faint, old style photograph of a woman in a dress from the 1800s turned out to be a picture from a magazine taped to the glass and hung on the wall. It reminded her of the picture of her own mother.

She pulled her picture out of her briefcase. Sam stood next to the counter and gazed around holding the picture. Her eyes wandered to the stairs going up. She envisioned her mother walking in on her.

"Larou, what are you doing?"

"I'm taking a bath, Mom."

"In the middle of the room?"

"Mom. Do you see any doors?"

"Well, this is … build some doors! Build some walls for God's sake."

"Mom, I have to replace ten more tables, restructure part of the floor, and pay for a new range. When am I going to have the time or money to build walls? I can't even afford to replace the bathtub!"

"Where is the tub anyway?"

"The last owners took it with them. I'll bet it was nice—a whole claw foot affair..."

"Well this is just disgusting. What if you had a visitor?"

"Oh yeah, Mom, I'm going to bring in a man, then say, 'Just a moment while I freshen up darling,' and then go pee in the middle of the room in front of him. Again, I don't have time to go looking for a man!"

"Oh, Larou."

"Oh, Mom."

Sam put the picture of her mom on the counter. She made sure it was straight and leaning properly on its little cardboard peg.

"I miss you, Mom."

Her mother wasn't the only thing she missed. Sam got sick of eating pizza. She thought almost fondly of the terrible chicken they ate on the base overseas. She just couldn't think of anything else, and nobody else delivered. She had no way to cook and no water yet. There were restaurants, but not close, and she didn't want to spend that much money anyway. The convenience store was pretty much a joke for food. She didn't want to touch the refrigerated sandwiches there, by way of the fact they didn't even seem to have an expiration date.

She went back to the restaurant and was searching eBay for ranges when her phone announced, quite rudely, that she was over her data limit. She swore. It was another thing she hadn't thought of. Internet. She lived on it!

She looked everywhere for a cable, a phone line, something. She found a phone line tucked away behind a shelf but no cable line. She sat down and huffed in frustration. She felt like an angry five-year-old who wasn't getting her way. She wanted internet, and she wanted it now! She decided to increase her data limit to find a range. She came across an oven just a few miles away. A restaurant was replacing their old oven. It was gas, it had six rings, a griddle, and two ovens; it was perfect. She decided to pay them a visit.

The front door attendant wrinkled his nose at her, "Uh, no."

"I need to see your head chef; I'd like to take the old oven off your hands."

"Not through this door you don't. There are customers in here. Around the back."

Sam felt a little like a whipped puppy as she knocked on the back screen. From inside came sounds of cooks' voices, rattling and banging of pots and pans, yelled orders, and the scent of something heavenly.

The oven that she supposed was the one advertised stood next to the door, and she took a moment to look at it. A man in a white apron splashed with flecks of red sauce answered her knock after a few minutes, wiping his hand on an immaculate rag.

"What do you want?"

"I'd like to take this oven off your hands."

"Eighteen hundred."

Sam snorted, "I'm not stupid; you paid two thousand for it ten years ago when it was brand new. I'll give you three hundred."

"Five."

Sam pulled out her card, "Take a visa check card?"

The chef looked at it, "Where did you get this?"

Sam stared at him incredulously, "It's not stolen! I can provide identification if you like."

The chef waved a hand at her and offered the card back. Stubbornly she took out her wallet and provided her military I.D. "Look. It's me. There on the I.D." The chef started to turn away.

"LOOK, DAMMIT!"

He turned with an angry look on his face and then saw the I.D.

"A military I.D. Well, I'll be damned. I thought you were just one of those jackass thieves who tries to buy old restaurant equipment with stolen cards and sells them for the metal cost."

Sam gritted her teeth together. "If I were doing that, why would I fucking pay? You have the range sitting right out in the open. No one is watching. I could have just pulled up in a truck and taken it!"

"All right, all right. I'm sorry. You're obviously real. What do you want the range for? Why don't you just buy a new one?"

"I don't have that kind of money. It's why I bargained you down to five hundred. I'm trying to reopen a restaurant on First Street."

"First Street? You're not going to get any customers there!"

"There's a whole neighborhood...look, I don't want to argue about this. Are you going to sell me the damned range or not?"

The chef nodded, "Come on in; I'll run the card."

She stepped inside, feeling distinctly grungy near the chefs who were pouring their hearts into their pans. Her mouth watered at the smells as she passed.

Inside his office, the chef pulled out a machine and ran the card, waiting for the slow connection.

"So you were a chef in the military?"

Sam gave a well-practiced speech.

"No. I was a liaison between the Marines and Army. I designed systems."

"But you have experience cooking."

"No."

The chef looked at her and shook his head, "You are insane."

"Why?"

The chef took off the slip of paper, and she signed it. He printed another for her.

"There won't be a lick of profit off that place until the city decides to rezone the original section, which will be never, or until they renovate, which may be close to the same time."

Sam clutched the receipt, "The building needed me."

The chef threw up his hands, "As you will, crazy woman. Where's your truck? I'll help you load."

"Truck?"

"Yes. Your vehicle. To get the range back to the building that needs you?"

"Shit."

"You don't have a truck."

"I...didn't think about it."

"You must have made some liaison."

Sam felt a fluttery desperation seize her chest. She laughed a little hysterically, then covered her mouth. The chef raised an eyebrow.

"Look. I'll tell you what, Miss Larou. I'll cover up the range with a tarp and stick a couple of trash bags on it. You go arrange for a vehicle. It may still be here by the time you get back."

Sam nodded and turned away from the office. As she walked through the kitchen, her stomach reminded her it was time for food. The thought of pizza made her feel a rush of nausea. She took a deep breath before walking out the door, as if the mere *scent* of fluffy rice, steamed vegetables, and Chicken à la King could stave off the hunger. Outside the door, she made sure she put the card away and cast a last long look at the stove she hoped she hadn't wasted five hundred dollars on. As she started walking away, she heard, "Larou."

She turned around, and the chef put a styrofoam box into her hands. She opened it, and the scent of fresh food made her eyes water.

"Thanks."

The chef nodded and went back inside. It was some of the best food she had ever eaten, hands down.

It wasn't until she was putting the receipt in her briefcase that night that she took a close look at it. The chef had only charged her three hundred.

8

New Things Don't Fall Off Trees

The truck problem actually had an easy solution. U-Haul was probably one of the businesses that had the most custom going. Sam managed to get a pickup truck for nineteen bucks. One of the dishwashers helped her load up the range. When she got back to the restaurant, she rigged up two sturdy 4 x 4s to take the weight of the back two legs as she slid it down. She used two flat dollies to roll it to the doorway and then clenched her fists when it wouldn't fit through the doorway. She removed the door and still wound up with two gouges in the frame when she forced it through. She made sure to use the dollies to move the old range to the other side of the kitchen and put the new one where it was supposed to be before returning the truck. Her muscles were shaking from the absolutely titanic effort it took to move the monster by herself.

As she finished hooking up the gas line to the range and turning on each burner in turn to make sure it worked, she heard an awful noise coming from the walls. It sounded like a gurgling earthquake. Her stomach dropped into the ground. She wondered how the hell a grizzly got into her walls. She even wondered if it was rats. New York rats moved into her building. All of them. At one time. She stared at the walls in horror, wondering when they were going to explode. The noise moved up and down the walls, and then in a glorious *whoosh*, water blew out of the taps in the big, double stainless-steel sink that she had left turned on.

"WATER! I HAVE WATER!"

She danced around in joy. No more bottles! She could wash! She could clean!

She heard someone laugh behind her and whipped around. The chef from the restaurant was chuckling at her antics.

"I've never seen anyone so happy over water before."

She stuck her tongue out at him and turned the taps off, "Have you ever been without water? It's horrible!"

The chef turned around to look at all the still-dirty surfaces, smeared with her pathetic attempts to clean them.

"So I see."

"So what can I do for you, Chef?"

"I wanted to see the competition."

"Chef, I don't even have a coffee maker. I don't think I'll be competition for quite a while."

The man smiled drolly, "Well, that is a relief. Here."

Chef pulled out a thin catalogue and put it on the stainless-steel prep table. "That is a list of local suppliers. Vegetables, oils, cooking accoutrements, you know."

"Well, no, I don't know, but thank you. I appreciate it."

"You're welcome. Let me know if there is anything else of mine you'd like to steal. We'll talk. My name is Louis."

He was on his way out before she could ask if that was the only reason he wanted to stop in. She lost no time in continuing the cleaning process. The kitchen looked almost perfect by the time she stopped and thought of food again. Then she looked at the range and remembered: she had no pots, no pans, no silverware, no accoutrements. She hadn't even looked in the fridge yet. She wasn't sure she wanted to. Her dwindling account mocked her, and she stared at the credit card she had in her briefcase with real disdain.

There were still basics to buy...also city inspection costs. Her one saving grace was that she would be getting a military paycheck soon. It wouldn't be enough to cover everything, but it could keep her fed until she started bringing money in. She got a loaf of iffy bread and some butter along with a packet of ramen noodles from the convenience store and chowed down while flipping through the catalogue. She almost laughed at some of the prices. There was no way she could pay a convenience cost of forty bucks a week for any order under five hundred! And the prices of the "accoutrements" was out of her sight. Twenty bucks for a spatula, hundreds for plates. No. That would never do. There was that salvage store...

She cleaned up the crumbs from the dry ramen she had crunched her way through.

Where was she going to find food to start with? The credit card mocked her again. She pushed it out of her mind and locked the front door. It wouldn't be the last time she felt uneasy at what she considered a flimsy bolt. So many things left to buy and to do. New things don't fall off trees, her mother used to say. She believed her mother now.

She blessed the salvage store the next day. Plates, not all the same. Cups, again not all the same. Forks, spoons, knives, beat up but clean. Spatulas, spoons, a few pots and pans, again not all the same. She froze in front of a scratched and dented red ten-speed. She reached out to touch it. The tag said twenty bucks. She dumped the rest of the equipment she was holding and moved the ten-speed back and forth on the floor. The gears didn't seem to catch on anything and the chain was in good shape.

"Take me home..." she said in the bike's voice.

"Okay." she answered. She flailed a bit trying to handle the bike, the pots and pans, the basket of silverware, and the cups. She settled for taking the bike first and parking it next to the sales counter and then taking the rest of the equipment up. The girl was very careful about ringing up all the items, double-checking each tag before pressing total. Sam noticed that the girl spoke very slowly.

"Twenty and then seventeen dollars and fifty cents, please."

Sam felt confused and then realized that she had brought the bike up first. She glanced at the girl's name tag.

"You're very observant, Amy. Here, I'll pay both totals together with my debit card."

"Can I offer you another bag?"

"Oh...yes, please. I didn't think very hard before I started picking up all this stuff."

"I have to charge you five cents for the bag."

"That's fine."

The girl rang the card and carefully placed everything in the basket into a paper bag with handles. Sam thanked her, and, putting the bags on the handle of the ten speed, wheeled it out of the store. On her way out she noticed a poster in the hallway proudly proclaiming, "We Hire from The Opportunity Center."

A vocational center? The girl had been speaking slowly. Could she have a disability? Was that how the disabled got jobs? At the gas station on the corner Sam put some air in the bike's tires. She had never thought about the disabled working. She hadn't thought about the disabled much at all. She knew that they went to school. What did they do after they graduated from school? They wouldn't just sit around inside all day. Would they? A rather horrific memory of watching a documentary on asylums from the nineteenth century popped into Sam's head.

What was it like for someone with a developmental disability to work? Sam spent most of the ride home trying to imagine what life was like with a mental disorder. Then she felt dumb. How was she supposed to know what that felt like? She knew how to fail, but just having a developmental disability didn't mean they automatically failed at everything. Amy was decent enough at being a cashier. Maybe it was enough to accept that there were developmentally disabled adults. They were just another part of society. She wondered if there were still places like those asylums. It hurt Sam to think about it, and she put it to the side of her mind to think about some more later on.

9

Judgment Day

Sparkling windows, immaculate floors. The curved counter had been removed and was residing in front of the window next to the front door. A fleeting thought of filling the inside with soil and planting flowers crossed Sam's mind.

Sam had replaced the counter with a short table that held plates, cups, bowls, and silverware. She crossed the kitchen, idly swiping a hand across the top of the fridge. She smiled at her clean fingers. She had spent long hours sterilizing the fridge, though for a blessing the previous owner had cleaned it well before shutting it down. It currently had a grand total of one gallon of milk and a head of lettuce. She had wolfed down the bread, cheese, and bologna the previous night. Every surface was scrubbed, and the picture of her own mother had a place in the eating room. She tried to think of anything she had forgotten. All her paperwork was on a now shiny stainless-steel prep table in the middle of the kitchen. The rear storage area was empty of everything except cleaning supplies. The downstairs toilet was immaculate though a little wobbly.

Impatiently, she wandered the restaurant. The door opening caught her attention. A rather dour-looking man walked in dressed in a business suit, tie neatly clipped to his shirt. He was holding a clipboard.

"Man, does every single person still use paper here?" muttered Sam to herself as she went to greet him. She smiled and offered her hand.

"Hi, I'm Sam."

He took her hand without a change of expression, but Sam thought his nose twitched. His shake was perfunctory, and he withdrew his hand quickly. His eyes went to his clipboard.

"I'm sorry, I have a Lara Alamabod on my paperwork?"

Sam was thrown off balance slightly.

"Well, I am Larou Olabode, but I encourage people to call me..."

"Can you spell that, please?"

Sam's expression soured.

"Can you spell yours?"

The man blinked at her, "Spell what?"

"Your name. You haven't given it."

"What does that matter?"

Sam sighed; the atmosphere was getting rather chilly in the seventy-degree summer weather.

"You could be a rapist or a thief or anybody for that matter. You could even be a prospective customer whom I have to turn away, because, gee, the inspector hasn't shown up yet."

The man drew himself up, if it was possible, even straighter. He was slighter taller than the average man Sam had seen in this city. Close to six feet. His skin tone was very pale with few marks on it. Was he wearing foundation? Hair neatly trimmed and brushed to one side. The scent of VO5...wow. Sam hadn't smelled that in forever. His suit was pressed with perfect precision, his shirt was obviously good twill cloth. His shoes were so shiny Sam thought the Colonel would have been jealous.

"My name is Mister Nero Amelo. I am the city health inspector. Would you like me to spell that for you?"

"It's very pleasant to meet you Mister Amelo. Tell me, do you do your own paperwork?"

"Frequently. Why?"

"Well, I was just wondering how you could have possibly misspelled my name when I submitted it electronically."

Nero shifted from one foot to the other. Sam thought he looked uncomfortable.

"I usually make notes instead of just printing paperwork out."

"Very well, though I encourage you not to do that anymore. You understand."

"Understand what?"

"The misunderstandings that can occur. Now, about that inspection."

Sam smiled politely, having neatly gained what she considered the verbal upper hand. Nero sighed and rolled his eyes and then, beginning at one end of the restaurant, he painstakingly went over every inch. He marked down brand names and serial numbers, and when he at last opened the fridge, his eyebrows knit together in confusion.

"You don't have any food."

"I do have food. It's there."

"Milk and lettuce? Is that what you are planning on serving?"

Sam restrained the urge to snap, *What else?*

"I did not think it would be appropriate to order food that might not be served before I had a license."

Nero frowned, "Well, there will have to be a second inspection at any rate."

"Why?"

"A pre-inspection makes sure the site is suitable. Your second inspection will be in working conditions. Safety, orderliness, and so forth. After that there will be unscheduled visits to make sure you are maintaining an appropriate facility."

"Oh."

Nero turned abruptly to her, "Have you ever done this before?"

"Run a business?"

"Worked in a restaurant."

"Ah, no. I was in the military before this."

"It shows."

"The military job?"

"No. Your ignorance."

Sam flinched and grimaced as a pain shot through her stomach. She cursed the response. Nero's eyebrows rose in surprise, but he didn't say anything. Sam schooled her expression.

"Well, Mister Amelo. What can I improve upon?"

"You have no dedicated kitchen trash can; you do not have a fire extinguisher; your fridge is unsuitable though minimally acceptable; your knives must be in sheaths; one of your tables looks unsafe; have you had the fireplace inspected?"

Silently Sam gave Nero a copy of the fireplace inspection sheet. He nodded curtly and continued.

"I don't see soap for handwashing; you have no gloves for handling food; no instructional signs for the Heimlich maneuver; your cutting board must be replaced with a brand new one; the hood for your range is too old, though, again, minimally acceptable. Do you have any instructional paperwork for employees?"

"I don't have any employees."

"You are an employee."

"I have to train myself?"

Nero's eyes flashed in great amusement, though Sam didn't see him smile. She grunted.

"I fell for that one. What else?"

"There is no warming table..."

"I will not be keeping foods under a lamp; they go out as they get cooked."

"And do you know how?"

"How to what?"

"Cook."

"I make a decent BLT, and my food handler's license is in the paperwork I submitted to you."

"Joy. Now, aside from the extinguisher, the trash can, the gloves, the cutting board, the soap, and the table, your site looks fairly suitable. Can you fix the deficiencies today?"

"Can I get an extinguisher, a trash can, some gloves, a cutting board, soap, and remove the table today? Yes."

"Very well, I will take you at your word."

Nero signed a sheet and gave her a copy.

"I will register your service with the city. What is the name of the business please?"

"Name?"

"Yes, Miss Olabode, the name of your restaurant. What will people say when they complain to me about the terrible tacos?"

"I'm not going to have tacos!"

The inspector pinched the bridge of his nose.

"Please. I do not have time for this. I have three other inspections to do this morning."

"It's not mor..."

Sam stopped at the glare that emanated from the man in front of her.

"I'm sorry, Nero, I hadn't thought about it. I was so wrapped up in cleaning..."

Nero sighed,

"Mister Amelo, if you please. And to make it simple, for now I will write u slash k. You may change it at your convenience. Please make it soon. It's the name the paperwork will reside under."

"Yes, Sir."

Sam felt as if she should lower her eyes respectfully...or maybe curtsy. She wound up just letting the inspector out the door.

"Insufferable man."

She stared around her. She was legal. She was licensed. She could serve food. She was in business.

10
All This Time

Sam didn't know much about weather. She knew that spring turned into summer, summer into fall, fall into winter. The change in this particular city, however, didn't seem to follow that pattern. One day it was summer. Then, just a few weeks later, it was the dead crack of winter. Seeing-your-breath kind of cold and everything. In those few weeks of summer she bought food, she made food, and she was even getting better at making said food. But nobody seemed interested in eating her food. She continued to waste money as the weather worsened. When she stood in the doorway, no one would talk to her or even look at her. Most of the people living in the area went so far as to cross to the other side of the street, which was irritating.

The only people who didn't were the kids who waited for the bus in front of her shop every morning. She didn't pay much attention to kids. They were kids. They never had any money and never stayed long enough to eat. A few of them parked themselves on the round counter outside the window, but she didn't have the heart to tell them to get off her lawn.

From what she observed, the kids were unusually silent. They didn't horse around as she had done when waiting for a bus at that age. The boys didn't chase the girls, grab their hair, or tease them. The girls didn't stand in bunches whispering, giggling, and sharing secret notes. These children stood, or sat, silently. It was kind of eerie. They almost didn't seem like children. They filed quietly and quickly onto the bus when it arrived choking and sputtering black smoke from its tailpipe.

Sam noticed as it got colder, very few of them arrived with many more clothes than they had in summer. They arrived with jackets in various states of disrepair, and Sam had no idea how they avoided freezing to death. One morning Sam was leaning against the door, taking advantage of the clean air sweeping in through the open door to try to wash out the terrible smell of burned chilis from a failed morning egg experiment. The kids arrived, one by one. The smell of snow tingled Sam's nose. One girl turned very slightly to look at Sam. Sam's heart dropped to see the circles under the girl's eyes. The child glanced past Sam into the restaurant. Her eyes were haunting. Hungry. She seemed to clutch her coat a little tighter before she turned away. The whole day, Sam couldn't get the look out of her head. The girl was with her when she swept, when she cooked lunch for herself, when she went upstairs to her sleeping bag.

The next morning Sam kept the place closed, the lights in the restaurant off. She sat under the upstairs front window which she opened a crack. She shivered in her sweater and listened as the children arrived at the bus stop. Next to the door on the counter, she had left cinnamon rolls in a cardboard box. No icing, but plenty of raisins. She had found with great pleasure that she was actually very good at baking.

"Jeannie. Look. Do you think she just threw those out?"

"I don't know, what are they?"

"Rolls. They smell good, and they're still warm."

"Do you think we should take one?"

"What if they're poisoned?"

"I don't care."

The last words were followed by sounds of chewing. More children arrived, and when Sam heard the bus leave she went down. The box had been cleaned out. All twenty rolls were gone. Not even crumbs in the bottom of the box. She smiled.

She kept doing it for another four days. On Friday she opened the door and was surprised to see the box still there, with all the food in it, but an old man was sitting next to it biting into one of the small toast sandwiches she had made with canned tuna and cheese. He froze and looked up at her when she stuck her head out the door. She looked up and down the street, and then at him. He stared at her, eyes wide. She tipped her head at him.

"You must be cold. Would you like some coffee with that sandwich?"

The man didn't say anything but nodded very slowly. She picked up the box and went inside, leaving the door open but noticed he didn't follow. She turned around and went back to the door.

"It's warm in here. Would you like to come in?"

He moved slowly, seeming to be unsure if she was actually inviting him or whether she was playing some kind of trick on him.

"It's ok, really. Oh...it's a bit chillier than I thought. I can almost see my breath in here. Come on in and sit by the fireplace; I'll turn it on."

The cost of gas flitted through her head, but she shoved the thought aside and sat him at a table. She settled the box on the table in front of him. The man dug through one of his scrappy layered coats, and he pulled an old paper cup from a ragged pocket and offered it to her. She smiled,

"No, no. I'll get you one of my mugs."

She filled a mug with coffee from the pot she kept on the stove and gave it to him.

"I've been leaving the food out there for the kids who get on the bus every morning, but they didn't show up today. I don't know why."

The man, who was looking at the rest of the sandwiches, looked down at the cup.

"Well, as long as they aren't here, we may as well enjoy these, right?"

Sam placed another one on a plate and put it in front of him. He looked at it for some time before reaching for it.

"I'm sorry. I...didn't know they were for someone else."

Sam shook her head, "It's no problem. The children weren't there, and I would hate for food to go to waste."

She took a sandwich for herself, and they sat companionably in front of the fireplace as it warmed up, the logs beginning to change from dark brown to a dull red. Sam relaxed into the heat.

"So, what's your name?"

"Eli."

"My name is Sam. It's nice to meet you, Eli."

Eli ate quietly, sipping his coffee. It was the closest Sam had been to company since the inspector had been there. It was nice to have someone else in the room. A long while later, Eli dug in his coat again, and she saw him slide a quarter over the table. She started to refuse it, then an inner feeling seized her by the middle. This man was offering up something he wanted to part with. It was all he could afford. Sam took the quarter.

"Thank you, Eli."

"You're welcome. I should git now. I have to go find some cans."

Sam watched him get up from the chair, drain the rest of the coffee, and set the mug down very gently. Then he walked out the door and down the street to her left.

Eli couldn't have been younger than sixty to look at him, with deep lines in his face, bright blue eyes, and wild gray hair stuffed under a faded, flat cloth cap. Sam turned that quarter over and over in her fingers, thinking very hard.

She had envisioned a busy little corner restaurant, people coming in for reasonably priced meals. Instead she had gotten nothing. She had taken out an ad in the paper. The neighborhood couldn't possibly have missed her cleaning up and opening, the signs in the windows, but not a single person walked in. Eli was the first customer she had ever had.

Sam took the quarter and placed it very carefully in the small frame she had found for her good luck dollar. She snapped the frame shut and hung it on the wall. The quarter was more precious to her than any other dollar she had ever made.

Maybe there was a better way of doing business in this particular neighborhood. One that was less demanding, less strict. It bore thinking about. The next Monday, the children were there. She decided that each weekday she wouldn't open until all the children left. It gave her a bit more time to herself in the morning.

11

Unexpected

Eli came in once in a while but not regularly. Somewhere he got a battered coffee cup. Sam allowed him to use it, but only if he let her wash it before he poured coffee into it. Customers had trickled in, one or two at a time. It just barely kept Sam afloat.

Sam and Eli were sitting quietly one afternoon. Sam was trying to decide how to make cheaper fare that would last longer without buying canned food when a stiff, angry matriarch marched in with one of the children from the bus stop in tow. Sam got the distinct impression a cyclone had just blown in, and a house was hovering over her head.

"You! My Dinah says that you have been leaving food outside your door, and she's been eating it!"

Sam blinked and opened her mouth, but the woman kept going.

"Food costs money!"

Sam nodded.

"We have enough debt! How *dare* you put us further into debt! I can't afford for Dinah to be eating at a *café* every morning! I'm not spending hundreds of dollars per week. This is ridiculous. It's rude! You are a scam artist, and I will report you!"

Sam's heart was beating wildly, and she kept taking little steps back as the woman yelled at her.

She finally stammered, "I...I'm sorry, ma'am. I didn't mean...I didn't know...I'm not expecting you to pay me!"

Silence. The woman looked confused.

"What?"

"Really. I...She...All of them. They looked...I'm sorry."

Sam's brain shut down on her. She didn't want to intimate that she pitied the children and offend the woman. She had just wanted to do the right thing.

"Well. What's done is done, and I certainly can't pay that much for food!"

The words stunned Sam. Food was one of the main considerations next to rent! It was necessary for life! You couldn't skimp on food!

"What can you pay?"

Sam had no idea how that had come out of her mouth. The woman looked at her incredulously. Sam gathered herself mentally and motioned to Eli who looked very tense and ready to flee at any second.

"Eli pays a quarter for food and coffee when he comes in. If I made your daughter food, how much would you pay me?"

"I...I don't know!"

"Ok. Well. I'll tell you what. The food in the mornings is free. I offer it to all the children. It's ...good advertising. They tell their friends, their friends tell parents, parents come and eat here. If your daughter wants lunch or dinner, send her with whatever you can afford, and I will feed her. I cannot promise it will be great, but it will be food. I will serve her the same amount anyone else gets."

The woman looked conflicted. Finally she raised her chin, said "Fine!" and turned around and stomped out. Dinah didn't say anything during the encounter. She followed her mother silently with wide eyes. Sam felt run over and confused. Eli looked up from his coffee.

"Could I have another cup, Sam?"

Sam shakily gathered Eli's mug and got him some more coffee. She got herself some too.

"Eli. Why didn't I think of this before?"

"They don't think of you do they?"

"What do you mean?"

"Nobody thinks of no one else until they need 'em. That woman needed someone to yell at. It weren't your fault you were the target. Mebbe it were a bad day at work. If she hadn't gotten angry at somethin', you never woulda crossed her mind."

"But if I had thought of offering them what they could pay, would they have come in sooner?"

"Nope."

"Oh. I'm confused."

"Sam. Think about it. People, they don't like me. That's 'cause people here is one step away from bein' me. They think if they don't look at me, they don't have to think about it. If they push me away from the garbage bin, then they gots some control over part of their life, right?"

"That makes ugly sense."

"They're jealous of you. Got light, got heat, got food. So much food you're givin' it away. They don't even want to look at you until they need you. For either me or you, we don't exist until they need us. The difference is, they don't need me at all."

Sam patted Eli on the shoulder. "I need you, Eli."

Sam spent most of the next day searching for ways to keep going. She was only a few weeks away from having to shut down unless she either cut costs or made some money. She decided to do a small amount of subtle espionage. She went back to the restaurant where she got the range and asked for the head chef. The sous-chef wrinkled his nose at her and left her waiting outside. She had to wait in the snow for at least twenty minutes before Louis appeared. She was trying to stomp some feeling into her toes when he did.

"Hi, Louis!"

"My God, Sam, come in before you catch your death!"

Louis whacked his sous-chef on the head as they passed.

"Don't ever leave this woman standing outside again! Heartless ruffian!"

Sam smiled to herself as she passed. She refrained from sticking out her tongue at the man. They settled into Louis' office, and he insisted on pouring her a coffee with brandy. It was very luxurious, and she took the time for a long moment to smell the coffee before she drank it.

"Ah, a woman after my own heart. A true appreciation for coffee."

"That's only because I burn mine."

"Well, what can I do for you Sam?"

"I wanted to do some work on my building, but I need some boxes—good, stiff, cardboard boxes. Would you happen to have any?"

"Oh, yes, we get so many we have to pay to have them taken away. You are welcome to as many as you want. Here, I'll show you where we store them."

They went through the back of the restaurant to a storage closet where packs of the cardboard boxes were tied up. Sam chose a small stack. They walked back through the kitchen.

"Thank you so much, Louis. It's hard to find clean cardboard."

"Yes. Cleanliness is next to godliness in the kitchen, isn't it?"

"Oh...say, do you use your kitchen scraps?"

Louis looked shocked,

"Sam! You aren't seriously that hard up for food that you would take garbage and serve it to customers!"

"No, no, I don't mean your garbage, Louis, I meant your ends and trimmings. Carrots, onions, potato peelings. Do you use them?"

"No...no, we don't. Why would you want our trimmings?"

"Well, frankly, I think they make good soup, Louis. You have organic produce. Organic produce in the pot produces better stock. I've been reading. I won't be able to avoid canned food forever, but if I can make good stock, I can produce large amounts of good soup as a staple for my menu."

Louis smiled, amused.

"Reading is good, Sam. It makes you a better cook. You have a fine idea. Give me one of those boxes."

Sam chose a small one, but Louis made her refold it and chose another one, strapping it into shape with packing tape. He swept a whole pile of various produce off the stainless prep table where his sous-chef was working. The sous-chef didn't even flinch.

"Oh Louis, I didn't mean your good produce!"

The sous-chef snorted. Louis took Sam by the arms.

"Sam, this is the discard pile. We run a restaurant that caters to investors, credit companies. These individuals do not want a spotted carrot in their dinner. André is the best sous-chef I have ever had. He can pick the perfect produce and happily toss all the rest in the garbage. You may have the discards. André?"

André rolled his eyes. "I understand, Louis. When...she...shows up, I let her in, I give her coffee, and then let her take all the discards home. Are we getting a puppy too?"

Sam giggled; she couldn't help it. "Thank you, Louis. This is very...very helpful."

Louis smiled, "When you are ready to learn about chocolate, come back and see me. You can apprentice with Michelle. She is an artist who will only flay you once every time you screw up."

As Sam was walking out, Louis leaned in close, "There is a diner over a few streets. They are not as fine as we are, but if you tell them Louis sent you, they will give you their trimmings too."

Sam dropped the extra boxes and hugged Louis with one arm. He pecked her on both cheeks, "You are a good woman. Stay that way."

12

Strapped

"Your bill is now overdue by four months, we have added non-payment fees, blah blah...your total is two hundred three dollars. Thank you for choosing...blah blah blah."

Sam made a tearing noise, as if ripping the statement in half, and waved the paper at the fireplace before putting it in her lap. She picked up the next envelope and expertly ripped the top off.

"Thank you for paying...wait a minute. What did I pay? Who is this? Who are you?"

Sam turned the envelope over. "Oh, insurance."

Sam held the sheet up, "I shall place it on the wall and immortalize it! I paid a bill!"

"Would you like me to pin that on the wall for you?"

Sam scrambled out of the wooden chairs she had lined up to sit on with her feet up. Her heart was pounding. Dinah smiled from the doorway. It was a tiny smile.

"Oh, Dinah. I'm sorry. I wasn't expecting you. What time is it?"

"It's...um...eight. Is it too late?"

"No no! I have soup and sandwiches. Is that ok?"

Dinah blinked, "Are you kidding me?"

Sam shook her head on her way to the kitchen. She picked up the soup pot ladle.

"I'm not kidding, why?"

Dinah moved in a bit farther. "Well, I don't usually eat dinner."

Soup slopped over the edge of the ladle onto Sam's hand. She yelped and dropped the ladle back into the pot.

Dinah leaped forward as Sam floundered with the kitchen sink handle.

"Damn!"

Sam bumped the hot water handle on.

"Not that one!" Dinah yelled and turned it off, then wrenched the cold water handle forward. Seizing Sam's hand in her own, she shoved the growing red welt under the cold water. Sam gritted her teeth as the sting grew, then numbed, then grew again.

"I don't know why I am even surprised anymore," Sam muttered.

They stood there for a minute and then Dinah turned off the water and grabbed a clean rag. She dabbed Sam's hand.

"You're pretty good with wounds."

"Two little sisters. What are you surprised about?"

"Oh, the fact that kids here don't eat dinner. I'm not used to the thought of anyone's not eating. Here, I'll get the soup."

"No I can get it."

Sam grinned, "Careful, the ladle bites."

Dinah filled a bowl while Sam flipped two pieces of bread on the griddle and spooned a generous portion of tuna on both slices of bread.

"Um, Miss Olabode?"

"Yes, Dinah?"

"Can I have two more sandwiches?"

Sam shrugged, "Sure, I don't see why not."

She flipped two more slices onto the griddle and spooned tuna onto them.

"Dinah?"

"Yeah?"

Sam looked at her, "Why do you keep looking outside?"

Dinah looked startled, "I'm not! Why would you say that?"

"Dinah. Your face is turning red. I'm a trained security observer. I spent two years learning how to tell what a person was going to do before they did it. Why are you looking outside?"

Dinah fell silent and stirred the bowl of soup with a spoon slowly. A long moment passed while Sam waited patiently.

"She couldn't pay."

"Who?"

"My friend."

Dinah's voice was so low Sam had to strain to hear her.

"Dinah, did she get breakfast?"

"She doesn't take the same bus I do."

"You mean, your friend is sitting outside in the freezing cold waiting for you to finish and bring her something?"

Sam handed the spatula to Dinah. "Put those together, don't let them burn!"

"Wait! She'll only run!"

"I can catch her, Dinah."

Dinah watched helplessly as Sam opened the door to the restaurant.

Sam saw a flicker of motion to her right as a figure in a jean jacket fled. She sprinted forward and grabbed the jean jacket in her hand. "Stop! I'm not going to hurt you!"

Suddenly Sam was left with only the jacket in her hand and watched the teenager sprint away. She decided not to pursue the child and returned to the kitchen.

"Dinah, I wish you had told me she was out there."

"She just wanted something to eat. I thought..."

"Oh, it's not your fault. I should have had you go out there. Dinah. Let me make this plain. I am not angry with you. If your friend wants to share your dinner, then fine. I don't mind that. I just don't want her standing out in the icy weather while you are in here eating comfortably, okay?"

Dinah finished eating the sandwich and soup and slid a dollar across the table. Sam took it.

"Thank you, Dinah. And thank your mother. And remember what I said."

Sam handed the jacket and the extra sandwiches now wrapped in plastic to Dinah.

Dinah looked at Sam for a long minute.

"And call me Sam. It's my name."

"Okay, Sam."

Sam cleaned up for the night and put the soup in the fridge. She bit her lip and wondered about canning. Would she need to once people started paying her? She had stocked up on a lot of canned items already, and they would keep her going awhile. She would have to shut down her mobile phone the next day. She didn't have two hundred to pay the bill, and they would shut it down anyway. She could still use Wi-Fi for her phone or computer when she had to by sitting next to a place that had it. She could even afford a cup of coffee at a coffee shop now and then to use it legitimately.

She stretched the hand she had burned. It wasn't bad. An uneasy rumble in her stomach and a burning smell in her nostrils warned her a moment before the memory hit.

Flames. Explosions. Blood. Screams.

Sam closed her eyes. It's not real.

Tears. Vomit. More blood. Blood, blood, blood.

But it's not real.

Sam's brain refused to believe it. She opened her eyes when the sounds in her head stopped. The feelings continued. She was being attacked. She was going to die.

She was on her knees next to the leg of the prep table. Her nails clenched into her palms.

She struggled up the stairs, her legs aching painfully. The bottle of Xanax defeated her. She sat on her sleeping bag pounding it on the floor stupidly and yelling at it. She finally fell asleep with the tablets strewn on the floor next to her after the bottle broke open.

"Make it stop. Please make it stop. Go away. Please stop..."

13

Everyone Has a Place

The day started out with graffiti. Not the good kind. Sam surveyed the spray-painted...was it a G? An A? R, there was definitely an R. Maybe...GRR!...on her windows.

She scratched her head and looked around. Just...people. Of course, who the hell would just stick around waiting for her to discover the graffiti? Maybe someone owned this street other than the city?

"So the mob is waiting for me."

She realized how silly she sounded. She hadn't seen hide nor hair of anything she could construe as "gang" activity in this place. No little old ladies being knocked over for their purses. Nobody snatching cigarettes off trucks. Wait, that was the Mafia. Maybe she could convince the graffiti artist to move his work a little further down to the space that didn't have windows. She went inside to get a bucket of soapy water.

She cleaned off just the windows and surveyed the damage. The spatters that occurred on the wood around the windows looked a bit artistic without the windows being affected. Spatters of red and yellow, a little purple. It actually gave the side of the building some color.

She smiled wickedly to herself and went inside. She got out a sheet of paper from her briefcase and a marker. When she was done she taped the sheet up on the window from the inside. Then she got to work for the day.

The sign read:

"I wouldn't mind some unicorns. Thx - Sam"

She was briskly stirring a pot of soup when it occurred to her with some suddenness that she had not yet named the place.

"Oh, dear."

She let the pot warm up by itself on a low flame while she paced.

The Club. Sand Wiches R Us. The Soup Bowl...no, that was taken. Sam's Place. That last one appealed to her most. Simple, descriptive. But what if people thought she sold other things?

"Sam's place."

"SAM'S place..."

"Hm... Sam's PLACE!"

"It sounds good," an unfamiliar voice answered her.

"Oh...sorry, I didn't hear you come in."

Three men stood in the entryway.

"Oh, look at you, you're all cold, come on in and sit down! Here I'll turn on the fireplace."

She turned on the gas while the three scruffy-looking men got settled by the heat.

One of them turned to her after removing his gloves, "So, do you have a menu?"

Sam shifted a little uncomfortably, "Ah...sorry, no. I haven't had many customers, so I've had to cut down quite a bit. I have soup started, I can make you cold or grilled sandwiches, I have milk, water, and coffee."

"Um...soup and coffee sounds great, thanks."

Sam dished up three bowls of soup and snagged three cups on her way over to the table. She filled them from the coffee pot on the stove and started a new pot.

"Anything else? Water?"

"No, no, thanks, just a bit of something to keep going, that's all we need."

"Okay, then, just let me know."

Sam wandered back into the kitchen and scraped the already clean griddle for something to do, then hovered by the window, unsure what to do with herself with actual customers in the eating section of the restaurant.

Twenty minutes later she heard clinks signifying the end of the soup.

"Would you guys like some more soup?"

The three looked at each other with what seemed to be uneasy expressions, "Uh, no, thanks. How much do we owe you?"

Sam smiled, "What you can afford, gentlemen. It's how it works here. You get what you get and pay what you can."

"I...don't understand."

Sam self-consciously brushed at her jeans, "Well, this is not a high-class neighborhood, gentlemen, and I have come to the realization that if I demanded prices as high as those ten or twenty miles away, I would never get anyone to buy food here, so I am asking people to pay what they can afford. If you have a dollar on you, pay a dollar. If you have five, then it's five."

"How do you stay in business?"

"I'm actually pretty close to the edge, but I think everyone here is."

One of the men slapped the man who had spoken on the shoulder, "See? I told you Dinah wasn't lyin'!"

The man stood up and removed his hat, "Well...Sam is it? I have to admit I don't have any money on me. I'm very sorry. We, I, expected you to be some kinda scam."

Sam shrugged, "C'est la vie, Monsieur."

"I'm sorry?"

"Oh, it is what it is. Such is life. You got some soup and coffee; I'll still be here tomorrow."

As they stood and put on their coats, one man pulled a five from his wallet and gave it to her.

"I think you should expect some people for lunch tomorrow. If the soup is hot and the sandwiches generous, they'll be happy to pay you a bit more."

Sam took the five-dollar bill, "Thank you. You guys are welcome back any time."

They each took her hand and shook it as they left. She realized she hadn't asked their names. She put her head outside the door and wrinkled her nose as the air bit sharply,

"Hey, can I ask your names?"

"I'm Joe; this is Phillip and Mark."

"Mark, Phillip, and Joe. It's nice to meet you."

They walked away from her down the street and she wondered if those were their real names. The rest of the day was quiet. No one else came in. She finished off some soup, herself, and stared at the door in the back of the room. She couldn't afford a locksmith. She took out a paperclip and a nail file and fiddled with the lock. It didn't open, and she felt stupid. She didn't even know how it worked! She blinked at herself and then went to the door that led to the storeroom. It locked and had a key. She removed the doorknob and spent the next few hours fiddling, trying to figure out how the lock came out. She finally managed to slide the lock out of the handle and studied it carefully. It would take more than a paperclip, she decided. She needed some type of hook. Maybe a hanger bent at one end. She discovered a hanger was too thick. It needed to be flat. A flat metal piece hooked at one end. Suddenly she looked at the fireplace and dropped the lock on the table.

"I am an idiot. A complete and utter *moron*! How could I have not realized...ah!"

She took her screwdriver to the back door and within a minute the handle was in her hand. She pushed on the connector rod so the door opened.

"Sometimes...sometimes, POW, right to the moon, Alice!"

She pushed the door and found it was wedged against something or dragging. She pushed harder, and it took quite a bit of force before she managed to open it enough to squeeze through. There were boxes that had been piled, but fell against the door. She cleared them away and surveyed the twenty by thirty extra feet of space. It was concrete, covered in moss and algae. It was freezing cold, having no heating source back in this area. It was a very odd space. It was outdoors, but the top was covered by some type of tarp so the snow and rain couldn't get down here. Plenty of dirt though. There was a door at the far end but it had been covered by the facade on the outside. She shivered and went back inside for a sweater.

She spent the rest of the day rifling through some of the boxes. A lamp, silverware, pots, some plates and cups, a few pictures in frames. She brought the pots in. They were bigger than her own, real restaurant-sized types. She stuck them in the sink and closed the door. What was she going to do with that space? She shrugged and looked at her loaf of bread. Singular. Loaf. She sighed and struggled into her coat. Joe had suggested that she better have "generous" sandwiches. If there were more than just one showing up, one loaf of bread with ten slices left wouldn't cut the mustard. She groaned inwardly at her own joke and locked up, dragging her ten-speed out the door.

It was a quiet ride in the early evening. The traffic wasn't bad until she hit the larger parts of the city. Even then it still seemed kind of empty compared to what she had been used to in her life.

Three loaves of bread, a load of bologna, and a bag full of tins of some type of fish for fifty cents each, and she was headed back home. She stopped at a light and looked around at some of the regular family-sized homes. Light, warmth, television. Wow. TV. She hadn't watched TV since the motel. The cold urged her to get home quickly.

14

Convincing

The windows mocked Sam with their colorful swirls and paint smears. Sam moved the bucket filled with hot soapy water forward. Wringing out the sponge, she lifted it tiredly but stopped just shy of the window. She tipped her head and lowered the sponge which dripped a bit. The splash of orange in front of her looked…She stepped back further.

"Oh look! A Unicorn!"

She raised and lowered the sponge, feeling like an idiot. She was loath to get rid of it, but it was graffiti; still, she *had* asked for a unicorn!

She sighed and dumped the soapy water out in the gutter. It would stay. For now. The swirls of psychedelic orange and green and purple depicted a horned creature dancing amidst dots of white.

"The Psychedelic Unicorn…Nope, people would never step foot in here. Maybe when I'm rich I'll open a coffee shop."

Sam noticed marks on the handle of the door with dismay. Someone had tried to get in. Obviously someone without skill. She felt very uneasy. She couldn't afford a decent door with a decent lock. Couldn't even afford windows. These were those flimsy double-paned things, but the door was still a single-paned door.

She just knew she could feel the warmth seep out of the room through the cracks, but that wasn't as big a concern as the door lock.

It turned out to be a good day. A very good day! Men and women trickled in almost constantly from late morning through noon. Few of them met her eye, but they somehow had heard that they could pay what they had. She served; they paid. A few were fairly generous, covering their lunch and someone else's. At the end of the day Sam had well over a hundred dollars. She had also run out of lettuce. She served the last few sandwiches of cheap bologna with just mayo.

"Sorry guys, no more lettuce."

She got a few shrugs but no protests. The last customer to leave kept staring at her as if he wanted to say something. He finally spoke up when he got up to leave.

"If I gave you money before, could you make something I could take with me?"

"You mean like take-out?"

"No, something simple like a bag. You know something I could stick in my backpack before work?"

"Oh. Yeah, sure. If you like."

"How much?"

"How much food could I give you?"

"How much would you charge me?"

Sam smiled tiredly, "How much do you have?" She wondered how many times she'd have to say it before they would believe her.

The man frowned, "I don't feel comfortable…"

Sam abruptly sat down in a chair in front of the fireplace, exhausted.

"Come here."

The man hesitated and she snapped, "Come here and sit down, for God's sake!"

He glanced at the door, but turned and sat down across from her. She placed the hundred dollars on the table in front of her. A rather large pile of ones and fives.

"Do you know why I made this money today?"

"Because you gave people food?"

"I made it because I understood that if I tell people, 'Pay me this,' I give people a line in the sand. This far and no further, I say! If I tried to do that, people would never consider walking in here again. I did that for weeks before you guys walked in here today. It didn't work. I'm on the edge, because I did that. Today I have made more money than in all the weeks since I opened. If I change that now, all those people who came in here today will say, 'Oh look, it was all a trick! She didn't mean it! Screw her; we won't go back there.'"

She stared across the table at the man, who wore a fairly thick jacket liner that didn't match the jacket over it.

"When I say, what will you pay me? I mean it. It costs me just under seventy five cents to serve a bowl of soup and a sandwich. If you pay fifty cents, but the next person pays me a dollar, I break even. Some people only take the soup. I am basically gambling that people are going to give me enough to profit. I don't need a lot of profit, just enough. Today it seems that my business model paid off. If this happens every day, five days a week, I will make enough to live. Now, what will you pay me to make you a packed lunch every day? Keep in mind that I can only give you what I get. It's not fancy; it's just food."

"Lady, when you work hours cleaning bricks in a construction site, then more hours in an old age home, then more hours taking out garbage at a supermarket, and eat once in the whole day, you don't care what you eat as long as it's edible."

"Sam."

"What?"

"Please call me Sam. It's my name."

"Oh. Okay. Um, how about two dollars and fifty cents?"

Sam scooped up her hundred dollars.

"Done! I'll go get some paper bags today."

The man started out and turned again,

"Hey, Sam?"

"Yes?"

"My name is Lawrence."

"Nice to meet you, Lawrence. Tell your friends about me."

Lawrence chuckled as he left.

15

Plants From Hell

Sam stood in front of the vegetables in the store with dismay. The price of the lettuce had gone up. A lot.

"Two dollars and ninety-nine cents per head? Are you kidding me?"

A woman stocking nearby smiled ruefully at her, "Yeah, I know, outrageous, right? We changed over to a supplier from another state after the one we used was shut down with Listeria recalls all over the place. Safety first! But we have to pay more to get it here."

Sam sighed and left without the lettuce. She searched other markets, but they were all too expensive. One smart ass quipped, "You could always grow your own."

The thought percolated all day as Sam purchased meat that was close to its expiration date. She had the thought of chopping it up and making some type of conglomerated meat loaf with it. She brought it back to the restaurant and began experimenting. Her thought kept turning to the counter out in front of the restaurant and her idea for filling it with soil. She thought about filling little pots and putting them on the walls inside the restaurant. Plants would take away from the ugliness of the wallpaper.

Sam stared at the oven while the meat baked. It was a blended mixture of pork, chicken, and beef rib meat. It needed lettuce. Sam envisioned little lettuce cups growing all over the restaurant. It made her laugh, but she wondered if it wasn't such a bad idea. Plants needed light, and there was lots of light from the windows.

For a moment she had a vision of a jungle overtaking the walls of the restaurant and Mister Nero beating back piles of greenery to get into the room. Children peeking out of vines. No: children *swinging* from vines that had grown from the ceiling!

Sam was giggling madly when the kitchen timer went off. She opened the oven and stared in dismay at the grease practically overflowing the pan with the lump of meat in the middle.

"Crap."

She spooned out some of the grease into another pot before removing the pan. She ignored the stench of burning fat from the inevitable drips on the bottom of the oven . She removed the loaf to a rack and let all the grease drip off it before wrapping it up and putting it in the fridge. She stared at the grease, wondering what to do with it. She was loath to throw it out. Nothing was discardable in this game. She heard the door open and looked up from the pan of grease.

The city inspector stared at her expectantly. "You don't have any customers."

"Mister Nero, it is eight o'clock. It's not exactly the Compte de Triomphe. Nobody's lining up to make reservations."

Nero's expression didn't change, but his one blink spoke volumes.

"Do you mean the Prix de l'Arc de Triomphe?"

"What?"

"The...oh never mind. It's a famous racecourse."

LINDA DEAN

"It's not a restaurant?"

"No."

"Oh."

"So I was intending to see your dinner service. But it appears you don't have one."

"I don't usually. Fridays are exceptionally quiet here. The last person left an hour ago."

"And the name of the business?"

"Oh, that. You know, I usually have a big lunch crowd now. Maybe you could come back on Monday and see it!"

"Miss Olabode."

"Sam!"

Nero covered his face with his hand.

"Oh Nero, I'm sorry.."

"Mister Amelo please."

"Then why won't you call me Sam?"

Nero took a seat quietly and stared at her. Sam fidgeted.

"Miss Olabode, I require a professional atmosphere in which to do my job. I do not use first names, nicknames, baby talk, or any other unnecessary character mechanism in which to advance the purpose of my visits."

Sam sighed and poured the last of the coffee into two cups and sat across from Nero. He sipped warily and then visibly shivered.

"What is IN this? Tar? Yuck, there are gristly bits...asphalt??"

Sam shrugged, "It's eight o'clock on a Friday. My coffee is made in a stove top percolator."

For a moment they sipped coffee and stared at each other.

"Nero, your job is fairly simple. You come into a place, you look around, you judge people, you go back to your office, do some paperwork, and then you're done. You don't create anything; you don't risk anything. I certainly don't see you in the neighborhood when you aren't on the job. I don't see you at any of the supermarkets or walking around downtown. Do you even have a life?"

Nero drank the rest of the coffee in one gulp.

"I do not. But I take exception to the accusation that I do not create anything. I create safety and security. I create the paperwork trail that proves good businesses are good. I also create the paperwork trail that allows the legal system to keep track of bad businesses. Licensing is not as simple as you seem to think. I spend a third of my money on clothing so that people will take me seriously. This job is about image almost all of the time. I have to command authority the second I walk in the door of a business I am inspecting. I also don't fraternize with those whom I have a business relationship with. That's every business in this neighborhood. That's why I don't have a life. I don't take chances, because doing that would take chances with other people's safety."

Sam was taken a bit aback.

"So what's your favorite color?"

"Green."

"Favorite dessert?"

"Cheesecake."

"Ahh, so you're a human being. I do apologize."

"You...are...hilarious."

"You spend a third of your money on clothes? That's..."

"It's a personal choice."

Sam shrugged. Nero got up and handed the coffee cup to her.

"I will see you Monday at eleven a.m. I will expect you to have a name for me. If you do not, I will make sure your business is permanently known as u slash k."

"Oh. Okay. I was wondering, what are the rules about plants?"

"Plants?"

"I was thinking of hanging some plants."

"As long as the plants are kept dust free and there is no mold in the soil, there is nothing I would be concerned about."

"That's good to know."

"Well, goodnight."

"Goodnight, Mister Amelo."

16
Delivery Girl

"Hey..."

Sam turned around and stared.

"Oh...James!"

The scruffy-looking boy seemed a bit taller and wore a pair of coveralls. He also looked a bit humble.

"Well, don't stand in the door, come on in. Do you want some coffee? I know it's warming up, but...you know, everyone could use a decent cup of coffee."

James walked in a few steps, "No, but thanks. I was wondering..."

Sam nodded encouragingly.

"Look. I'm sorry about that...comment I made."

Sam knocked lightly on a table. Sometimes it was better to just give commands to the awkward.

"James Sutton. Sit down."

The boy sat. He was obviously uncomfortable. Sam sat across from him.

"Talk."

"If you hadn't given me that car, I wouldn't have gotten a job."

"James, I don't need a car I can't use."

"The tow truck driver would have given you four hundred for it."

"I didn't need four hundred dollars; I needed to get rid of the car."

"Well, if you hadn't given me the car, I wouldn't have been able to show my boss that I could tear down an engine."

"You tore down the engine?"

"I had to prove that I could fix the crack."

"You *fixed* it?"

"Kind of. I was able to weld the crack in the block, but one of the pistons is fused. I can't fix that."

"So…why did you weld the crack?"

"So I could prove I could do it. Bud wasn't going to let me do it on one of his customer's cars."

"Bud?"

"Yeeess?"

"Seriously. Why am I ever surprised?"

"Surprised by what?"

Sam laughed with a snort, "A car mechanic named *Bud*? It's like every show I ever watched as a kid. Some grease monkey with a wrench and delusions of grandeur calls himself Bud 'cause he can't pronounce his real name of Bartholomew. Ass-crack all hanging out of his pants when he bends over. The joke practically writes itself."

James blinked, "So you think all mechanics are like that? Like some dumb jock?"

After a moment James shrugged and continued, "Bud has a master's degree from MIT."

Sam went quiet all of a sudden and stopped laughing. She realized she'd fallen for the same trap that she judged others on. She flushed in embarrassment.

"Oh, well put like that it seems a little...no...*really* bad. I'll, ah, have to watch out for that."

Sam shuffled her feet uncomfortably, "So is the apology all you came in for?"

James lost his confident demeanor and looked at his shoes.

"Um, no. Could you...Um, crap."

Sam waited patiently. James took a deep breath and started over in a rush, "I wanted to ask if you could bring my grandmother some food while I'm working. She's really frail. She fell down and broke her hip a while ago, and she can't walk more than like ten feet right now. I don't want her to try to stand up to cook. She's taken care of me for a long, long time, and I just feel like I owe her, you know? Since I can't afford a whole lot, Bud told me to come down here and talk to you."

"James, I would be happy to bring your grandmother some food."

"Great, I'll let her know. Here's the address."

Sam watched James leave. Her brow furrowed a little. The next day she packed up a sandwich into some plastic wrap and took a bottle of orange juice with her. She knocked carefully and then realized that she hadn't asked James what his grandmother's name was. She stared at the door before she knocked again. She felt odd. Was she really a delivery girl? She had never even delivered pizza as a teenager. She knocked. Boldly.

"Hi there! It's Sam! I have lunch for you!"

She was a little concerned when there was no response. She turned the doorknob and walked in with a smile on her face hoping she wouldn't scare the old lady senseless.

Then her military training took over. She froze before she processed the scene. There was a man with a knife. He was six feet tall with a tattered tan leather jacket, a black shirt spattered with paint, faded Levi cowboy-cut jeans with the belt loops cut off, and solid black rubber-soled work shoes. Stubbled hair that looked like it had been shaven badly, beard growth, and blue eyes. Large ears. The knife was a Ka-Bar, Desert Storm variety. The jacket had several lumps that could hold any number of items.

In front of the man stood James. James had sweat on his face. He stood in front of his grandmother, who sat in a chair; her cane had fallen next to the chair. She was gripping the chair with both hands very tightly. James seemed like he was attempting to reason with the man.

"You have to give me the money, John."

"You don't understand. I don't know who. you. are. Please. Just leave. My grandmother and I don't have any money. My job hasn't even paid me my first check yet!"

Sam prayed that James didn't take his eyes off the man. They seemed locked in the grip of each other's eyes. This was good. She walked forward. Ten feet, Five feet, Two feet. Then Sam's heart froze. The man looked at her.

"Hi there. I'm Sam. I brought lunch for *James's* grandmother."

The man reached in his left pocket with his left hand and brought out a gun. It was a 9 mil. Beretta. Standard Navy issue. It had deep scratches where the manufacture number would normally reside. James grabbed the gun.

The only thing Sam could hear at that moment was her own breath. Her ears shut out the sounds of James grunting, the man swearing. It all faded into silence. One breath. Two breaths. Then Sam had her hand on James's hand. She wrenched the gun away with a twist. The man reached for his other pocket. She repositioned the weapon, pointed, and fired.

There was just as much blood as she remembered. She lowered the gun. James opened and closed his mouth. The man's eyes were still open. She knelt and checked his pulse. Nothing. Sam saw James's lips moving.

"You shot him. You shot him!"

One breath. Two breaths. Sound came rushing back at Sam.

Sam looked at James's grandmother. She knelt next to her. "Are you okay?"

The old woman nodded shakily. Sam turned to James. She was careful to speak gently but firmly.

"James. Get your grandmother a blanket."

Seconds later James returned with a blanket. They tucked it around his grandmother.

Sam took hold of James's shoulders.

"James. This is very important. The police are going to come."

"The police, oh God, he was…he was…"

Sam gave him a little shake. "*James*. Listen to me."

James pulled his eyes back to Sam's face.

"James. The police are going to come. They will handcuff us and take us to the station. Is there anyone who can take care of your grandmother?"

"No…just me…"

James's voice whined in his abject terror.

"Ok. I will have the police call…someone. James. You have to listen carefully. Do not say anything to the police. Do you understand?"

"Don't…what?"

"James. I want you…to stay silent. Don't say anything, no matter what they ask, no matter what they say. Don't. Say. Anything. Do you understand? You have to say it. You have to tell me you understand."

Sam finally got James to say he understood. She opened the door wide, took the gun apart, and placed it on the floor.

She had James help his grandmother into her bedroom very carefully. They tucked her up with plenty of blankets.

"What's her name?" Sam whispered to James.

"Ellie," he whispered back.

"Ellie," Sam said. "I know this is scary. I will have someone come to help you as soon as I can. Okay? Your grandson will be back very, very quickly."

Ellie couldn't do anything but stare at her helplessly. Sam went back to the living room.

"James. Empty your pockets onto the table. All of them. Right now. Do you remember what I said?"

"When the police come, put your hands up, don't make any threatening moves. Don't say anything. Do you understand?"

"I understand, Sam."

"Good boy."

Very soon the sirens came down the street. Too soon.

The rest was a haze. Police yelling. Handcuffing. She thought they knelt on her back. She didn't care. They led her to a car, a different car than James's. She hoped and hoped that James did as she said.

Then she was in a small cell. She was by herself. She curled up on the bench, and tears dripped down her nose onto the floor. The blood stayed with her.

17

Jail

Sam had a longer wait than expected. She'd been fed and given standard-issue gray coveralls and a health kit that included soap, a washcloth, and a toothbrush with toothpaste. Then she was left to her own devices. Nobody spoke to her. After she had slept, she created a comforting routine for herself. A small amount of exercise, eat whatever food was given to her, wash, then sit quietly and think. She wanted to sort out the conflicting angry emotions before she had to appear before anyone.

Her thoughts were not kind. She found she couldn't remember the face of the man she'd shot. It was strange, as if he was there, but not there. With great reluctance she decided to think back further and test her memories. She took a firmer seat on the bench, sitting up instead of slouching, both feet flat on the floor.

Her team had been ordered to create a safe zone in a dusty village. The village was a major weapon trafficking hub. In order to infiltrate the area, they would have to remove a minor leader who had a penchant for selling local children to fund his activities. Sam and her team had lain for two days on a hilltop waiting for him to take his usual walk out into the scrub. With great pleasure she had been the one to place him fully in the sight of her weapon.

"Go," came the almost inaudible whisper from the team leader, and she had squeezed the trigger. A vicious explosion of excited joy washed over her. She remembered clearly the man's choppy hair, his large nose, his deep walnut-colored eyes, and that chin that tilted arrogantly. She remembered his surprised expression and the hole that appeared in his head. Even as he began to fall, his hand twitched upward, but it was too late.

The memory was completely clear. She remembered the man's name, his profile, the fact that he had no family that would care to search for him. Sam blinked and took a deep breath. There were other targets, other places, that she remembered with the same clarity. Yet, when she tried to think about the man in the apartment. all she got was a mixture of confusion and guilt. A blurry memory of movement with only moments of clarity. Why? Was it just the human tendency to remember specific points with clarity? Was she even remembering correctly? A tremor ran through her.

Sam stood up and brushed her teeth, then stretched to relieve the pent-up energy that was giving her cramps. There was no way to know what time of day it was. She didn't even know how long she had slept. The tiny room seemed to press in on her, but she stretched again to take away the feeling, forcing the claustrophobic tendency back. She settled onto the bench again and began playing a number game with herself that would keep her mind occupied without stirring up dark and angry emotions. She had to keep control. If she had a panic attack here, it would be a disaster.

Panic attacks. They hit without warning. There was no reason or rhyme to their coming and going. Sometimes she could think back on her military experience with fondness. Other times, just the thought of getting into a military transport or getting a can of green beans caused her to think that people were going to kill her.

Green beans. That day in the store when she had no idea what a panic attack was, that was the worst day ever. Just standing there in the supermarket on a vacation day picking up cans of vegetables, she thought she heard boots. She looked around. No one there. She picked up another can and froze. A tingling sensation of terror ran down her spine, and she found she couldn't move. The sound of boots walking toward her froze her in place. She kept thinking "It isn't real!" Then she started to doubt. Was it real? She thought she was going crazy. Hallucinations made her sure they were right behind her with guns drawn, aimed at her head. Tears sprang to her eyelids. The store faded away, and she closed her eyes, convinced beyond a shadow of a doubt, she was going to die. Her heart raced. She had faced real death half a dozen times with more aplomb than this! It wasn't until she had made an appointment with a doctor that she learned she had suffered something called a panic attack.

It was a terrible prospect. Every time it happened it removed her from the real world and plunged her into a paralyzing place where fear ruled with an iron hand. She had no control. The doctors told her she wasn't the only one. Many people who had been through terrible experiences had panic. People who were raped, people who were beaten, people living in war zones, even people who had been humiliated or robbed.

"It is the mind's way of trying to protect us, to keep us from getting into those situations again. In any case where the mind feels threatened, it sends a flood of hormones through the body telling you there is danger. You interpret this as real danger. It's very confusing, because it may seem to have nothing to do with the situation you are currently in. It's like setting off an alarm clock at random intervals, and it seems like the alarm can't be shut off."

And that was panic. Luckily Sam had gained some control. Some. And the medication helped, as did discussions with people who could help sort out things in her head. It didn't just go away though, and Sam hated the fact that she felt weak for falling apart.

After a day, Sam began to feel more than just the guilt and

confusion from the memories of the shooting. Weren't they going to question her? It was obvious she had shot him. What was going on? Why wouldn't they talk to her? Food appeared at intervals, but the police made no eye contact. They merely left her in the cell, which to her own judgment was their "drunk tank."

Were they going to turn her over to the state prosecutor? But they had to charge her first.

Didn't they?

She was handcuffed for her interview, which was short, but telling. Her interviewer was a man in his forties. His hair was speckled with gray but immaculately clean, trimmed, and combed. Unlike the officers, he wore a suit. It was well tailored to fit him. Sam took note that this was a detail-oriented investigator. He did not smile and kept to the point. He asked her name, her social security number. For all intents and purposes it was an interrogation. She received short, noncommittal responses to her own questions. She spoke only of the facts of what happened, nothing of motivations. She displayed no emotion. Days later when Sam finally found herself in the courtroom, she sat uncomfortably for a very long time. It was a tiny courtroom—no furniture in it but two tables in front of the judge's desk. James was nowhere to be seen. An hour passed, and then the judge came in. The bailiff announced him, and Sam started to stand, but the guard pushed her back in her seat.

"Not you. And keep your hands in your lap or on the table."

Sam was confused. The judge spent long minutes shuffling through papers.

"This hearing is an arraignment for...Lara...Olamad?"

"Larou Olabode, your honor."

"Miss Olabode. How do you plead?"

"I do not have a plea, your honor."

"Oh really? Why not?"

"I have not been provided with legal representation. I have also not been accused or charged, your honor."

The judge sighed heavily. He looked sour, as if he wished she hadn't mentioned that.

"I took the opportunity to do some preliminary background checks on you, Miss Olabode. It appears that the only thing I could find was that you have military service."

Sam didn't say anything.

"I believe I was a little more than surprised when I received a call from the Department of Defense."

Sam didn't say anything. A quiet moment passed.

"Would you happen to know anything about that?"

Sam felt a nudge. The guard glared at her.

"I have not been provided with legal representation, your honor."

"The Department of Defense seemed to make it quite clear that they did not approve of this research. They also did not approve of our questioning you."

Sam didn't say anything.

"So I dug a little further."

Sam didn't say anything. The guard nudged her.

"I have not been provided with legal representation...Legal representation, your honor."

"Yes. So you said. Apparently the Department of Defense objected to *that* research even more."

The judge stared very hard at Sam. She kept her eyes on the table.

"Miss Olabode. You are clearly an honored veteran of the military forces. You have no outstanding warrants or complaints against you. There is very little reason to believe that your actions were anything other than defensive. I choose to release you from custody. Guard, remove the hand and ankle cuffs. I will be ordering a continuing investigation into this matter. Stay within the physical limits specified on your paperwork."

Sam looked up at the judge, "Your honor, may I ask a question?"

"I am extremely tempted to say no. I am, however, impressed with your ability to hold your own tongue in my courtroom; so yes."

"The boy. James Sutton? May I ask what happened to him?"

"What do you know about Mister Sutton, Miss Olabode?"

Sam sighed and looked at the table. The judge banged his gavel on the block. It sounded impatient.

"This session is adjourned."

Sam rubbed her wrists and stood up.

"Miss Olabode."

"Yes, your honor?"

"He was released."

"Thank you."

The judge left the room, and Sam walked through the small courthouse to a desk near the exit to retrieve her belongings.

When she got to the restaurant, she was mildly surprised to see James waiting for her.

"Hey."

"Well. Hey."

"They kept you a long time. They wouldn't let me in. What happened?"

Sam opened the door, "I was going to ask you the same question, James."

James followed her in. She cursed the fact she had no coffee ready and put some water on to heat. She wished she could just kick him out and go take a shower, but she needed to know what happened.

"I swear, it wasn't my fault!"

"James. Just start from the beginning."

"When they took me?"

"No. Before that guy showed up."

"Okay. I was at work. I had a break, and I decided to check on my Gran."

"Is she ok?"

"Yeah, she's okay. She's still pretty scared, but she's ok. Anyway, I decided to check on her and went home. There was a knock at the door, and I thought it was you. When I opened it, this guy just stormed in, slammed the door behind him and shoved a knife at me. He wanted my money. I gave him the ten dollars I had in my pocket, but he wanted more. He kept insisting there was more! He kept calling me John. I didn't know what to do. When he made a move toward my Gran, I got in between them. Then you came in."

"James. You've never been in trouble before, have you?"

"No."

"Well. It's not over. We will still be questioned, I'm sure."

"They tried all night to get me to say something. They threatened to take my Gran away and everything."

"Did they send an advocate in with you?"

"A what?"

"A child advocate. James, was there anyone else in there besides you and the police?"

"No. Why?"

Sam reached for the pot that was now whistling and poured the water through the coffee filter and grounds. She watched it drip into the coffee pot.

"You did exactly what you were supposed to, James. I'm glad you did."

"You thought I'd break, didn't you?"

"Yes. I did. I was very worried."

"I'm tougher than they are. Those bastards can rot in hell before they'll get anything out of me."

Sam tried not to smile. She was almost successful.

"As I said James, it's not over. I will make sure that they assign you a child advocate before you are questioned again."

"I'm not a child!"

Sam lost her smile and frowned at him as she poured out two cups of coffee and gave him one.

"James Sutton, you are an idiot."

"What the hell is that supposed to mean?"

"You dropped out of school to go work at a mechanic's shop to take care of your Gran. While that is admirable in theory, you are being extremely shortsighted, aka stupid."

"How do you know I dropped out of school?"

"If you'd been in school, you wouldn't have been working at nine in the morning."

"What if I had late classes?"

"James. The first day I met you, you were picking the lock of my piece-of-crap Oldsmobile. You obviously have no knowledge of value or taste. You just aren't that good."

"That's harsh, man."

"The truth hurts. I'd shake the hell out of you and throw you out the door in a fit of pique, but one, I'm tired, and two, I don't want the police to take even more notice of me than they already have."

"Oh."

"James. Before the advocate gets to you, there are some things you have to do."

"I don't have to do shit."

Sam put her cup on the table. Her nose twitched. She got up. James cringed a little as she came around the table and very carefully seized his collar. Sam lifted him until his feet just barely touched the ground. Then she propelled him toward the door. She heard his coffee cup hit the floor. She kicked it out of the way.

"What are you—ow! Stop that! What are you doing??"

Sam got to the door and flung it opened and propelled James onto the sidewalk. She took a glance to the side to make sure the people on the street would see her and then nailed James with her eyes. He was still struggling to break her grip. She lifted him and shook him. She raised her voice so that a healthy proportion of people would hear her as well.

"No. *This* is what is going to happen, Mister Sutton. You will go back to school. You will sign up for as many classes as they will let you take! You will maintain your job at the auto shop, and I don't care—*I don't care* if you have to work every second of every day for the next three years. I don't care if you don't *sleep* for the next three years. You are *going. Back. To. School!* Now, do you understand?"

Sam liberally punctuated her remarks with shakes. With great ceremony, she unceremoniously flung James onto the sidewalk, *"Answer me!"*

James nodded at the terrifying vision leaning over him and scrambled backward on hands and his butt to get away from her.

"I understand! Okay! I w--I will!"

Sam turned around and went back inside, slamming the door and locking it. She stomped up the stairs and peeked out the window. James had picked himself up. All the people on the street were now staring at him. Sam's lips lifted in a malicious grin. There was no way anyone had missed that. She decided she could bathe in good faith.

Sam had surrounded the tiled portion of the floor with a hanging plastic sheet and plumbed the stubs to provide hot and cold water. It hadn't been very hard, but she had to be careful not to actually shake the pipes that weren't attached to anything. As long as she didn't let too much water out of the faucet head, it didn't overflow the tiled area. It was still better than anything she had experienced overseas on missions. She stepped into her "shower" area and simply stood in the hot water for a while before carefully stretching her muscles one at a time. As she touched her side, she felt the long, thick scar that ran the width of her ribcage. She swallowed hard as she thought of James again. It was hard not to let her mind dwell on all the possible scenarios. How it all could have ended.

"James is safe," she told herself.

"You are safe," she told herself.

It didn't stop the rivers of blood she saw when she closed her eyes.

18
Help!

"I'll have some coffee. No food thanks."

"Oh, God, I'm sorry, I'm out."

"You're out of coffee? How can you be out of coffee?"

"I wasn't expecting this many *people!*"

For the first time the entire restaurant was completely packed. Every table was taken, and she had run out of seats. Sam actually had to wonder what her room capacity was supposed to be. She was frantically flipping sandwiches on the grill when the inspector walked in.

"You have a lot of people here!" he shouted.

"Yes, it's very busy!"

She surreptitiously slipped on some gloves before moving the sandwiches to plates and bringing them out.

"Here we are! For you and you and you."

She spent just a moment watching everyone bite into the hot food before turning back to the inspector.

"You weren't here when I arrived last Monday."

"I was...busy."

"So it goes. I almost left you a notice shutting you down."

"Well, that would have been unfortunate. Pardon me..."

Sam continued to try to move as smoothly as she could.

"If you could just stay out of the way...thanks..."

Sam dashed milk into three small mugs and brought it to some smaller kids who were clustered around a table.

"Milk for you guys. Sorry--you girls!"

Sam snatched the dirty dish bin from its resting spot and went to the sink to unload it.

"Your kitchen is dirty."

"I haven't finished lunch rush yet."

"But you're planning on sweeping?"

"And mopping."

"Well, there is that. How is your fridge doing?"

"Um, it's still running. I think I have enough money from today to buy a real coffee machine!"

"I am ecstatic. How about the name?"

"You have my name!"

"The name of the restaurant."

"Oh, God--" Sam winced visibly.

"Well then...u slash--."

"Give me a second!"

For a mercy, the inspector fell silent. Sam put her hands to her head, then removed the gloves and washed her hands.

"The...uh...lettuce cup. No, no, too cute--"

"The Lettuce Cup it is!"

"No! Wait! That's not it!"

Nero wrote firmly, the pen making three copies.

"The...Lettuce...Cup. I assume no silly spelling on that...an eight for a u or any of that childish nonsense?"

"Crraaaaaaaap. Look. I have to finish lunch!"

"Oh, I'm done! Have a good day! Here's your copy right here on the prep table. Don't forget to make a daily deposit. All that cash— wouldn't want it hanging around."

Sam watched the now smiling inspector leave the building. She picked up a ladle and plunged it into the soup, stirring viciously. The Lettuce Cup. Lovely.

Four hours later she melted into a chair. The soup was gone, the bread was gone, she had one slice of her special meat loaf left. She had a handful of vegetables and had to open a can of chili for the last customer, who was just now finishing.

"That was pretty good. Thanks."

"You are more than welcome."

"You should get some help in here. You could use it."

"I've never been this busy. Ever."

"I don't think you'll get less busy."

"What makes you say that?"

"Oh, common sense. You should go buy that coffee machine. You'll need it. And uh, if you need help, give these people a call."

Sam took the card that the man handed to her.

"Work Resource Center. One break at a time."

She smiled at it.

"Thanks."

"You're welcome. I left the cash on the table. Have a good one."

Sam cleared up quietly. She gathered bills and quarters from each table as she went. When she got to the man's table, she picked up the bill, and her mouth went dry. The clean, crisp $100 nearly squeaked at her.

"Sun shines on a dog's ass once in awhile," she whispered to herself. She hoped it was real. A swipe with a cash marker assured her it was.

She sat in the coffee shop to use their Wi-Fi while she ordered a coffee machine and potting soil along with a second-hand commercial toaster that needed a teeny bit of work on its rack. Then she bought all the rest of her groceries. She flipped through the pages of a second-hand cookbook in the salvage warehouse. When she was done she had ten whole dollars left. She made it to the bank just as the security guard was about to close the door and went to the teller to deposit it.

"You could have done this at the machine you know," the teller told her.

"I know, but it's the first time I've had any profit from the business. It seemed special."

The teller smiled. "Yes, it is special. Here is your receipt."

Sam left the bank feeling good. She struggled onto the bus with seven bulging bags. The evening was a long, eventful one filled with burned crusts, hollow loaves, and much frustration before she finally made a few loaves of bread worth calling "bread." What happened to her baking mojo? She couldn't believe it the next morning when she opened the door to put out the tray of muffins for the kids on the bus and saw a line.

"I'm so sorry. I'm not open. I don't have anything yet."

The four people standing around grumbled and walked away, but they seemed fairly good natured about it. Sam was mystified. After being ignored for so long, suddenly it seemed she was definitely the hottest place going. She hurriedly made a lunch for James's grandmother and brought it to her. Then back again to the restaurant where she began making coffee and heating the ovens. She had discovered a discount freezer *filled* with frozen pizzas the night before. She had bought them all for half the half price when she mentioned the expiration date. The manager was only too happy to get something for them. Soon the restaurant was filled with the scent of melted cheese and sausage. Just like the previous day, the place was packed, and she ran out of what she had to serve. Her own few well-made loaves of bread were eaten with great enthusiasm. By the time she finished cleaning, she felt like she was going to cry. She couldn't keep this up. It had only been two days, and she thought she was going to drop. She needed help. Right now. But she couldn't afford help.

In desperation she went back to Louis with a gift firmly wrapped in aluminum.

"Louis, I need your help."

"Ahh—are we really in competition now? You are going to try to steal my secret recipes."

"No, no, really. I need to hire help, but I can't afford it. How do I get help if I can't hire it?"

"Work longer hours? Charge more for your food."

"Louis. I work from five a.m. to ten p.m. every day, and I don't charge."

"You—are you crazy? I do not understand what you are saying."

"People pay me what they can give me. It's working, but I can't do it myself."

"Then you must find someone to invest in you."

"Get people to invest money in me. How do I do that?"

"Well, I had to ask my mother," Louis gestured toward a portrait in his office of a lovely old lady in a dark-patterned dress.

Sam patted Louis' hand, "I wish I could, and I know that my mother would have been all too happy to help me. Really, she would have if she were still alive, but I don't have any relatives."

Louis tapped his fingers on the desk, "Let me think for a while. Can I get back to you?"

"Yes. Oh yes, here. I made this for you. I know I'm just a beginner, but it turned out so nicely I thought you might enjoy it."

Sam gave Louis the aluminum-wrapped bread loaf and left. She was a few steps down the street when she heard ferocious arguing in French behind her. She turned around and saw both Louis and Andre run up to her. Louis had the loaf of bread opened and they each had large hunks in their hands.

"Sam! Sam! You have to tell us how you did this!"

"Did what? Made bread? Don't you do it all the time?"

"No, *this* bread. This is amazing! It's tangy!"

"It's sweet!"

"It's... "

A flurry of what could have been complimentary French; Sam couldn't tell.

"I used flour and yeast…"

"You have to come back to the kitchen and do this again."

"But I can't! I have to buy groceries! I have to get ready for tomorrow! I have to bake bread at *my* restaurant!"

More ferocious arguing. Suddenly Andre turned and walked off. Louis stared at Sam.

"I will come with you."

"What?"

"I will come with you and see what you do to make the bread."

Sam folded her arms and looked stubborn.

"You don't think I'm going to *steal* your recipe do you?"

Sam lifted her nose just a hint.

"All right! I will...get you patrons!"

"Patrons? What is that?"

"People who will give you money to help you run your business."

"But those people are your customers, Louis!"

"No. Not these people. These are new people."

"Straight out of the oven?"

"Sam, please?"

"Fine. We have to go to the store."

"Which store? I'll drive."

"I can't..." The thought of the bus, the heavy bags, everything, intruded. She changed her mind. "Thank you, Louis."

Sam directed Louis to the store. As they parked, Louis turned to Sam.

"Sam. Are you buying all your groceries from here?"

"Yes. Why?"

Louis put his forehead on the steering wheel.

"Sam. You are wasting an incredible amount of money."

"What? How?"

"Sam. You are paying more than full price for everything at this store."

"But I get the discount stuff, I've saved a lot of money!"

"Sam. How busy are you every day?"

"Well, for two days I've been packed."

"Right then. Bulk foods it is."

"I don't have that much money!"

Louis started the car."I will show you."

Sam received a hurried lesson at a bulk store in how to tell a good deal from a bad deal and how to purchase for a week instead of a day.

"Louis. I hope I didn't make Andre angry."

"Sam, Andre is only angry because you wouldn't tell him how you made the bread. He thinks you owe us that."

"I do owe you that, but I don't know what I did to the bread to make it so good. The customers seemed to like it."

"You asked for nothing that we could use, and you paid for the range. You do not owe us."

"But your kindness..."

"Sam. No one should owe another person just because they received some kindness. That is something that should be spread freely, without reservation, without price."

Sam smiled. "I agree."

Sam found that a side benefit of being busy was getting to know some of the other business owners in the neighborhood. As it became warmer, people stopped rushing from place to place so fast. Sam could sometimes stop for a moment to talk to them. The man who owned the convenience market was a wizened little seventy-year-old who had also been in the military. The man with the hot dog cart had aspirations of being a comedian. The insurance salesman swore he was going to drink himself to Heaven by starting a brewery.

Teachers, construction workers, pet store owners, laborers by the dozens. Sam couldn't remember them all, but for brief moments she could do something for them that some hardly ever had time to enjoy. She could listen. And even when she heard things that were outrageous, silly, stupid, condescending, whiny, or even offensive, she remembered Louis' words and let them talk. It was a kindness she could pass on without reservation.

19
Tito

Sam had watched Tito set up outside her door every day for a month. He would walk up with a box, big and bulky and square. From the top of the box a flimsy looking folding chair with a clean cushion appeared. Within moments, he folded the box to become a black painted step stool. He dug out a cloth, flicked the dust off the step stool, and sat down. He would wait. Eventually someone would walk up. Sometimes they would sit on the top of the box, sometimes they would just place their foot on the top of the stool. If the shoe material was shiny patent leather, Tito would get out his wax and shine away. It never took long for shiny leather, and Tito got one or two customers a week with these at most. Most people had work boots. Tito would start with a stiff brush, getting all the dirt off the boot. For nylon boots, a paste of laundry spot remover. It stayed on just a minute or so, then got wiped down thoroughly followed by a squirt of waterproofing. For leather boots he'd use soap, then the boots would get a rubdown with a good cleaning cloth that had been lightly oiled.

After watching Tito for a few days, she brought out a cup of coffee to him. He took it silently, and she sat down next to him while he waited.

"How long have you been doing this, Tito?"

"Since I was sixteen."

His voice was not what Sam expected. She thought he'd be soft spoken, shy, deferential. Instead he spoke in a strong, steady tone. He had no trace of a Mexican accent. She wondered how to ask him about his life. She was still thinking when he decided to talk.

"Trouble started when I was ten. Couldn't read. That teacher kept on trying and trying. Told me I was just being lazy. Kept me for hours after class. Over and over. Got a tap on the hand every time I got a word wrong."

Tito stretched out his hand. The wrinkled skin had faint white marks by his wrist.

Sam gulped back a gasp, "Tito, that doesn't look like a tap."

"Yeah. They were big taps really. Puffed up red and black. They finally stopped trying. Called me retarded. Told my mama something wasn't right in my head."

Sam tipped her head at him, "Tito, have you ever seen a doctor?"

Tito took a gulp of the coffee, "Oh yes. A few years ago. They told me I have Dyslexia. Told me it's fixable. Not like an operation or anything, but that I gotta have the right teacher."

"So what did they do when you were sixteen?"

"They decided I had to have some type of trade. Something to make money with. So they took me to the shoeshine guy down on the corner, right? Biggest man I ever saw. Black as the shine he put on people's shoes. My parents paid him to show me how to shine shoes. The first thing he ever told me was, "Keep it simple, Tito. Don't use shine if the shoes are already shiny. Just spit on em and give them a good rub. Use the right color for the right shoes, Tito. Brown for brown, black for black, white for white. I don't see many white shoes anymore. Shug, that was his name, Shug. His teeth were white as sugar. He never saw any of these fancy work boots. I had to figure those out on my own. Shug taught me that if a woman stepped up to my seat I was supposed to take out the standing cloth. That's a thick scarf. Let her rest her feet on the scarf and do the shoes by hand."

Tito chuckled to himself, "Shug never saw any woman in their military shoes, either. Gave me quite a fright the first time I saw it. Woman just up and sits down in my chair with those pretty patent leather shoes. 'Well, are you going to shine them up or aren't you?' she says. I stared at her like I was a simpleton. I did them shoes. Right on her feet. First time for everything, I figure. I figured right. My mama, the schoolteacher, the administrators, they all figured wrong. I wasn't retarded at all. I just couldn't read. I can solve problems, though. And you know, once you know a trade, you know that trade the rest of your life."

"Have you ever tried anything else Tito?"

"No. I think I just got so used to shining shoes I didn't really want to do anything else anymore."

"How about cooking. Do you cook at home?"

"I cook my own dinner, yes. I can make my own food. Some of it's pretty good, too. Nothing like the smell of cornbread and chili in the middle of the snow. I like pasta better though. I like making it. Really simple pasta, just flour and egg. Roll it out, cut it, and then boil it. Sometimes I fry it after that. It's good fried."

"Tito, I think you know more about cooking than I do."

"Me? Nahhh, you own a whole restaurant."

"Well, I'm pretty good at baking, but I tell you, I burn pasta, and don't get me started on what I do to rice. The last time I tried, I almost had to throw away the pot."

"Ohh, rice ain't hard at all. I could show you that."

Sam patted Tito on the shoulder, "I'd appreciate that, Tito. You come tomorrow morning. I'll give you breakfast; you show me how to cook some rice. Now, don't take any wooden nickels."

"Ohhh, you are a tease Sammie! I'm not blind! I just can't read. Not yet anyway."

20

Reality Check

Along the path to running the restaurant, Sam had envisioned grateful people pouring out their love for her. Hopefully in fives and twenties. A rude dose of reality caused her to grudgingly (but with some good humor) accept the love in ones. She smoothed out the pile of ones and smiled to herself. She was earning a living. A living that didn't involve killing people—that brought no pain or tears. Wait. She had cried when she ran out of food. She burned herself, which was painful, and she had to take a shower before bed every night, because the griddle on the range made her smell like the Hulk.

But, of course, there the dream ended. She looked up from her pile of ones at the pile of women who were staring at her. She transferred her smile to the women.

They had not directly accused her of anything, but she knew that "We have some issues" couldn't be an accusation that her coffee was bad.

"Issues?" she asked in a neutral tone.

"You don't make people pay," was a prompt response from one woman.

"You have a generous amount of customers," said another.

Gaining confidence, the other women nodded at each other.

"And not all very nice types either."

"...Must be something else going on here."

The women now began speaking faster and over each other. They sounded like a bunch of arguing chickens. Sam held up her hands before the conversation went any further, "Whoa!"

The women's voices went quiet, and she looked at each of them. She wanted to make sure she acknowledged each of them.

"You obviously have a problem with me. I do not think, however, the problem is that I have *some* customers who don't pay. And owing to the fact that I never billed myself as a restaurant that catered to a specific class, I don't think that the people I serve offend you all that much. I think the problem is with me, Sam. Am I right?"

The first woman who had spoken up cleared her throat, and Sam turned her full attention to her.

"Your unorthodox management style is unsettling. I have been a business woman for nearly half my life, and I have never seen anyone break rules like this unless they had some other reason for doing business."

Sam responded, "I'm afraid I don't follow you very well. Could you elaborate on these other reasons?"

The woman's tone was now tight. Her words clipped, as if she didn't want to let them out. The other women stopped looking at Sam.

"Well, money laundering, drug dealing, commercial espionage."

"Commercial espionage?"

"It happens. You could be out to ruin this neighborhood. I personally believe you could be trying to set up a ready market for drugs. We won't stand for that in our neighborhood! Our children are too important to us to be ruined like that."

They had accused her of being a drug dealer. It was almost as bad an accusation as being called a whore. She carefully considered what she was going to say to them. While she was considering, she folded the ones in front of her and very conspicuously placed them in the bank bag. After a long moment, another one of the women broke into her thoughts.

"You couldn't possibly be making enough money off of this ratty little place you call a restaurant."

Sam turned her attention to the speaker. She wanted to ask how the woman knew how much money she made. In fact, there were many questions roiling in her brain. The babble in her brain made Sam close her eyes for a brief second.

"Ok, no. You know what? No. Come with me."

Sam walked toward her stairs, motioning for the women to follow. Not one of them moved.

"Look, you have to see this for me to explain my situation to you. Nothing will hurt you, but if you feel threatened, grab the baseball bat off the wall there. Just be careful with it. I think it might be from 1920 or something."

One of the women took the bat that hung from a couple of pegs as decoration and advanced behind her. Sam's back prickled in warning as she turned away from them, but she forced the feeling to go away. She walked up the stairs into her upstairs living unit. They followed and arranged themselves in a neat semicircle next to the stairs.

"Ladies, you see before you the grand sum total of my living arrangements. My sleeping bag, my piles of clothes there on the floor, and my bathroom, which is the toilet and the curtained off area there."

"What is this supposed to prove?"

"What am I supposed to be spending my money on? Stereos? Hot tubs? Bling? More drugs? That sleeping bag is the most expensive thing I own."

Sam didn't mention the $7000 laptop in her briefcase.

The women milled, uncertainly, looking for all the world like a bunch of restless chickens.

"You could be hiding it!"

"Hiding what? I don't have a closet or an attic. There's less than six inches of space between me and the rain in that roof. Do you think I'm stashing my boy toys in the fridge?"

Sam took a deep breath, "Look. I have been feeding kids in this neighborhood for over six months now."

"That's the problem!"

"Apparently!"

Sam stomped her foot in her frustration.

"I am doing something that you are finding difficult. Something that is out of your control. This hurts your pride. I don't care."

"If you don't care, then why are you showing us all this? Why not just throw us out?"

"Trust me, I thought about it, but the people who show up to this restaurant need to feel that this is a place they can count on. If you go around spreading rumors that I'm dealing drugs out of my home, that won't happen."

"But you're..."

Sam turned her attention to the woman who spoke, "Yes? What?"

Silence.

"Now we get down to the real reason. Let's go downstairs."

Sam didn't wait for them. She walked down the stairs and angrily slammed four cups on the counter in front of the coffee pot. It was the brand new coffee pot. A 12-cup BUNN brewer, all brushed stainless steel with a hot spot on top where she kept an extra pot. The machine was kept busy during the day. She loved it. She took a moment to breathe deeply before pouring the coffee. The women came down the stairs, eyes still flashing, but a little more uncertain. The woman with the bat had left it upstairs.

Sam put the cups on the nearest table.

"Now. I am what? Come on, speak up. What were you going to say?"

Silence.

"Black," Sam said. "That's what you were going to say. Or maybe not say, but it's what you were thinking. Yes? She rolled her eyes. "And everyone knows that black people listen to rap, collect bling, and deal drugs. Is that it?"

The four women looked at her. Sam was surprised to see several of them had real hate in their eyes.

"I have a news flash for you, *Ladies*, I am biracial. I do not identify with being white *or* with being black. I am human. That's all. I am human. I am a human being who is running a restaurant."

"Look. We're just not used to...this."

More uncertainty. Sam took the opportunity to really sink her teeth in and take a bite out of them.

"You know, I'm pretty sick of this small-town attitude when you people are *not* in a small town! You are right next to a city that is *trying* to grow! Have you ever thought of growing along with it? Have you? Because it seems to me the only thing you are trying to do is go *backward* on the evolutionary ladder. Drugs. I'm sure there are plenty of drugs on this street, but you won't find them in this restaurant. What you will find is me, working ten to twelve hours, sometimes twenty if I decide to make something better! For fuck's sake, I can't even afford to offer sugar with the coffee! I am not going to convince you all to stop hating me because of something I can't change. I'm absolutely sure of that, but if you can't find something concrete to hate me for, then just leave me alone. The arrangement with this community stands. When someone walks in that door, they pay what they can afford for the food that I offer them. If you choose to take me up on that offer, I am more than happy to have you walk in that door, sit at my tables, and eat my food. Now, if you will excuse me, I am going to go to the bank to deposit my GRAND total of one hundred nine dollars and....seventy five cents. You know, for the WORK I have done? The coffee is on the house."

Pointedly Sam collected her coat from the coat hook and opened the door. As the woman who identified herself as a business woman approached, Sam looked at her, and she hesitated. Sam spoke directly to her.

"All this infighting isn't doing anyone in this part of town any good. I can overlook graffiti. I can overlook people hating me because I look different from anyone else. I can even deal with a business that is constantly on the edge of going down. I will be damned, however, if I allow children to go hungry when I can prevent it. You may have pride, but I can shove mine right down into my boots if a kid needs a meal. If you don't like it, stuff it where the sun don't shine, sister, because that's how it's gonna be."

The women all walked out, and Sam followed, closing the door firmly and locking it. Without a backward glance she walked away.

21

Sugar and Spice and Patrons

"I got you a box of sugar packets!"

The small boy was very pleased with himself. Sam thought that ten-year-olds shouldn't look that pleased. This particular ten-year-old was known for his practical jokes. Sam opened the box very carefully. Inside lay piles upon piles of little white packets.

"Little Joe, I want you to tell me where you got these."

"At the hot dog stand! Isn't it great? There's so much sugar there! Can I have some now?"

"Plain sugar out of the packet? No! You'll rot your teeth out. Joe, you can't just take stuff from the hot dog cart. Phil owns that cart! He's going to be mad."

"No, he's not! He said I could have that box. I earned it!"

"Really? We'll see."

Joe grinned impudently at her. Sam watched the boy run off and picked up the box. She walked the three blocks to where Phil kept his cart and supplies. Phil spotted her just as he was pushing his cart into the tiny space he rented.

"Hey, Phil."

"Sam. Uh, sorry, I still can't give you my stale bread…"

"Oh, ha. No, thanks. I don't need it. I just wanted to return this…"

Sam held up the box of sugar.

"Oh, is that the one that I gave Joe?"

"You gave it to him?"

"He earned it."

Sam blinked; she wondered if she'd heard him right, "He earned it?"

"Yeah, I had all my stuff delivered early this morning. The delivery guy was a real jerk. Just dumped everything on the ground. Joe jumped right in, snatching boxes like a little tornado. Got done in half the time, so I said he could take one of whatever he wanted."

"Really?"

Phil shrugged, "You know how it is. No cash, lotsa crap. It seemed like a fair trade."

"Well…thank you."

"Yeah. Tell Joe he can come back any time he likes and help out. I'll let him have all the sugar he wants."

"Sure."

Sam walked back slowly. She turned it over and over in her head. Little Joe was one of those kids that couldn't help but take a pot shot at a BMW. He dug his initials into benches with a belt knife. Cookies regularly disappeared from bakeries when he passed. He often had to stand in class because he tipped backward so many times that the teacher finally sat him in the desk/chair combo to keep him from breaking his silly neck. Since he didn't want to just sit, he wound up standing at his desk. Sam put the sugar on her prep table and began getting out items for dinner.

"Hey, Sam. You look shaken."

"Tito! Oh, I'm glad you're here."

"What's wrong?"

"I don't know. No, I know what's wrong. Joe brought me sugar today."

Sam motioned to the box.

"I didn't believe him when he said he earned it. I feel bad."

"This is the same boy that graffitis your window every week and you feel bad?"

"Joe is the graffiti artist?"

"You didn't know? How could you not know? Who else would graffiti unicorns and teddy bears?"

"I didn't think of that. Well, I have to start the rice. Tell me again, how much water?"

"Sam. Haven't you written it down?"

"Yes! But I still screw it up!"

"I'll do it myself."

"Thanks. I'll start the chicken."

Sam felt tears prick the back of her nose as she took out handfuls of sugar packets to put in a bowl next to the coffee maker.

Joe was her graffiti artist. He could have sold that sugar, but he gave it to her. She didn't know where he could have sold it, but he could have. Joe was her graffiti artist. Sam stopped pulling packets out of the box. Joe had begun thinking of someone other than himself.

Sam wiped her nose with a tissue and set the rest of the box of sugar under the counter. She heard knocking at the door.

"What the...who knocks?"

She opened the door to see a rather elderly couple standing there. They were dressed dinner-party style. They were definitely out of their element.

"Hello. The door is open; you're welcome to come in."

"Oh, thank you, dear. We didn't know when your dinner service was, and there were no times on the door."

"Here, let me help you with your jackets. I don't have times; I usually open some time after ten unless you're under 18, and then you get breakfast and pick up a sack lunch that was made the night before. But you aren't under 18, and I'm babbling. I'm sorry. Would you like some coffee?"

"Do you have tea?"

Sam took a deep breath. This was the part she had been dreading. The first customers who would give her more than a dollar at a time and she had to tell them she didn't have what they would normally expect from a restaurant.

"I'm sorry. I don't have tea. I do have milk and sugar for the coffee though. If you like."

"Well, where would you like us to sit?"

"Where--oh! You may sit wherever you like."

"How novel."

"I'm just going to check on dinner. We're having rice and chicken tonight."

"Lovely. Can you sit with us for few minutes?"

"I would love to; let me just make sure that the chicken gets into the oven."

Sam flung the chicken into the roasting pans and slipped the pans in the ovens. She spared a glance for Tito who raised his eyebrows at her. She shrugged her shoulders, washed her hands, and went back to the table the pair had chosen to sit at with two cups of coffee in her hands.

"How are you doing? Here is some coffee for you. It's warming up outside, but it's still pretty chilly."

The man smiled and took an appreciative swallow. The woman clearly instigated most of the talking.

"Oh, thank you, dear. We heard about your restaurant from a friend of ours and decided we'd come down and see you. You're just starting out, aren't you?"

"Well, six months now, and, yes, it feels like it's just yesterday. I've learned a lot and gained a lot of business, but I don't have money for extras, hence the modus operandi."

The man looked up from his cup, "I'm sorry, modus operandi?"

"Yes, sir. My mode of operation. I can only buy what I can afford, and the people who eat give me what they can afford. No set prices. The food is plain but good. I try not to use canned foods, but that's hard when I don't have access to very much fresh food.

There have been quite a few canned chili nights. I have learned, however, to make my own bread, and that seems to make all the difference."

"Fresh bread, Jacob! Oh, I think that's great. So who are your customers?"

"Oh, people from all walks it seems. Although you are, I must admit, the most affluent we have seen."

The couple both smiled at her.

"Well, Sam. You are Sam, correct?"

"Oh yes, Ma'am. I am Sam," Sam winced inwardly.

"Ha! That was fun. The pun—oh, now I'm doing it. Sam, I am Mary Lynn. This is my husband, Jacob. We invest in new startups, small ones especially. You seem quite the new startup."

"Mary Lynn...like the scientist from Georgia Tech?"

"Well, I would have said Mary Lynn as in Mary Lynn Rajskub, the actress, but I much prefer to be associated with a scientist. Do you know her?"

"The scientist? Oh, no, I just read about some of what she researches. Polymers, Nanostructures..."

"You seem to have a wide range of interests, from cooking to science."

"Yes. Although I wouldn't describe cooking as an interest. Before I started the restaurant I think the biggest dish I ever created was mashed potatoes with fried onions for Thanksgiving, and that's only when my mother wasn't looking."

Mary Lynn chuckled, "Adventurous, then. I like that. Jacob?"

"I highly approve. How about your clientele, Sam? Can you tell us a bit more about them?"

"Well, Tito, who is helping out in the kitchen, is one of my regulars. He spends about two days a week helping me, and the rest of the week he's shining shoes. I have a bevy of schoolchildren come in throughout the day; men and women who work on the buildings and at the concrete recycling center come in; I get the occasional housebound request. Lunch is busiest for me. Then I do get customers who are covered by the other customers' orders."

"Covered? I'm afraid I don't understand."

"Well, if someone can't pay, I don't push them out the door; I feed them, too. Since most of my meals cost under a dollar to make, anything over a dollar can cover those customers' meals. Most of the time I break even with just a hint over the top. I do wish I could make more."

"And you keep thinking if you could fix the place up a bit more, you'd get more customers."

"Well, it is true that the neighborhood would trust me more if I had what looked like a more modern restaurant. Nothing really fancy; that might scare them into never showing up again, but this wallpaper is hideous; the tables really need to be replaced; I have a section of flooring that needs to be replaced, too, and I—well, that particular wish is a long way off."

"No, do tell. Everyone has something they want to do."

"I'd like to turn the back area into a hydroponics station. Fresh lettuce, herbs, maybe some veggies. But even the most basic equipment is just way too expensive for me."

"How do you fare during lunch?"

Sam smile wanly, "It's a wreck. I really need more help, but, again, I can't afford to hire anyone. Even Tito works for free. He likes to cook, and I feed him."

"How ever did you get started?"

Sam sighed, "Oh, you know, same old story: woman gets restless and leaves military, woman goes for a drive, breaks down in a new place, gets fed up with going places, and restaurant calls woman's name. Woman gives in and starts business."

"Sounds complicated."

"Only a little."

"Well, Sam, I won't keep you from your job any longer. We'll just sit here and converse until dinner is ready if you don't mind."

"Not at all. Please feel free to get more coffee if you'd like."

Sam felt fidgety. Did these people want to give her money? Why would they do that? She would probably never be able to pay them back. Soberly she mixed flour, salt, and a cup of bread machine mix in a large bowl, whisking gently and carefully. Tito picked up her box of bread machine mix.

"Is this how you do it Sam?"

"Do what Tito?"

"This must be what makes the bread so good."

Sam shrugged, still in the throes of uncertainty where Mary Lynn and Jacob were concerned. Were there actually other people out there willing to give her money, too? Why would they pick *her* of all people? And what was Tito staring at her for?

"What?"

"Sam. You really have no idea how good this bread is, do you?"

"It tastes like bread to me, why?"

"Where did you learn how to make it?"

Sam dug her phone from her back pocket. She rarely used it for data anymore, but every once in a while she wanted a recipe or something new to read. She brought up the recipe on the device and started the video, then handed it to Tito before going back to the bread. Warm yeast mix and milk went into the bowl. Tito listened to the video, puzzled, and then started laughing.

"What?"

"Sam! You figured out how to make bread from this garbage?? It's a chef's nightmare!"

"The cook clearly stated…"

"Hydroxyls, alkaline something mixture--this is chemistry!"

"It's a formula! The box of machine mix had the same ratio of ingredients!"

"Only you, Sam."

"Only me what?"

Tito gave the phone back to Sam.

"Sam. Only you could be so detail oriented that you would take a lecture on how the best bread in the world is made and take it for a recipe. You translated all that gobbledegook...into English."

"You're making me uncomfortable, Tito."

"I'm sorry, Sam, but it's true. You should really be working at some fancy restaurant. You could make millions."

"Tito, I don't want to make millions!"

"Then what do you want?"

Sam stuck the dough in the corner of the table and covered it with a damp cloth and plastic wrapped the bowl.

"I—don't know. I guess I just want to be useful."

"You don't have any big plans? Save the world? Become an award winning something?"

"No. I never thought about it. I really kind of stopped thinking too far in the future when I started the restaurant. Everything became "Right Now.""

"Maybe not everyone has to have big plans, Sam, but you do have potential."

"Oh, Tito, go back to the rice!"

Sam looked over to see Mary Lynn smiling at her from the doorway of the eating area. She flushed at the smile the older woman was giving her. Her voice was soft, but held a wealth of emotion.

"Useful is good, Sam."

Sam didn't know what to say.

"Useful is what this city needs. There is so much apathy because of the economic breakdown. People feel there is no place for them. People like you are a bit like a torch. You provide something they can't find on their own."

"Mary Lynn, are you really considering giving me money?"

"Yes. I am."

"Why?"

"Well, I came down here because someone asked me to. I didn't pay the request too much mind; I go lots of places that need money. Most of them don't make it. They just aren't ready for the long haul. You've made some pretty hefty mistakes. You started out with way too little money in the first place; you purchased the wrong things; you had no plan. You're struggling because of it. I think it can be improved. I think you have a good chance to turn this place into something successful. For some reason, your attitude draws people in. Whether you know it or not, you are addressing the root of a problem. Whatever it is about you, people here need it. That's why I am considering giving you money."

"I hadn't originally intended on starting a restaurant."

"I don't think that really matters."

"I wanted to start a security business."

"But you changed your mind."

"Someone said something—I don't know. It seemed like a restaurant was more useful."

"Sam, that shows flexibility. That is another admirable trait."

Sam leaned against the prep table.

"Mary Lynn, I would be very grateful if you were to invest in this business."

Mary Lynn's smile was bright and cheery, "I'm glad. Now, about dinner?"

The rest of the evening was busy. Mary Lynn and Jacob watched for a few hours as Sam handled the dinner service. It was a bit nerve-wracking, but Sam had been inspected by generals far more intimidating than this older couple and handled herself with the same good grace as she ever had with a weapon. In the end, she received not only money from Mary Lynn, but every single person who showed up. Breathing room never felt so good.

22

Storytime

The severity of the JAG officer's expression was fairly scary as Sam walked into the office for her legal appointment.

"Oh, uh. Hi. I'm—I'm Sam."

She swallowed. She hated the legal department. The officer motioned her to a chair. She sat. The office was sterile. A functional desk, a functional chair, no pictures on the walls. She felt so stiff she could have been wearing her formal uniform. Nobody intimidated her like legal. She never knew what to expect.

"Well, Chief Olabode..."

"No."

"I'm sorry?"

Sam found her voice. This response was natural to her.

"My name is Sam. I am no longer employed by the Navy. I am not a Chief."

"But your name isn't Sam," the JAG officer replied.

"Nevertheless, that is what you will call me."

The JAG officer leaned forward on his desk.

"Look. You know the reason you are here. Your court case has raised quite a bit of a fuss. Shooting someone has consequences...Sam."

"No."

The officer frowned sourly, "Why do you keep saying that?"

"Because you are getting it wrong. I didn't shoot someone. I killed someone. He was dead by the time he hit the floor. I know that."

"Well, the consequences of that action means that I need to go to court with you."

Sam nodded and responded curtly.

"I have questions."

The JAG officer sat up. He hadn't identified himself. He didn't need to. His name was on the nameplate outside the door. Sam didn't ask that question and ignored the fact that he had a name.

"First, I would like to know why I wasn't questioned at the station."

"They weren't allowed to."

"What? Why?"

"Sam, your security classification still holds. I know it doesn't make sense to you, but when your social security number is identified in the computer system by someone requesting legal information with it, the request automatically flags an alert to military legal. We call the facility you are being kept at and inform them as to their rights concerning you. Any questioning must be done by us, not them. This is to avoid any possible information leaks."

"Why didn't they perform any drug or alcohol tests?"

"That, I do not know. That would have been within their rights. Perhaps because of the situation they thought it didn't matter."

"Didn't matter? But that doesn't make sense at all! How are they supposed to know whether I was affected by some illegal substance when I grabbed that weapon?"

Sam stopped talking and took a deep breath. She remembered every single piece of advice she had ever gotten about talking to legal. Don't show emotion. Don't show frustration. Don't speak in anger or fear. Questions concerning facts are good. Keep it factual, not personal. She let out the breath calmly. She started over. In as few words as possible, she described what had happened all the way through the confusing arraignment hearing. She didn't ask why a JAG officer hadn't shown up then. It was obvious that they had known it would be dropped, and so no one bothered offering her representation. That was efficiency. The officer made notes as she talked, but since Sam knew she was being recorded on camera, she didn't question why he didn't write everything down.

"Thank you, Miss Olabode. I think I have everything I need."

"Very well. Just give me a call and let me know when the court date is. I'll show up. I'm sure there's nothing else I need to do."

Sam got up and went to the door. She stopped before opening it.

"You know, the hell of it is," she said, not looking at the officer, 'there was no mention of what happened to that man. No mention of who he was. I couldn't even get his name."

Sam turned and faced the officer. She could feel herself growing uncomfortably hot.

"Every person I killed while in the military had a name and a history. They were people. This man was not a person. He was nothing more than a reason for lawyers and courts to make money and to try to fix a social problem. In this case, the military is going to give the courts and the lawyers money. The police didn't have to solve the problem by shooting him themselves. That man had no name, no history, no *life*. He was just an excuse. It's disgusting."

Sam opened the door and walked out. It was ridiculous. There were protocols, things that should have happened, that she expected would happen. They should have questioned her. The judge should have questioned her. Even the JAG officer should have asked more questions than he did. The situation wasn't spelled out, it wasn't elucidated, it wasn't *real*. She should have been faced with a grand jury that would have decided whether she would be tried. The public defender would have told everyone who the man was, why he pulled a weapon, what the situation had been. Instead, it had all been so hurried, swept under the rug. Uncomfortable. It was like she had been reading a book, and the book just stopped senselessly in the middle of the storyline.

She felt numb and hot. Time ceased to have meaning anymore as she walked. It could have been minutes or hours that passed since she walked out the door. She found herself facing what looked like a combined bookstore and coffee shop. She went in without feeling anything and tucked herself into the furthest nook she could find. She sat on a stool. She ran her finger along the spines of the books in front of her and chose one at random. She held the book to her chest and used it as a shield to keep it from heaving. She closed her eyes and rocked back and forth in small motions. She could see the weapon. She knew she had three choices. The young boy standing bravely in front of his grandmother, his hand outstretched. James took the gun and she took it from him. She had two choices. Then the man did it. His hand moved to his pocket.

One choice. Just one.

Please. Please don't do that.

She aimed straight for the only spot that would make everything stop. It had to stop.

"What the—Hey, you! Hey—are you okay?"

Sam shook her head and struggled to stop the tears. She held the book with one hand and the other stretched out in front of her toward the memory of the man.

Stop it. It had to stop.

"Oh, wow. Must be a really bad day. Just—wait there."

Sam had no intention of moving. A few minutes or a few hours later, Sam couldn't tell, a hot cup of something was pushed into her numb fingers. She looked up and saw the concerned face of an elderly gentleman. She sucked in an ugly breath.

"I'm sorry. I'm so sorry. I tried to stop it. I tried to. He's a person. He really is!"

Sam couldn't help it. She began sobbing. The cup trembled dangerously, and the man rescued it. Sam took her hand back and cradled both of them against her chest.

"Ok, okay then. Not ready for tea..."

Sam began to shake. She couldn't stop, It was cold. She couldn't make it stop.

Her chest got tight and she wheezed.

Two firm hands gripped her arms.

"Hey. Hey. Look at me. Right here. Yes. Look at me."

Sam made the effort to lift her eyes to his through the blurry tears.

The man's voice was calm.

"It's not real."

"But—it has to stop."

"It's not real. Look here. The book in your hands is real. Look at it."

Sam lifted the book, but her hands were shaking so badly she thought she would drop it. The old man's hands covered hers.

"Look at it. Concentrate on it. I want you to tell me what's on the cover."

"I—" Sam took a shuddering breath between sobs. Every word was painful.

"I see an elf."

"That's good. What's the title?"

For a long time, Sam just concentrated on breathing, then the words on the cover seemed to clarify. The tears no longer blurred her vision.

"Champions of Falural."

"There we go. And you're breathing again. This is good. Here just put the book in your lap and take the tea now."

Sam took the cup of warmth in fingers that were now tingling. The tightness was gone from her chest, and although she had an overwhelming sense of sadness, she knew that air was moving in and out of her lungs.

"I'm sorry."

"Don't apologize. Panic attacks are not something to apologize over."

"I'll buy the book."

"Oh sweetie, you can't do that."

"Why—why not? Isn't this your shop?"

"Oh no, this isn't a shop."

Sam gasped as she looked around herself. There were nothing but shelves, and books. A few tables. Couches. No wonder she thought it was a coffee shop.

"You live in a library!"

"Oh, no, this is just part of the house."

"What is the rest of the house filled with? Giant eagles? Panthers?"

"You have an imagination."

Sam giggled and wiped her eyes. She felt hysterical.

"Okay, drink that tea now."

"No, I should go."

"No."

"Wh...why?"

"Right now, you are my guest. When I am done conversing with you, you may go. Right now I would like you to finish your tea."

"And then what?"

"Well, I suggest you take the book with you and finish it."

"Okay."

The man was kind. Sam wished that everyone were that kind. She remembered very few times that people recognized what was happening as a panic attack. Standing in the supermarket aisles trying to look calm while inside her a storm raged. The employees and other shoppers had not recognized the panic. This man recognized the agony and responded with the one thing that could help, patient acceptance. It didn't make it all go away, but it made her functional again. After the tea, after sitting quietly for a while, Sam was able to walk and talk again. That night, she settled down with the book and opened it to the first chapter:

Ashan looked down at the young elf who sat quietly, eyes closed. Her posture exuded a small amount of trepidation.

"Are you ready, Turl?" He asked

"Yes." said the young girl.

Very gently, Ashan placed the tiny, squirming bundle of fur into Turl's arms. Her eyes flew open in surprise.

"Oh! It's..."

"A kitten. A kitten who will grow with you, Turl. What are you going to name her?"

"Her?"

"Oh, yes. We would never pair you with anything less than the best kitten. The best kitten for a hunter is female. This kitten will never give up and never give in. She will be with you through thick and thin. All you have to do is be kind to her and show her what you want her to do."

Turl cuddled the baby to her chest. The bundle of fur mewled.

"Oh, she's hungry!"

Ashan chuckled deep down in his chest, "Ah, a good, good start! I will get your new friend some strider meat."

Turl gently scratched the baby's neck. When Ashan returned she took a chunk of meat and held it to the baby's nose, but the kitten only sniffed at it and then went back to curling up on her lap.

"Ashan, what am I doing wrong?"

Ashan knelt down, "Turl, the baby needs to know she is special. She needs to be excited about eating. The first thing you have to do is tell her your new name."

"My new name, but what's wrong with the name I have now?"

"Your name now only reflects you. It needs to reflect both of you. Trust me. I know you've already picked a name, right?"

Turl nodded.

"Good. Hold her up in front of your face so she's looking right at you. Then tell her your name."

Turl held up the kitten in front of her and waited until the kitten had locked eyes with her.

"Hello there, baby. We're going to be partners, and I want you to know that I give up my child name of Turl, and now I will be known as Tigurl."

Turl didn't hear the soft noise of wind through the clearing, but Ashan did. The soft twinkle of magic centered itself in Tigurl's hands. Suddenly her face went still and then broke out into a broad grin.

"Ferala. Her name is Ferala! Oh, Ferala, you're so hungry. I'm

sorry. Look, I have meat here! No—no milk. You need to eat grown-up food now. Just try it; I promise you'll like it."

Ashan slipped out of the clearing to let Tigurl and Ferala have their first moments together privately.

Over the next few months, Ashan watched the kitten and the girl grow up together. Within just a few weeks, Tigurl was teaching Ferala to pounce. Within a year they were hunting together. Then Ashan had to show them the truth.

He lifted Tigurl onto the back of a giant eagle and got up behind her. Tigurl twisted around to look anxiously at Ferala. "But...Ferala!"

Ashan put a comforting hand on Tigurl's shoulder. "Trust me. Just watch. Ferala has a few tricks that you don't know about."

Ashan signaled to the eagle, and Tigurl had to work to keep her neck from snapping forward as the bird leaped straight up. Once in the air, the eagle expertly swooped back around until it was headed straight for the big cat. As they swept overhead Ferala took a few running steps, leaped up, and vanished.

Tigurl gasped and then suddenly felt a hefty weight settle onto her chest. She looked down and saw a silver figurine hanging from a necklace that hadn't been there before. The figurine was a tiger, paws outstretched.

"Ferala?"

A wave of triumph came from the tiny figurine on the necklace.

"Ferala!"

Ashan leaned forward to speak above the wind.

"You can summon her once we are on the ground again!"

They arrived at the seashore, and the eagle's claws dug into the sand. Tigurl hurried to dismount and summon her partner. Ferala was just as happy to see Tigurl. Then they both turned to look at Ashan, who was not smiling.

"Tigurl, I brought you and Ferala here to see what you will be facing in the very near future. It is not a pretty sight. When this began to happen we fought as hard as we could, but even our best mages have failed against this corruption. It is an outside interference with the magic of nature. We don't know what it is, where it comes from, or how it works. You are one of many young elves who are being asked to find out."

Tigurl and Ferala followed Ashan to a high bluff and spread out before them was the ruined carcass of a village. Its once-grand buildings were now covered in some type of evil magic that could be seen from the bluff itself. It made Tigurl ill to look at it. Next to her, Ferala panted heavily and snarled as though there was an itch she couldn't scratch. Ashan dropped a hand onto Tigurl's shoulder.

"As hard as it is for you to see with your elf eyes, I want you to look through Ferala's eyes at the corruption. I want you to see through the eyes of nature itself. We've done this before. Just close your eyes and think Ferala's thoughts. Then open your eyes."

Tigurl closed her eyes, and Ferala bumped her knee with her large feline head. Her heavy rumble went through and through Tigurl until their thoughts began to mix. Until Ferala and Tigurl were one and the same. Then Tigurl opened her eyes again.

There were—creatures. Creatures that were sucking the magic out of the village, out of the ground, the buildings, the trees. They were eating the essence of what was here! And all the time growing larger, and no way to make them stop. They were brought from somewhere, somewhere else, she couldn't tell where...

"Tigurl, come back. Come back, child!"

Tigurl slowly and painfully tore her thoughts away from Ferala's, and, falling to her knees, she burst into tears. All the people who had lived here. They had died terrible deaths! No one could help them. They were undead now, wandering spirits forever and ever. Only stopping the source of these creatures would stop them from destroying the world around them.

Ashan held the girl as Ferala licked her face anxiously. Ashan reached out to caress the big cat's head.

"Find their home. Find them, the both of you. Make them stop. You and the others are the only hope we have left!"

Reluctantly, Sam closed the chapter. She didn't want to read it all at once, but she wondered how Tigurl and Ferala, as young as they were, could possibly find the source of this great menace and stop it before it destroyed their entire world.

She snuggled into her sleeping bag. This reading thing was a good idea.

23

Ripped

"I'm sorry, Tito; between eight and nine I need to take a drug test. Somewhere between nine thirty and twelve is the court appointment. Between one and two I need to be at the Work Resource Department, and then from two until whenever I am making bread. If I make enough for a week I won't have to worry about it."

"So you are not going to open tomorrow?"

"No Tito. Tomorrow is very full."

"It's just..."

Sam set the scrubbie down and turned off the hot rinse water, "Tito, what's wrong?"

"I don't want to shine shoes anymore."

"Oh, Tito."

Tito studiously kept his eyes on the dish he had dipped in the sanitizer and put it on the drip rack.

"Tito, look at me."

Tito's eyes were very uncertain. He dried his hands mechanically on the towel he was holding.

"If you don't want to shine shoes, don't shine shoes."

"But I don't have any other way of making money."

"Have you tried getting another job?"

"What kind of other job?"

"A cooking job, Tito."

Tito snorted, "Who's going to hire me?"

Sam reached in her pocket and brought out a dollar, "Tito, go get a newspaper. Then I will give you a piece of paper. Write down everything you can do. Everything. Even if it's not cooking related. I think you're going to be surprised. Then look through the paper to see who is hiring people with those skills."

"Sam. Who's going to hire me?"

Sam pushed the dollar into Tito's hand, "You won't know until you look."

"The dishes aren't done."

Sam stared at Tito and blinked.

"Right. I'll go to the convenience store now."

While Tito was gone, Sam sat down to look at the "informational package" that the JAG officer had sent her:

"Do not speak unless spoken to by name. I will handle questions directed at your case. Have all proof of identity and drug testing results with you as well as a copy of your DD214. Do not respond to any requests for any other military records. I will handle it. Do not ask any questions."

Sam felt a particular pang at the last sentence. Do not ask any questions. That's right. Never question your superiors. Don't ask why you have to do that job. Don't ask why that happened. Don't wonder why life isn't fair—or even reasonable. Don't try to change it. Just don't ask.

She tried to ignore the dark feelings behind the sentiment and slid all her papers back into the manila envelope. She wished, again, that she could handle everything with her laptop, but the world was not how she wanted it to be, and this particular city was still apparently paper-happy. No laptops, tablets, or even phones in the court room.

When he returned, Tito seemed surprised to see that Sam was right about the length of the list he wrote up. Sam only corrected the words that didn't make any sense. He had come a long way in his efforts to learn to read and write. She sent him home with instructions to look through the paper and circle in red all the jobs he thought he could do, even if he was unsure.

The next day she took a very deep breath and dressed in her business suit. She put her hair in the soft style she had worn the day she had inquired about the restaurant. She spent a few minutes trying to fight down the tears. They could take everything from her. In two minutes, that's all it would take. Two minutes for the judge to decide he really didn't like her and sentence her to jail. She showed up for her drug testing on time and then sat in the court hallway staring at the wooden wainscot across from her. She was careful not to think of anything. She was aware of the JAG officer walking up and sitting next to her.

"Do you have everything?"

Sam held up the envelope.

"I will refrain from asking if you got the drug testing done. You wouldn't miss that."

Sam didn't say anything. *I'm getting good at this,* she thought.

"You didn't miss it, did you?"

Sam looked at the officer. He sighed.

"This city court is absurd. They said a plea hadn't been entered."

"They didn't enter one."

"What?"

"They didn't give me representation, so I didn't enter a plea. They sent me home."

"You mean they didn't charge you? Why didn't you tell me this?"

"You didn't ask. You didn't call. You just sent me a packet."

"You walked out of the office without a second glance before I could tell you anything. Oh, this is ridiculous. If they haven't pressed charges, it means the case is going to be dismissed."

"No."

"This again. What now?"

"It means there was never a case to begin with."

"You...are right...and wrong. Backyard investigation is not uncommon."

"It wasn't a backyard investigation. The judge told me they were going to investigate."

"Another good detail that I should have known."

"Just do what you were sent here to do. I will do what you told me to do. It will be over."

"Yes. It will."

And it was. The judge was nonconfrontational. He didn't even refer to her as a defendant. He spoke about the docket number. Not even a case number. He didn't look at Sam at all.

"After due investigation, this docket is being filed with no charges. The prosecuting attorney has recommended that, because the victim was under an extreme drug influence, and self-defense would be strongly indicated. I concur. Are there any follow-up remarks?"

The JAG officer stood, "No, your honor."

"Very well then. Dismissed."

And that was that. Sam made her way out, ignoring the fact that she didn't feel any better at all. The victim wasn't even called by name. She had no idea how much that had to do with her military classification and how much with the fact that there were hundreds of druggies on the docket waiting for trials. Maybe she had just helped justice along a little. For an hour Sam sat at a branded coffee shop and drank, very slowly, a coffee she didn't taste. The memory of the psychiatrist she had seen in the military came back to her.

"Conflicting feelings are normal, Sam. More than normal. You know these people are dangerous, but you still see them as people, and it hurts. But you know, beyond a doubt, that your team is more important. Their lives are more important."

Sam throttled the rage that wanted to build up. Why? Why are the lives of the people she killed less important? Why should Eli or Tito or the victim be any less important than the people who decorated with antiques or paid their bills on time?

Tired. She was tired. But she didn't have time to be tired, and she didn't have time to be angry. She had enough time to get across this sprawling hunk of a city with its new parts and its old parts and get someone to help her out. She noticed, as she threw her empty paper cup in the trash that nobody looked at her. She, too, was unimportant in their world. It was too much to think about, too much to feel.

The Work Resource Center was a chunky building with a long sloping roof. Brick. Sam liked the brick. It looked functional. She liked functional in this instance. The interior smelled clean and for some reason that relaxed her. She especially liked the receptionist. It was as if she had walked into a place that wasn't hiding something. She smiled inwardly as she took a seat. It was like slipping into a warm bath. Even the argument that occurred right in front of her between a superior and an employee seemed..honest.

"I was promised fourteen an hour!"

"Jane, you have not completed the minimum working hours for fourteen dollars an hour."

"I have to pay for school!"

"Jane. I cannot talk about this now. Make an appointment and we will talk. We can get this worked out, I'm sure."

"It's not fair!"

"Perhaps, but right now I have other work to do. Please make an appointment."

The superior, a woman in a slightly rumpled suit, walked away from Jane and approached Sam. Sam stood up as the woman offered her hand, "Hello there. I'm the case coordinator for the Work Resource Center; you are Sam, right?"

"Yes, ma'am, Sam Olabode. I would like to hire one of your workers."

"Well, that's good. Sorry about that argument you had to witness. Some of our workers haven't yet learned the etiquette here. Now, have you read some of the information on our workers?"

"Yes. I know that most of them wouldn't be hired if it weren't for you."

"That is putting it kindly, Sam. Most of the rest of society would like to see these people go away permanently where they couldn't see them."

The coordinator led the way to her office which was small and packed with tall metal file cabinets. Sam took a seat across the desk from her. She decided to be the instigator of discussion.

"So what kind of challenges do the workers face? Your website stated you can't just send anyone; you have to match the person to the job, right?"

"Yes. Well, we have to take into account some of the same things any employee would face. We have to make sure they have the right education for the job and that they understand what the job involves. Our workers can have anything from physical disabilities to learning or other mental disabilities. We want them to be successful, so we do a lot of the legwork that people on their own would do by themselves."

"Well, I run a restaurant. It's on First. Not a big restaurant, but since I have started I have gotten more customers than I can deal with, and it's starting to hit my profit line, which wasn't big to begin with. I can serve more people if I get some help to do some of the basic stuff: clear tables, bring food out, prep in the mornings, clean up in the evenings...maybe do some dishes or pack lunches."

"That sounds like a good job to me right now."

Sam smiled, "Well, if you are available for minimum wage, I can hire you."

"Ha! That would be a step up for me. Unfortunately, I am under contract and can't leave for at least six months, so how about..."

The woman rifled through some notecards on her desk.

"Any monetary transactions? Money handling of any sort?"

"They would bring the cash that is on the table to me after cleaning, but they don't have to count it."

"So handling but no counting, okay. You said prep. Measuring?"

"Some, yes. Cups, Gallons, handfuls...pinches? Oh, and whatever I make up on the spot."

"Flexibility...okay, I have a woman named Elizabeth Gardner. She does not speak well and can be slow in learning but is steady and reliable. She is also very friendly, which we consider a great asset."

"My customers can be a bit surly sometimes. Would that put her off?"

"No, I don't think so. I see Elizabeth is actually working here today. Would you like to meet her?"

"I would be happy to."

Sam was a bit nervous and took a brief moment while the woman was out of the room to check her breath. She stood up as Elizabeth came into the room. Elizabeth was shorter than Sam. Sam's eye for detail noticed that Elizabeth's smile was lopsided. Her face seemed slightly flattened but very round.

"Elizabeth, this is Sam Olabode. Sam, this is Elizabeth."

Sam held out her hand, and Elizabeth took it very gently.

"Hello Miss Gardner."

"Hello. Pleeeze call me 'lizabeth. Mittth Gardner is my mother's name."

Elizabeth's syllables were sometimes drawn out, and she spoke very carefully. The woman was right; Elizabeth was very friendly, and Sam took a shine to her after just a few minutes.

"Elizabeth, I have a restaurant, and I am looking for some help. If you are interested, I'd like to offer you a job."

"I would like that a lot. When would you like me to start?"

"Is tomorrow good for you?"

"Yeth. Tomorrow is good."

"Thank you, Elizabeth. I am very grateful for the help."

Elizabeth went back to what she had been doing before while Sam started filling out paperwork for the supervisor.

"That was well done, I have to say. You actually offered her the job."

Sam looked up, startled.

"Well, I did need the help. She seemed to fit. Why wouldn't I?"

The woman shrugged, "Most people don't know how to approach our employees. They think they have to walk on eggshells or treat them like babies. At worst, they assume that we do everything and treat them like some type of work horses, looking them over and then telling us that they'd be fine and contact them when they are ready to come to the job."

"That's horrible. No, really. That's a horrible way to treat another person. Your employees are people. They aren't some type of circus animal to be trotted out."

"Ah, and there you have hit the nail on the head. Many companies use our employees as an advertising tactic."

Sam remembered the poster at the salvage center. The name wasn't the same, though. Sam wondered how many resource centers in the area offered work to challenged workers. She signed the payment contract, which stipulated the minimum required payment, appropriate raises, and that payment would be issued through the resource center for the employee. Perks were to be offered by the employer. She handed the completed packet of papers to the woman.

"Well, I can't say that I don't have some nervous questions running around in my head, but I am a skilled supervisor, and I can figure those out quite nicely on my own. Once the customers start getting taken care of, I can relax a bit and start improving the place. Elizabeth will certainly not be a marketing tactic or a circus animal. I really need her."

"Good. She needs you, too."

24

Elizabeth

Sam breathed a huge sigh of relief seeing Elizabeth walk in the door.

"Hello, Elizabeth!"

"Hello, Sam!"

"You can hang your coat there by the door. Let me just wash my hands."

Sam noticed Elizabeth was wearing a delicate flower print dress with bright red leggings, and her shoulder-length golden hair had almost perfect ringlets. Her coat was the same bright red as her leggings and was made of a thick wool material. She moved with exaggerated care. Sam realized she was nervous.

"Do you drink coffee, Elizabeth?"

"No. I drink water and milk and tea sometimes. No soda, no beer, no juice."

Sam didn't catch all the words and busied herself with some water for the both of them.

"Let's talk for a bit before we work. Is that ok?"

"Sure!"

They sat down at a table. Sam felt her palms sweat a little.

"Well, first I have to tell you I'm nervous. Are you?"

"A little, yes."

"Whew. Well I'm glad I'm not the only one. I'll start by telling you something about myself. I started this restaurant just a little while ago. I had never thought of running a restaurant, but I think I like it pretty well. I have a lot of people coming in now."

"What did you do before the restaurant?"

Sam had to stop a moment, as she couldn't tell what Elizabeth had just said. At all. Then it hit her. The nervousness was because she didn't understand all of what Elizabeth said.

"I'm sorry, Elizabeth, I didn't understand what you just said. Can you say it again?"

For the next half hour, Sam apologized a lot and asked Elizabeth to repeat many of her questions. By the end of her own story, Sam finally got the hang of how Elizabeth spoke.

"How about you, Elizabeth? Will you tell me about yourself?"

"I am thirty years old. I like to work. I like food."

"What kind of food?"

"Hot food!"

"Hot like...spicy?"

"Yes, hot pepper on pizza!"

"I love pizza. How about work? What work do you like to do?"

"I like to talk on the phone, but I'm not good at it, because my jaw is twisted."

"Does it hurt? Your jaw?"

"No. But there's not enough money to fix it. It will cost lots and lots to fix it."

"Well, is there anything you'd like to ask me before we get to work?"

"What do you want me to do today?"

"I'll show you."

Sam started Elizabeth wiping off each table and chair first. Little by little, Sam noticed that her own nervousness was fading away. Elizabeth was very quiet at first, but after about fifteen minutes Sam noticed that she was humming to herself. Although she hummed off tune, it was a pleasant sound as Sam filled paper bags with sandwiches. By the time people arrived for lunch, Sam had introduced Elizabeth to several other tasks. She found she needed to repeat certain instructions, but Elizabeth asked questions about details that Sam had taken for granted or didn't think about at all. Did the bag lunches need to be facing the same way to make room on the table for more bags? How many forks would fit in the fork box? (Because she had more forks than box space.) Maybe the tables should be set with forks and napkins?

Other than forgetting to use sanitizer on the tables after cleaning them when everyone left, Sam couldn't find anything wrong with Elizabeth's work. It had been a successful, busy day.

Sam sat down after everything was clean and took a deep breath.

"That was a good job, Elizabeth. How many times a week can you do this?"

"I'm not allowed to work more than twenty hours a week right now."

"Oh man. So part time. How about making more of you? I could use about three more workers just like you."

Elizabeth giggled. Sam smiled at the sound.

"I know your mom will be picking you up soon, but here, sit down, and I'll pour us both a treat."

Elizabeth sat down, and Sam poured some hot chocolate into two cups.

"You did say you drink milk. You did NOT say you don't eat chocolate, so I made us some hot chocolate. Ok, well, warm chocolate, because hot chocolate burns the roof of my mouth."

"I love chocolate."

They sipped for a minute.

"You are a good worker, Elizabeth. I'm very happy to have you here. It's going to take me a little while to understand everything you say, and I'm sorry I'm so slow in understanding you sometimes. The customers liked you, too."

"I have downs. I'm slow."

"Downs? Oh wait...Down Syndrome?"

"Yes." Elizabeth nodded soberly.

"I don't know anything about Down Syndrome."

"It makes me slow, and I get angry when I do things wrong. I do a lot of things wrong."

"But you didn't do lots of things wrong today, Elizabeth."

"My other boss said I was stupid."

Sam stopped drinking her hot chocolate and set the cup down.

"Did I...I didn't hear you right. What was that again?"

Elizabeth slowed down a bit, and Sam noticed that her face flushed.

"My other boss, Steve, he said I was stupid."

Sam's nose twitched.

"Steve was wrong, Elizabeth. You are not stupid. Yes, you are slower than me, but I don't need someone who is Speedy Gonzalez. I need someone who can help. You're fine. You listen and do what I ask you to do. I like that. And trust me, when you are allowed to work more than twenty hours a week, I will give you as many hours as I can afford!"

Elizabeth smiled.

"I didn't like Steve. He told me I was fat. I'm not fat."

"That is true; you are not fat."

The sound of the door distracted them.

"Elizabeth, are you ready?"

A gray-haired woman with a tired expression stood in the door.

"Mom, this is Sam. I'm working for her now."

The woman nodded at Sam. "I remember. Did you enjoy work today?"

"Sam is nice."

Sam picked up the cups of hot chocolate, and because she didn't know Elizabeth's mom's name, she voiced her opinion in a familiar tone.

"She's hedging her bets, Mom. I heard about Steve."

Elizabeth looked nervous. Elizabeth's mom sighed.

"Oh, Elizabeth, I'm not going to yell. Sam seems like a perfectly nice person."

Elizabeth didn't look convinced, so her mother turned to look at Sam.

"I'm sorry, really. I went a little nuts when Elizabeth told me about what Steve said to her."

Sam walked over and held out her hand to Elizabeth's mom. They shook hands solemnly.

"Elizabeth was a great learner today. The only thing I would like her to do is to remember to wipe down the tables with sanitizer at the end of the night. Other than that, she was great. She made sure every time someone got up that the next person would have a clean table. She made sure everyone who needed a lunch got one. She even wrote names on the bags for kids who wanted her to. The customers like her. Not having to wipe tables as my last thing to do is going to give me a whole half hour to do something for myself."

"Thanks."

"You're welcome."

Sam sat down with her pile of design magazines after Elizabeth left. She wasn't nervous anymore. Elizabeth seemed to be so...normal.

Normal? Of course she was normal! She was human! Sam felt a

wash of guilt. She flipped through a catalogue of curtains. No pink. No blue. Tan was nice but very thick. Maybe yellow.

She had twelve hundred dollars. Twelve hundred free dollars to use to make the restaurant look nicer.

Was it the way Elizabeth looked that made her feel nervous? Wait...no. What were all the things she had heard about those with disabilities?

Retard.

Moron.

Spastic.

Stupid.

Simpleton.

Freak.

They should be institutionalized.

They're all unpredictable and dangerous.

Who the hell wants to see that in public?

They're just lazy drama queens.

Genetic abnormalities don't belong.

They should be killed when they are born.

It's immoral *not* to abort those babies.

Sam put a hand over her eyes. All the shows she had watched that said how delicate these people were and how they couldn't mix with normal people. All the hate directed toward them, as if they would ruin everyone else's lives. As much as Sam thought she had avoided it, she had been affected by it. It had influenced her perceptions. She had been more than willing to hire Elizabeth but had never realized how much others' thoughts had affected her own feelings. She felt wrenched. She knew Elizabeth was a normal human being. She belonged just as much as Sam did. Was she wrong now? Would the nervousness start up again? Would she treat Elizabeth differently? The horrifying thought that she might almost terrified her.

No. The only way to treat Elizabeth was to continue to let her work. It wasn't Elizabeth's problem. This was a Sam problem. The only way to get over that problem was to continue to get to know Elizabeth, herself. There was no reason to think Elizabeth would ever hurt her. She wasn't a mass murderer; she hadn't waved dangerous knives around. There was no reason to think she was dangerous to anyone. There was no reason to think that anyone from the Work Resource Center was dangerous.

The customers liked Elizabeth.

She had worked hard.

She had smiled.

She was truthful.

Elizabeth was the kind of person whom Sam would love to get to know as a friend—just as she knew Tito, or James, or Charlie, or Anna, or any of the host of adults and children who had strolled through the restaurant.

Sam looked at the picture of her mother on the hideously papered wall.

"You cannot allow a problem to fester, Sam. You can't shove it under your feet, either. You have to confront it, deal with it.

Decide if it's your problem, or whether it's a problem you have with someone or something else. Make a plan to deal with the problem. Don't shy away from problems that are inside you. If you are to blame, fix yourself."

Yellow walls with a tan wainscot and lace curtains. So bright, so inviting, and they would make the place inviting for pictures hanging on the walls. Yeah. That would be great.

25
Water Everywhere

Sam and Tito stared at the wallpaper in dismay. Most of the paper had been ripped off the walls, but the paper above their heads remained.

"We didn't think this out so well, Sam."

"Yes. So I see."

Sam turned slowly. The paint under the wallpaper was a pale green with cerulean stencils of broken flowers. Sam wondered who painted the stencils. Who picked the color of the paint? Who had decided to cover it all with wallpaper?

"Are those...roses?"

Tito looked around very confused, "What?"

Sam walked up and pointed at one of the stencils, "Here."

"Yes. They could be roses...or carnations?"

"I think carnations are fuzzier."

Tito looked at Sam out of the corner of his eye.

"Sam?"

"Yes?"

"Is there a reason you mentioned the flowers?"

"Yes. I want to keep them. I also want to keep the wallpaper."

"You want to KEEP the wallpaper? But we just tore it all down!"

"We only tore most of it down. I want to keep the rest of it."

"Sam. This looks horrible!"

Sam nodded, "True! Very true! But think about it, Tito. Someone decorated this place before I did—probably more than one person. I don't want to get rid of their efforts. I just want to make them look better."

Tito still seemed confused, "But it's going to look ridiculous."

"Tito. The name of the place is the Lettuce Cup. How much more ridiculous could it get?"

Tito shrugged, "You have a point."

"I have no idea what to do. I'm just not good with decorating! I mean, basic stuff is okay, but this is complicated."

"We need help."

"Yes, we do."

"Where can we find a decorator?"

"On any street corner along with the..."

"Tito!"

"Well, it's true. They're just as out of work as anyone else. Can we afford one?"

Sam sounded a little sulky as she said, "No."

"Can we afford anyone who knows anything?"

"No. But we can learn."

Tito folded his arms suspiciously, "What do you mean, learn?"

"The craft store has classes."

"It's still in business?"

Sam flipped open the newspaper she'd been reading to the advertisement enticing enrollment for courses in learning to "decorate on the cheap."

"Oh. So, barely," he said dismissively.

"Tito, we have twelve hundred dollars. We can't spend half of it on one person who will only tell us what to do."

"We're going to need more than just the two of us."

"Elizabeth can help."

Tito rubbed at his face and jaw before responding, "Are you sure?"

"Yes. I'm sure. I'll teach her how to do the bread, and we'll go back to doing soup and sandwiches while we decorate."

"You're going to teach Elizabeth how to do bread?"

"Tito!"

"What? She's...you know."

"Is this a fucking conspiracy or something?? Elizabeth is not stupid, Tito. She's slow, but she can do it."

"If you say so, Sam."

"And don't you *dare* say the word retarded in this restaurant, do you understand? I will tear you a new exit hole in your underwear!"

Tito held his hands up and backed up, "I get it! I get it!"

"Right, then. Tomorrow there's a paint class. It's at seven p.m. We'll go together."

"Okay."

"Hey, Tito."

"Yeah, Sam?"

"Have you gotten any responses from your applications?"

"Yeah. About fourteen no thank-you's."

"Don't worry Tito; it'll happen."

The next day Sam explained to Elizabeth how she made bread.

"We're going to mix all the dry ingredients and the wet ingredients separately. Then we're going to warm up the yeast, and we'll combine everything. When it forms a nice ball, we'll keep adding flour and pushing on it, kneading it, until it feels really, really smooth. Then we'll let it sit on the counter next to the range until it gets really big. Once that's done, we'll cut the whole batch into four pieces. Each part gets formed into a loaf and then we let it get big again. Then we bake them. Now, I know it's a lot to take in at once, but I have it all written down, and we'll do it together, okay?"

Elizabeth looked nervous but nodded.

"Let's start with measuring out all the ingredients."

Elizabeth turned out to be fantastic at measuring. She was so detail oriented that she spent an inordinate amount of time making sure the exact amounts went into the bowls. Sam wiped down all the tables.

"Okay, Sam! I'm done!"

"All right, what's next on the recipe?"

They worked together to mix everything. Elizabeth really liked kneading flour into the dough. After the dough had risen, Sam turned the dough out on the prep table and then handed Elizabeth a knife. Elizabeth promptly froze.

"Elizabeth? What's wrong?"

"The knife. Mom doesn't let me hold knives. They're dangerous."

Sam carefully took the knife from Elizabeth and put it down on the table.

"Okay. Let's talk about this. You mean, you've never held a knife?"

"No."

"How do you cut your meat when it's on the plate?"

"Oh."

"And when you were working in the office, did you ever use scissors?"

"That's not a knife."

"Actually it's two knives. They're held together so they can cut things."

"I didn't know that."

"So do you agree with me that there are some times when a knife is okay?"

"Um...yes."

"Well, this is one of those times."

"But it's a big knife."

"The size of the knife doesn't make it more dangerous. If we are careful, then the knife is just a tool."

Elizabeth didn't say anything, but she did touch the handle of the knife. Sam waited patiently.

"What do I do?"

"Ah, now we're getting somewhere. I want you to cut the dough in half. Take your time. It's okay."

Elizabeth picked up the knife and tried to figure out where the exact half was. Again, Sam waited patiently. Finally Elizabeth cut it in half.

"Now cut each half in half again so that there are four pieces."

The same slow process happened.

"Now wipe the knife carefully with the sponge and put it back into the block. Good. Now we need to make those pieces into round balls. Like this."

Elizabeth followed Sam's movements, stretching the dough under itself and placing it onto the baking sheet. Elizabeth did the last two by herself. They were a bit chunky and not at all perfect, but Sam declared them acceptable.

Elizabeth helped to wash all the dishes while the loaves rose. Elizabeth frequently stopped to check on the dough. When the dishes were done and put away, they put the bread into the oven. Sam had to once again convince Elizabeth that it was okay for her to get near the oven. She even had her put on the oven mitts to put the tray in. They waited patiently for the twenty-five minutes it took the bread to bake, sitting with cups of hot chocolate. Sam put the recipe page into a plastic jacket and sealed it up with glue.

"Now you can use this every time we make bread, okay? Don't worry about spilling on it. You can just wipe it off when you're done."

"I can't do it by myself!"

"Well, I think you can, but I'll be here whenever you make it, so you can always ask questions, okay?"

"Okay."

When the bread had cooled, Sam had Elizabeth wrap up all four loaves. Just in time. Elizabeth's mother and Tito walked in as they were finishing, and the woman took a deep. appreciative sniff. "Oh, it smells so good in here!"

Sam grinned, "I know, I love bread days. It makes everything smell wonderful! Oh, Elizabeth, don't forget to take one of those loaves."

"But it's not mine; it's yours!"

"No! You made it. You deserve to take part of it home with you. Trust me, you always want to taste what you make. And if you want it to taste differently, we can talk about your ideas, okay?"

"Mom, look! I made bread, and Sam taught me how to handle the knife too."

Elizabeth's mom looked at Sam. She seemed puzzled, "You taught her to make bread?"

"Yes. I need someone else to know how, and Elizabeth is so careful. She made great bread."

For a moment the woman shook her head before leading her daughter out.

Tito and Sam spent the next few hours learning the difference between water colors, pastels, oils and acrylic paint. Sam quizzed the craft teacher about stenciling and came away having bought tracing paper, thick card paper, and an Exacto knife.

"Don't forget, next week is texturing!"

Sam stayed afterward and helped pick up some of the materials they had used.

"So are the lessons making you some money?"

The craft teacher looked tired. She nodded.

"Yes, enough at least. I just don't want to close this place. I dreamed about doing crafts for a living since I was a little girl. My mother thought I was crazy. I worked for three years as a waitress, overtime almost every day, taking every shift no one else wanted to get enough money to start. Boy I hated that job. I wore a tee shirt so tight you could tell what religion I was."

Sam couldn't help it, she laughed.

"But, unfortunately, that isn't enough anymore. Half this city is still falling down, and the lower half falls down faster than the upper half grows, but I'm hoping that I can hold on long enough for it to fix itself."

"Yeah, me too. I have help, but I don't know if it's going to be enough."

After a few classes, Sam and Tito figured out that they could texture the walls so it looked like grass. Then they stenciled the roses onto the walls and made it appear as if blue water was dripping from the ripped wallpaper at the top onto the stenciled roses. The result amazed them. Across the wall at one point Tito had insisted they paint the restaurant's name, "The Lettuce Cup," in bright, almost fluorescent green. It hurt Sam's eyes to look at it, but it was certainly noticeable.

When the walls were finished, Sam put her growing plan into action. A bunch of small cups had been painted by the kids who came in regularly. Mostly flower motifs, but some were just random colors. They filled them all with potting soil and slid the cups into holders along the walls. Then each cup was planted with an herb seed or a few lettuce seeds. When they were all done, Sam stood back to look at the redecoration effort. Several of the children hugged her. She was immensely grateful for their efforts. But the cups were not the whole of her plan.

She cleared out the back area and scrubbed it so clean you could eat off the concrete. She repaired holes and patches and installed brand-new clear sheeting over the top of the yard area. Some of the old boxes had fallen apart, and most of the junk that was in them was that—junk that went in the trash. Then she began to set up long supports at hip height made from two-by-fours. Set into the boards were rectangular fish pond liners made of hardened plastic. She drilled drain holes into these and set up pumps that would fill the pond and then drain it when it hit a certain level. The water would then cycle back through the pumps and into the system again. After only a few minor leak problems, she carefully filled each tub with hard clay pebbles and began planting in the system.

The new hydroponics took up a huge chunk of the change that she had asked for from her patrons, but she felt a deep sense of satisfaction that, at last, people would be able to eat more fresh food and less canned crap. That was, if it all worked as she hoped. It was during several points in the process of setting everything up that she realized she was short of breath. It felt like a panic attack, but there was no fear involved, just a bone-deep tiredness that came from not getting enough air. She would have to sit down frequently. She tried stretching exercises, but they didn't work very well.

She started sitting on a stool when she cooked on the grill, which made Tito look at her very oddly.

"Why are you sitting down?"

"I'm just tired from doing everything lately. And we're starting to get more customers in than ever. I'll be okay, but I think I need more sleep."

"You should see a doctor. Doesn't the military pay for that?"

"Oh, Tito, you're like an old nanny goat."

Tito smiled uncomfortably and went back to experimenting with the pasta for the big dinner they had planned.

The breathlessness went away after a few days of getting some extra sleep. By the time the patrons' dinner was served, Sam felt like her old self again, enthusiastic and energetic.

26
Ain't Got Time For That Crap

Sam found that there was very little she wouldn't do for the people of the neighborhood she had invested in. Though she was still using some of her own money to survive on, the restaurant made enough to operate and occasionally allowed her to do some extra things. It was getting better. She eventually got her phone service back. It was an unremarkable day when she met Eva at the bus stop. Eva struggled with three children—the oldest, who couldn't have been more than three, a younger toddler, and a baby. Watching her get them wrangled onto the bus was like watching a rodeo. Sam almost wanted to cheer for the toddler who was determined to escape her fate at all costs. The older child was too curious about the bus stop sign itself to listen to her mother, who held the large armful of baby and wheeled her shopping cart while attempting to snag the toddler. Sam remembered trying to wrangle marines who had been cooped up on a ship for a month and took pity on the tired-looking mom.

"May I help you?"

When Eva nodded, she scooped up the younger toddler in one arm and the older child in the other.

"Come along now. Your mother doesn't have that many arms."

She nodded to Eva and stepped on the bus with the children, who seemed to be too surprised at the strange person holding them to do anything about it. As Sam sat down across from the woman, the children still firmly ensconced in her grip, the three-year-old's lip trembled. The woman leaned the folded shopping cart against a seat, readjusted the baby into one arm, and waved the child toward her. Sam handed the older child over to her mother but kept a firm grip on the toddler. The child twisted on her knee to look at Sam. Sam blinked.

"Hello."

The youngster didn't say anything. Sam looked at Eva.

"Long day?"

"Just startin'."

"So a long day."

This woman had an accent Sam hadn't heard from anyone in the area before. It was a mixture of "inner city" and "southern belle."

"New to the area?"

The woman shook her head, "Oh, no. Been here all my life. Born in the same apartment I live in today."

"Really? I've never met anyone who has lived in the same place their whole life."

The woman didn't say anything. The child on Sam's knee patted at Sam's face and then at her own. The child was gentle, and Sam didn't stop her.

"May I ask you how many times a week you have to go shopping with the cart to get enough food home for all of you?"

The woman seemed surprised, "Ah...a few times a week. Maybe three?"

Sam felt stunned and shook her head, "With a thirty-minute ride and three children every time?"

The woman shrugged, "We all get along fine most of the time."

"You know, there is a restaurant on First if you are interested in getting rid of some of these trips."

The woman made what looked like an uncomfortable snort.

"Yeah. I've heard about that place. You run it, don't you?"

"Yes."

"Yeah. Look. I ain't got time for that crap. Sure, for a few weeks I don't pay nothing, or just a little, and then all of a sudden you're telling me I gotta pay, or you are reducing your portions, or you're late with cooking, and then I'm out of my schedule, the kids are cranky, and problems just pile up. Even worse, you ask me to do things I can't do, like work for you. I gotta work three jobs! If I am late for just one of them, one time, I get fired. I can't afford a scam."

Sam sighed internally, "I can understand those concerns, but if you find yourself completely out of options or out of time, it's there.

A chunky man from a row back piped up, "What Eva needs is a man!"

A few other men around laughed, but Eva rolled her eyes up toward the roof of the bus.

"A man ain't gonna solve my problems. I'll do that myself, thank you very much! I trust myself. My life is hard, there's no getting around that, but I do *not* need someone else to fix it for me. If I have a problem, that's how it goes. I gotta fix it, so I just do. I had no water for six months until someone finally turned it back on for the whole block! There's me pregnant and everything. What did I do? I go get bottles of water and bring 'em home. Walked across the street to fill 'em from the tap. If I had waited for someone else to fix it, I woulda died of thirst."

Eva turned her gaze back to Sam.

"And you come along, offering everyone a supposed free meal! No. No, I do not need that kind of crap. No man or woman is going to solve anything for me. Only I can do that. I stand on my own two feet."

Sam nodded, "That's an admirable way to live."

Eva looked startled and slightly suspicious. Had the woman never had a compliment?

"Thank you. It does for me," she responded quietly.

Sam fell quiet for a while. It was hard to understand Eva's anger. Feeling uncomfortable, Sam looked around the bus at the adverts. When Sam felt the toddler's head droop to her shoulder, she looked at Eva uncertainly. Eva shrugged and smiled.

"She does that all the time. It's the movement of the bus."

The atmosphere became a little more relaxed. Sam leaned back a little in the seat. How could she get a better sense of who Eva was without making her suspicious again? Asking her directly where she worked would probably sound bad...but...

"Do you have to travel far to get to work?"

Eva shrugged, "Only for two of the jobs. I do the third from home."

"Oh? Transcription?"

"Do I look that educated? I stuff envelopes."

Sam matched Eva's shrug, "There's no way to tell how educated you are until you decide to tell me. You seem to be confident and perceptive. Those are both qualities that are good in a transcriptionist."

Eva laughed, "I don't think so. I barely made it past eighth grade. I clean laundry for a living."

"Have you ever wanted to do anything different?"

"Sure, who wouldn't?"

"There are plenty of opportunities for education."

"It ain't like I got a lotta time on my hands. I can't be running around the city with three little kids. You see how much trouble I have shopping."

"How about online?"

Eva rolled her eyes, "Does it look like I have a computer?"

Sam sighed, "I can't tell anything about you just by looking at you. There are several colleges that offer scholarships and free computers."

"Technology is not going to solve my problems."

"It could help."

"Yeah, like it helped two of my jobs disappear, because they didn't need me anymore."

Sam frowned, "I don't understand.."

"The first job I ever got was as a knitter. I was really good at that. I could follow a pattern and turn out pieces really quickly. But the company got a machine that could do it faster. It took the place of fifty workers. It wasn't much better at my next job, which was to sort mail. A machine took that job too. Anything I can do, a machine can do it better, faster, and cheaper. No one really needs ME."

"But education makes you more valuable!"

"Valuable? Do I look…" Eva shook her head in exasperation before she finished the sentence and started over.

"I am not an antique. It doesn't matter how valuable I am. What people see when I walk up to apply is a poor black woman with three kids, and they don't need my kind of trouble. Who's going to watch your kids? What if you have to work late? I have been asked all of it, and it's all equally humiliating."

"You could learn to do something from home that isn't stuffing envelopes."

Eva let out a disbelieving snort. Sam decided to go for broke. The woman seemed to appreciate honesty.

"Look. The truth is, the world is changing in ways we don't want it to. In a very short time there won't *be* any jobs that you can do anymore. They are all going away; you've already seen that. Unskilled labor isn't necessary in the public sector anymore. You're getting pushed to the fringe of society. There is only one thing you can do, and that's to make them want you, or offer them something they don't already have. Learn something that they want to pay you for."

"Reality check, woman. Even if I find a job that pays more, I lose my benefits. I can't afford to lose those. If I was working a full-time job, I would have to pay for the children's medical, and I can't afford that. After paying my rent, I got just enough left to buy food. With a full-time job, I have to pay taxes that take away more money than what I get for food now, *and* I have to find someone to take care of my kids. It ain't that I don't want to work more, but even if I did, how would I survive?"

It seemed a catch-22 to Sam. She wanted to argue for better education, but this was far from a perfect world for these communities. Sam understood the anger just a little better now. Idealism and practicality didn't always mix well. Certainly not where people who just wanted to live were concerned. It was easy for Sam, who was familiar with technology. She doubted Eva even had a telephone. Putting herself into that position was an almost impossible task. Take away the certainty...take away the resources at her disposal...Sam had gotten a touch of that desperation while setting up the restaurant. Imagine if she hadn't had her disability. That cut a thousand dollars from her monthly allowance. If she had no disposable income as well, she wouldn't have been able to get a new stove, which was her main tool for making food. What if she had other people dependent on her for food, for clothing, for warmth? She would never have wanted to expose children to what she had gone through. What if she hadn't had a choice? She looked at Eva with new respect. She could never know for sure how it felt, but it had to be pretty scary.

When the bus reached the grocery outlet store, Sam let go of Eva's toddler after looking at the child very seriously and saying, "Stay close to your mom. She needs you." She was glad to see the child nod soberly.

They all got off the bus, and Sam watched them walk away. She continued on past the grocery outlet store and spent a lot of time wandering around some of the new buildings that were going up. There had been lots of progress since she had first seen them. She even recognized two of the workers from her neighborhood.

She would have tripped over him if he hadn't moved. She saw the movement from the corner of her eye as she was looking up at the building. She grunted and did a hop-skip-jump maneuver to avoid kicking or trampling him. She wound up just shy of his leg and felt like an idiot for almost stepping on him.

He was dressed in a gray coat and had wild hair under his knit cap. He had a cup next to him but he didn't seem to be begging; she thought she saw coffee or some type of liquid in it.

"I'm sorry. Excuse me," she said. "I wasn't paying atten..."

She stuttered as she saw the look in his eyes. He was terrified. The fear was blatant. His nostrils were flared, and he had abruptly curled up, hugging his knees. Sam knew that look. She shivered. She had seen that look in the mirror. The stark, unreasoning panic. Her heart fell like a stone. She reached out toward him.

"Hey, are you okay?"

He scrambled away from her and took off. His footsteps pounded the pavement away from her.

"Well, that was entirely the wrong thing to do," Sam muttered to herself. Suddenly her interest in the buildings had waned, and the air seemed a little chillier. She couldn't fix it all.

Sometimes the difficulties got a whole lot more personal than just how much food she had to purchase for the restaurant or the differences in the people who lived around her. The argument started when Evette came in and flopped into a chair across from her sister.

"I can't believe Mom won't take me with you guys. Just because she wins a ski trip to Colorado. Can't you talk to her?"

"No!"

"Why not??"

"Because you don't deserve it."

"What do you mean I don't deserve it? I'm part of the family too."

"You live with Grandma."

"So?"

"Mom won that ski trip, because all the people in the house helped her. You didn't help! You never help! You didn't even think about Mom until she won it."

Just a few moments later they were screaming in each other's faces. Sam got in between the two bristling teenage sisters, arms outstretched between them. Katie had tears streaming down her cheeks and had her finger pointed at Evette. She pushed her chest lightly against Sam's fingers.

"You! You have *no* idea!! You witch! Complaining. *God*. What kind of selfish person *are* you? Mom and Dad tried for years to talk to you. Years! All you could do was put on that act. "Oh I'm so hurt. Nobody loves me. I'm going to kill myself!"

Katie stopped as her voice became ragged and she sucked in a sob.

"We all *loved* you! You didn't care at *all* that we loved you! Four times we wound up in the hospital hoping you wouldn't die. I don't know how Mom did it. Standing there watching you. All you could do was smile. You smiled, and went out and did it again. Boys, drinking, drugs, stealing. You almost killed Dad. He had to work so hard to keep you out of jail he almost went to jail himself."

Katie pounded on the table nearest her, but the pounding was weak. She finally just sat down.

"Now you're complaining that you don't get to go skiing with us? Come *on*! When—when did you ever earn that kind of a trip? You've been with Grandma for two years! She's given you everything! We didn't have what you had, and you have the guts to come to me and whine! No. You know what? No!"

Katie stood up and shook her finger at her sister again, "No! Never again! If you want to be a part of this family..."

Katie slapped her own chest for emphasis "Part of *my* family, you have to show us you mean it! We're not doing that again! We— no."

Katie finally stopped yelling.

"We love you, but you're going to have to find some way to tell us that it's okay to love you. You're not hurting Mom and Dad again, and no, you're *not* coming on this trip with us. You stay behind for once. You stay behind and learn what it is to be left out. That's the consequence. If you're here when we get back, we'll talk, but not before. Don't knock on the door, don't go see Dad at work, don't try to see me at school. I will have you arrested if you do! You have a whole month to think about it. A whole month to yourself!"

Lowering her arms, Sam warily watched Katie grab her coat and walk out the door before she finally relaxed. She turned to look at Evette who stood with her eyes cast down at the floor, her face red with anger and shame. Evette quietly picked up her chair and set it by the table. Every person in the restaurant had been stunned into silence. Evette quietly collected herself, wiped her nose, and laid some money on the table.

"Thank you for the food," she whispered and headed for the door.

Sam watched her close the door behind her and rubbed her eyes with the heels of her hands.

"Sam, I don't understand, why didn't you stop them?"

Sam put her hands down. The question came from another teenager.

"What do you mean?"

"Last week you made me and Eugene sit down and talk when we were fighting. Why didn't you make Katie and Evette do that?"

"You asked for help."

"No, we didn't!"

"Oh yes, you did. You asked me to decide which one of you was right. I just made sure you guys could decide between yourselves."

"What's the difference?"

"Have you ever tried to make someone do something they don't want to do?"

"Not really."

Sam considered her words carefully.

"I used to ride horses as a teenager. I was on a trail with one of the ponies one day when he refused to go any further. I decided I had to make him do what I wanted. I hit that pony pretty hard. More than once. In the end it didn't do any good; the only thing that pony learned was to be scared of me. He still didn't go the way I wanted him to go. He also gave me problems every time I ever rode him afterward. People are like that too. If you force them to do what you want, the only thing they learn is resentment. The only thing you get out of it is a load of guilt."

"Hey, weren't you in the military?"

"Yes."

"The military is all about forcing others to do what you want to do, isn't it?"

"No. A good military is about appropriate response tactics to keep a population safe."

"So it's not about oil or land or religious control?"

"Weren't we talking about personal conflict?"

"I guess."

Sam drummed her fingers on the table.

"Look, what we really need to keep in mind are the things that are in our power to change. Katie made her choice. There was no way I could have changed her mind."

"But they almost got into a physical fight!"

"Which is why I got in between them, but unless they ask for help, I still won't tell them how to fix their problem."

The girl looked very dubious.

"It may hurt us when someone makes a choice that we don't like. And we can offer to be there for them, but we can't make them take our help. It's each individual's choice what to do with their life."

"What if it hurts someone else?"

"We can try to prevent the hurt to someone else, but we still can't make that person change."

The kid shrugged, "I still don't think it makes any sense."

"Does your mom make you clean your room?"

"Yeah."

"Are you looking forward to the day when you move out and you don't have to?"

"Yeah!"

"Your mom can offer to teach you to clean up all the days you stay with her, but when you move out on your own, cleaning up behind yourself will be your decision. There won't be anything your mom can say or do that will make you clean up if you don't want to. Do you think your mom would visit very often if you had a filthy apartment?"

"Well I'd clean up if she—oh."

"Yeah. There it is. Your motivations will be what make you change, and that's different for every person. Only you can decide to make that change. We can make kids go to school, but we can't make them decide to learn. We can only offer the opportunity."

That discussion stayed in Sam's brain, especially the part about offering an opportunity.

27

Dinner

Sam and Tito spent days preparing for the Patrons' dinner. The new tables arrived that morning, which made Sam shudder in relief. She really didn't want to have the people who gave her money sitting at tables that were ready to fall over.

They were not fancy tables, but they were at least sturdy and meant for commercial use. Long slabs of recycled wood had been sanded and finished and just needed to be bolted to their supports. No two were the same. The kids who came in for their packed lunches oohed and ahhed over the tables that had yet to be put together. There would be more space at each table for the customers but still plenty of space for Sam, Tito, and Elizabeth to walk around.

"Hey! Hey, guys, as you come in, don't forget to read the page here! If you would like to help tonight, I can guarantee treats! Yummy yummy goodness that is not dinner!"

Sam hadn't met most of the patrons that came to the dinner. The only people she *had* met were the elderly couple who had wandered into her restaurant "accidentally on purpose" with help. Luckily, they arrived first.

The older woman took Sam aside for a moment and gave her a sheet with all the patrons' names on it.

"I have to warn you that most of my friends have never been to this section of town. There was one couple whom I couldn't convince to come, no matter what. They were positive that they'd be mugged, raped, and left for dead the second they left their car."

"Oh. How...disappointing."

The older man walked over with a glass of water in hand, "Don't worry, they aren't all like that. Most of them are quite decent."

"Good to know. Oh, I hired some of the kids from the neighborhood to help serve tonight. It's a Wednesday, which is very busy around here for dinner, so I figured I really would need the help. And Elizabeth is here; she's from the Work Resource Center. "

"Oh, please introduce us around, dear. I would love to meet all your friends!" The elderly woman seemed genuinely eager, and Sam smiled at her enthusiasm.

"Here we go. Hey, guys, come on over here. This is my good friend Mary Lynn. She's the one who arranged for me to get some money so I could paint the walls, buy new tables, and get chocolate for the brownies today."

"Brownies!"

"We have brownies?"

"Where?"

"When can we have them?"

"Can we have them now?"

Sam grinned at the questions that were thrown at her all at once and put her hands up in defense.

"Hey, hey, slow down! Here we go. Mary Lynn, I would like to introduce you to Shanna, she's the tall one; Gary is the boy there in the back; then we have Chris; Sloan—not his real name, but I'll find it out eventually; Gary; Ann; Jennifer; Jake; and, of course, Elizabeth is in the kitchen. Elizabeth, come and meet Mary Lynn and Jacob."

"I'm busy!"

Sam nodded, "Trying to tear Elizabeth away from a job is very difficult and not always wise. She should be done soon, though."

Mary Lynn nodded and shook hands with each youngster. They ranged from ten up to eighteen years old. "It's very nice to meet all of you. How do you do? Now let me ask you, how do you like The Lettuce Cup? Is it nice here?"

The youngest girl spoke up first.

"It's warm in here, especially in the winter. I like the bread."

"Sam is nice; she lets us have as much food as we want. My mom can even get food for us if we're sick."

From behind them came a boy's voice.

"She can be real strict though. She made me go back to school."

Sam flushed when she saw James behind them. Mary Lynn looked at him soberly.

"As any responsible business owner should be doing, young man. What is your name?"

Mary Lynn was very forward, and James had no choice but to step up and offer his hand to her, though he looked like what he really wanted to do was bolt.

"Well, this young man looks like he's wanting for either some dinner or some work. Which is it, young man?"

"Well, my Gran is watching TV with a friend, so I don't have anything to do. I guess if you need help, Sam, I can help. I wouldn't mind something to eat, though. I forgot lunch."

Sam clouted the boy gently on the shoulder and smiled at him.

"Go get some of the sliced bread and help Elizabeth, would you?"

Shortly after that, people started arriving. The patrons themselves sprinkled in with the regular customers. A few of them were quite nervous and didn't understand Sam's plan of pay what you can.

"You don't have set prices? How do you know what your prospective is for the next month?"

"By prospective you mean potential profit?"

"Yes. Oh, and how do you know how much to spend on food?"

Sam took a deep breath, "That is...complicated. What I have been doing is taking how many people come in each day and then average that with the amount of money each night. That tells me approximately how much is being spent per person. If that number is greater than the food cost, I have made a profit. I also know how many people I can afford to feed the next month if I know how much groceries cost and the dishes I am planning on making. The taxes come out of net pay each month, and then I pay electricity, water, and gas, as well as purchase groceries from net pay after taxes."

"Have you ever had your prospective exceed your pay?"

"Yes."

The man raised his eyebrows, "How do you deal with that?"

Sam held up her hand, "Just one second. Amy? May I ask you to come over here, please?"

Amy was a woman of about five foot five with long curly hair and a round face. Sam especially liked her for her "can-do" attitude.

"Amy could you please tell this gentleman what you do when the bills get bigger than your pay?"

Amy shrugged, "I work harder."

The man looked confused, "What do you mean work harder?"

"I get another job; I ask for more hours; I make something to sell. I work harder. It's not like I can afford to fail. It's my family."

"Thank you, Amy."

The man watched her go back to her seat, "I'm not sure I understand."

"It's what we all do in this neighborhood. We work harder when we have to. We get up earlier, go to bed later, find something cheaper. Make a way to spend less."

"And this—works?"

"With lots of soup? Yes. Most of the time I do break even. A few times I have gotten a generous profit, but not often."

"But why do you continue to operate if you are operating on nothing but a line with no real profit in sight?"

Sam thought carefully.

"When a prospective employee starts, they usually start at minimum wage, correct?"

"Yes."

"And thus their family will be starting at minimum wage. Now they will struggle for a while. Say six months down the road they are good employees. You are a fair supervisor as well. Barring any company disasters, you both continue to improve. You give the employee raises based on their satisfactory performance. Their performance increases your profits given optimal market conditions. Do you have a reason to expect that they will suddenly become unhappy and quit?"

"No, not really. I provide comprehensive health benefits and a reasonable vacation policy for my employees."

"Ah, wise decision. A happy employee comes to work eager and willing. What happens if an employee doesn't eat in the morning?"

"Well, I can usually expect a grumpy employee until lunchtime."

"What happens if they don't eat lunch?"

"They get hungry. Very hungry."

"And cranky, and tired, and their work performance goes down."

"Yes."

"The people of this community are no different from a company. Every person has a job in it whether they think they do or not. If they are hungry, they are going to snap at each other and make each other's lives more difficult. If they have a reliable source of food, even if they are cold and tired, these people in the community are more likely to be kind to one another. The machine continues to work. A happy, well-fed person in the community is an asset. The community prospers. Right now, this community is broken. It can heal, but slowly. If I, at my own expense, make sure that this community has one part of their lives they don't have to worry about, namely reliable food, then they are going to be more willing to invest in their community. They will be happier with each other. Even if I, personally, do not profit right now, everyone profits, and when they come in happy, willing, eager to go to work, I will have done my job. I don't need a Mercedes. I just need people to trust me."

"How very socialist of you."

"Socialism is a tag word to express disgust for those who dare to do things differently. It no longer retains the original intent of the word. Do you truly want the government to own and manage all the industry? No, of course you don't. You want people to stand on their own two feet and contribute to society so you don't have to feel resentment that you're hefting their share of the work."

Sam stopped for a moment to take a drink of water and to really look at Joshua before she continued. He was looking at her slightly warily, as if she was voicing the thoughts he hadn't wanted to share.

"From our very beginnings, we as a species have learned to cooperate so that all of us might survive. That meant sharing our knowledge, our cultural beginnings, and our resources, like food. Utilizing competition to thin our ranks was useful a long time ago when we had not yet learned how to form permanent communities, when we did not have the medical technology to understand how our biology worked, when a weakness meant death for the group. But we are not unreasoning animals anymore. Cooperation and understanding gets us a whole lot further as a species. With all these resources at our disposal, it's not about scarcity any more.

We are redefining what it is to be human. It's a struggle. I would rather support others in their struggle than force them to undergo unnecessary deprivation just because of my views of what I think others 'should' be doing."

Elizabeth chose that moment to bring hot, freshly sliced bread to the table. She looked at Sam a little sheepishly after she had served everyone, "I don't have the little bits finished yet."

"That's ok. Elizabeth, I would like you to meet Haley and Joshua and their son Scott."

"It's nice to meet you." Elizabeth was very careful to pronounce her words. Scott looked up from the bread.

"Did you make this, Elizabeth?"

"Sam taught me how."

"It is really good. I love fresh bread more than anything."

Haley spoke up, "It must have been all that German Zweiback I gave him as a toddler."

They laughed before Sam moved on. No other conversation was quite as involved, but each was intense. Questions ranging from how Sam thought of letting people pay what they could to what Sam could cook.

The customers and patrons alike were treated to Tito's special pasta sauce with the egg noodles made with flour and egg, along with fresh salad. After dinner Sam took the patrons to the back of the restaurant. All the customers turned to stare. They all knew what was back there, but Sam had purposely not told the patrons about the hydroponics. They were instantly transported from a restaurant to a green room filled with fresh smells and the sounds of running water. It was so peaceful that the group seemed to hold their collective breath.

"Here is one of my big plans. This is how I will make the community better. As you can see, only half this space is used right now. When I can afford it, I will set up the other half of the room in the same fashion. I can grow up to forty heads of lettuce right now as well as climbing bean vines. I would like to grow tomatoes, potatoes, onions, and melons. In fact, I would like to purchase the property in back of me and use their facility to grow enough to supply the entire community with fresh food. This is the first step. All the salad that you ate tonight came from this unit. You can see where we cut the lettuce heads just this evening before you arrived. "

Sam went on to talk more about the hydroponics, what she had learned, what worked, and what hadn't. The rest of the evening passed with plenty of respectful glances from the patrons.

28

Failing Is Hard To Do

"The hardest thing I ever had to do was to buy something from the store by myself. I was really scared. We went into the store. My mom said I could get whatever I wanted. I was really hungry. I got some butter rolls and some milk, 'cause I like bread and milk. There were lots of people. I couldn't choose which line to go to. Everyone was bigger than I was, and I was scared. A lady asked if I was lost. I told her no. She let me go ahead of her in line, and when I got to the front of the line, I could see my mom waiting for me a little way away. I waved to her and gave my money to the man who put my bread and milk over the machine.

The machine beeped. The man gave me some money back. I put the bread and milk in my yellow bag. My mom said I did good, and I was happy."

Sam clapped as the little girl stopped reading from her paper.

"That was very good, Jen! It's a wonderful story, and I think your class will like it very much. Do you want to read it again?"

The little girl shook her head and sat down at the table where her snack was. Sam stood and stretched. They had about fifteen minutes together before Jen's mother came to get her. Sam had learned that in the late afternoons before dinner some parents would pay her a little extra if she let the kids sit in the restaurant until they came home. They could stay dry in the rain, do some homework, or play a game or two. Sam was lucky that she had enough experience with disruptive behavior to mediate disputes. Even when two children were angry enough to fight, Sam could keep them calm long enough for their tempers to die down. Sometimes Sam felt very sad, because she knew why the children were angry. They saw it at home, and how do you teach a child not to solve a problem violently when that's how mom and dad do it?

Her sense of responsibility twinged at her when she thought about what she used to do for a living. But she took heart in some of the Colonel's words.

"We're getting more and more people leaving, because they can't handle the job anymore. I don't think it's coincidence. I think we're going to have to do some serious thinking about how we are solving these situations. If we keep dropping people like this, special units won't be useful anymore. It's all going to come down to the political, because the fact is, fewer people want to be tough military anymore. The climate is changing. It's hard to see someone as the enemy when you can talk to them over the internet and view them as people. Instead of seeing the terrorist as a target, people start to wonder how they became so hate filled, and then it's hard to hate them like they seem to hate you."

Someone interrupted Sam's train of thought as she stuffed an apple slice in her mouth.

"We're sick of homework! C'mon, Sam, tell us a story!"

"A story? What, are you three?"

"You were in the military, you must have some pretty darn good stories."

Sam leaned against a chair and considered.

"Oh alright. Lemme think, lemme think...ahhh, I know. Ahem."

Sam took a sip of water before she started.

"Looking to get kidnapped was not what I had in mind when I went walking through the desert, but I knew it was a possibility. Now, standing across from the mafioso-type chieftain, I awaited his "judgment." Around me, many men with guns. Their clothes were rags...it was obvious some of them hadn't eaten in a while. Their darting glances gave them away.

The chieftain walked over to a corner and returned carrying a bottle and two glasses. He thumped the bottle on the table, sat down next to me, and muttered to the man who was translating for me.

"You can drink?"

I shrugged, "I'm a slow drinker, and I'm thirsty, so it'll be slower."

One of the men next to me barked out in laughter and spoke derisively. Unfortunately, the translator kept on translating.

"She drink slow, but she die fast! These American whores cannot *drink*!"

The rest of the men laughed at that man's joke. I pinned him with my eyes. He stared back at me with a glare worthy of the The Undertaker. I never dropped my gaze, just set my jaw and stared at him. His nose finally twitched, his eyes were just glaring in fury, and he started to step up to me. The boss next to me started to get up, too, but I decided I'd had enough. Either I was going to win and die, lose and die, or I was gonna get a chance to drink. I grabbed the man by his wrists and twisting my hands dropped to my knees. He was forced to wrench his gun in another direction to keep from shooting the boss, and suddenly I had the weapon in my hands. I smacked him across the face with the butt of the weapon and as he put his hands up, I hauled it back and nailed him in the nose. Then I did it again, and again...and again. Then I turned the weapon around, shoved the muzzle into his eye, flipped the safety, and fired a shot into his brain.

Then I turned my mind off. I would pay for that later. I would pay so dearly, but right now I had to stay alive. I just threw the weapon to one side and ignored all the other men with weapons. I sat at the table and took one of the shot glasses from the boss and poured it full. I took a long, slow, exaggerated sip.

"I drink slow."

Sam looked around the table where the faces were staring at her in various phases of amazement. She heard a small voice,

"What...what happened then?"

Sam tipped the chair casually, letting the front legs thump down on the floor.

"I drank. Three days later, they negotiated for my release, and I never heard of the boss or his men again. They just seemed to walk away into the desert and disappear."

"How did you pay?"

"Pay?"

"Yeah. you said you'd pay for that later. How did you pay?"

Sam got up, making sure they all had to look "up" at her while she spoke.

"I pay every single time I remember how it feels to kill someone. Taking a life means taking away that person's every choice they will ever have from that moment on. It means depriving someone of a family member, a loved one, a brother or sister. It also means depriving the human race of whatever that person may have been contributing, be it genetic material or their thoughts. After you kill someone, nothing is possible for that person ever again."

The silence was deafening as that thought percolated through the layers of consciousness. Sam walked away. Tito leaned over to her as she leaned against the oven,

"You didn't really do that, did you?"

"Nope."

Tito breathed a sigh of relief. Sam turned her eyes to his. Her eyes held a bit of ice.

"But I didn't think it would be appropriate to tell about the time I saw a seven-year-old blow himself up in a public mall because his religious leader told him to."

Tito looked ill, and the children weren't done with her quite yet.

"Sam, have you ever failed?"

"Failed? What do you mean?"

"Have you ever not done something you said you could do?"

"Oh yes. Lots of times."

Just as the last child left, her second employee from The Resource Center walked in.

"Hi there, Tony, come on in. We're just about to get ready for dinner."

Tony was quiet. So quiet, in fact, Sam felt a flutter of uncertainty. It was one thing to be able to communicate with strong-willed Elizabeth, but Tony was far more self-effacing. She had liked his respectful demeanor when she watched his video at the center. She thought he would be great for greeting customers at the door.

Sam showed Tony each table and told him which tables were good for which types of people. He nodded when she asked him if he understood the job. He still hadn't said anything when the first people arrived, but his broad smile to them from across the room seemed very promising, and the first customers took to his personality, chattering to him and to each other comfortably. Sam escaped into the kitchen and began filling plates. Tony showed up for each plate with satisfying promptness. The restaurant filled rapidly with people.

Now and then, the customers seemed to pile up at the door, but the jam would clear on its own. Then at one point the entire room got quiet. Sam stopped what she was doing and looked at her customers. All of them were turned toward the front door. There was a small cluster of people there. Tony was nowhere to be seen. Sam yanked her gloves off and wiped her hands on a towel, moving toward the front door. She wedged her way through the cluster of people.

Tony huddled by the front door. A woman was trying to get him to get up. Sam took charge.

"Okay, everyone needs to back up. If you haven't been seated, please take whichever table you like. Come on, please give Tony some space!"

Reluctantly the group moved away, and Sam closed the door to further customers. She sat down on the floor and waited patiently. Tony eventually looked up from where he was huddled. His face was wet with tears. Sam held out the towel to him.

"Here you go, Tony."

He took the cloth and sat back against the wall. He was gulping back semi-sobs. Gradually Sam heard the conversation in the restaurant return to normal. One of the regular customers had started snagging plates for other customers. Sam didn't mind. They could help themselves for now.

Tony finally calmed down and was breathing normally again. Sam breathed a sigh of relief.

"It was too many people, wasn't it?"

Tony nodded.

"I'm sorry, Tony. That was my fault. Would you like a different job to do?"

Tony sniffed and shook his head.

"Would you like to go home?"

Tony nodded.

"Well. I can understand that."

Sam got up and offered a hand to Tony. He didn't take it but got up by himself. He glanced at her and, still not saying anything, opened the door and left. Sam put her face in her hand. What had she told Jen? She had failed many times? Add another one. She took out her phone and stepped outside. The message box for the resource center rang through.

"This is the Work Resource Center. Please leave a message at the tone."

"Hello. This is Sam Olabode at The Lettuce Cup. There was a problem tonight at my restaurant. I hired Tony to work for me, but I'm afraid that he had to leave early. Please have the coordinator call my number. Thanks."

The rest of dinner was subdued. Sam piled the dishes in the sink and scrubbed them soberly. It was awful. The hot rinse water comforted her a little but not as much as she would have liked. She took her medication and slid into her sleeping bag feeling crushed.

The coordinator from the resource center got back to her promptly the next morning.

"Hello, Sam; can you tell me what happened?"

"Oh, crap, it was really all my fault. I think I just assumed too much. Tony was so quiet, I kind of rushed him through what he was supposed to do and then left him to his own devices. The crowd got too much for him, I think. I'm really sorry."

"Sam. Try to calm down just a little. I'm not sure I understand. Could you start from the beginning?"

"Well, when Tony arrived, I told him how to greet the customers and seat them. He nodded that he understood. But when the crowd got really thick, I think he just felt overwhelmed. He finally stopped what he was doing, and I found him huddled in a ball by the door. I think I really should have paid attention to that bit of uncertainty I had when he came in and didn't say anything. Did I mention how sorry I am?"

"Yes Sam, you mentioned that. I saw Tony this morning, and he seemed okay. He didn't file a complaint about you. Did you ask him to leave?"

"No, I asked him if he wanted a different job, but he shook his head. So I asked him if he wanted to go home, and he nodded, and I let him go. I couldn't just make him stay after that."

"Ah, I see. Well. I do agree that you probably made some mistakes in the beginning there, but knowing Tony, I think he made a mistake or two as well. Sam, I don't want you to think that you have to treat Tony like he's a piece of fragile china. He might have been overwhelmed, but I know he can still work for you. I'd like to send him back to you. I promise you, he does talk. I think that was one of the problems. He didn't tell you he didn't know what was going on, and he should have."

Sam nodded to herself. She was relieved, but she had to admit she was even more uncertain than before.

"Are you sure Tony will want to come back? I don't want to force him to come back to a place that was so uncomfortable for him."

"Well, I think that Tony really needs to come back, Sam. Tony is actually a good worker, but he does tend to shy away from complicated situations. When he didn't complain to me this morning, I knew that he was still thinking it over. I'll have a talk with him, and if he agrees, I can have him back again tomorrow. Is that ok?"

"As long as it's his choice to come back, I guess I'll work on it."

"Perhaps a less interactive job would be a good idea. Cleaning, washing dishes, things of that sort."

"Well, that definitely needs to be done, so yes, I can easily give him that job to do."

"Good. Give me a call tomorrow and tell me how it works out."

Tony showed up again the next day. This time, Sam set up a comfortable situation for him to communicate in.

"Hello Tony. Come on in. How are you today?"

She waited for him to respond, and he smiled at her.

"I'm better than yesterday, thank you."

"Good. Would you like to do a different job today?"

Sam thought she saw relief in Tony's face.

"Yes, please."

"Well, there are lots of jobs here to do. The first one is to make sure the entire floor gets swept before lunch. We have to put the chairs on top of the tables to do that; then after the floor is swept, all the tables need to be wiped with sanitizer. Let's do the floor together and it will go faster."

Tony had a keen eye for detail. He noticed dirt on the floor trim and dust in the window sills. After the floor was clean and the tables were wiped, Sam had him lay out cutlery at the tables.

"Now each time a customer leaves, all you need to do is bring the plate to the sink, wipe the table, and put new cutlery down at each place that was used, okay?"

"Okay, Sam."

Nervously, Sam went back to work in the kitchen, and she noticed the crowd get bigger, but although Tony was pressed into constant movement, he didn't seem to be overwhelmed. After lunch Tony did the dishes with Sam and then swept the eating room floor by himself while Sam cleaned the kitchen. It was a far more successful day, and Sam lost her nervousness bit by bit. By the time Tony was ready to leave, Sam was sorry to see him go.

29
No Longer U/K

Bread was no problem for Sam anymore, neither was finding new recipes or understanding how to cook them—unless they included rice. Slowly the plastic-covered pages of recipes began to conglomerate into a book-sized pile.

She looked up from flipping through the pages to see the inspector walk in the door. She grinned.

"You just keep turning up like a bad penny, don't you?"

The inspector's mild expression turned puzzled.

"Oh? How is that?"

Sam picked up a dirty baking dish and took it to the sink to wash it.

"Well, you're ugly as all get out, and no one wants to deal with you, but you are that fraction of society that is intrinsically important to our self-evaluation. Like a penny, you give us the ability to express appreciation in smaller amounts. So even though you frustrate the hell out of us, we need you."

Nero slipped on a glove and began walking around the kitchen while Sam washed the dish. He idly swiped the glove across the top of the refrigerator. Sam watched from the corner of her eye. He didn't seem focused on finding anything, just making the display of searching. He nudged the trash can from its usual position, then finally stopped "inspecting" and turned to her as she lifted the dish from the sanitizing solution.

"Well, your economic metaphor needs some work, but I think I understand the compliment. I'm not sure why you offered it, though."

Sam placed the dish carefully on the drying rack and wiped up the water on the counter and dried her hands.

"Mister Amelo, would you care for some coffee?"

Before he could begin to wrinkle his nose, she smiled and pointed toward the new coffee machine.

"Don't worry, I've improved."

Nero sat at a table and ran his hands across the smooth, solid, surface. He turned to look at all the new tables, the chairs, the inventive stenciling. Even the corners were swept of the slightest trace of dust. The tiny herb plants on the walls were delicate reminders of the nature of the business. Every part of both rooms was organized, clean, had purpose.

The cup of coffee Sam handed Nero was not gourmet, but it had a robust freshness. The same aroma that invited one to get up in the morning. Inviting. That's what this restaurant had turned into. The sun streamed in the clean windows, obstructed only by the shadow of the graffitied flower in a corner of one of them.

"You have improved your business quite a lot, Miss Olabode."

Sam smiled and sat in a chair across from him.

"Yes, it has improved, hasn't it? It's been a long row to hoe, but I'm getting there. I have good prospects with regular business. If I can start getting more cash flow, I'll be able to expand someday. I've managed to hire some reliable help, too. My days are full now but not overwhelming."

"I can't say I am not surprised, but it is a pleasant surprise. What are you planning on doing next?"

"Getting a real bed to sleep in."

"Oh, really?" He smiled, almost a laugh for him. "Wait...you aren't joking?"

Sam shook her head, "Sadly, no. I have been sleeping in a sleeping bag—a comfortable one—but on the floor. I would really love a bed. Even a bad one! The money to buy one has been tied up in the resta...in the Lettuce Cup."

Nero nodded, really surprised now.

"I underestimated your dedication: learning to cook, finding money to get new equipment, hiring help. I didn't think you'd be around this long."

Nero held up the coffee cup, "I hope you are around for a good long while, Miss Olabode. We need more dedicated business owners like you."

"Why, Mister Amelo, I deeply appreciate the compliment."

"Likewise, Miss Olabode. Keep learning. It will help you as you expand."

The two enjoyed another cup of coffee together. The antagonism was gone between them. Even Nero's tense anticipation was gone. He crossed his legs and wondered what Sam had up her sleeve next. Whatever it was, he was sure it would be for the good of this run-down section of a city that had its sights set on gunning it down. Just by existing, Sam had set up a small beacon of light in the middle of the whole mess.

30

Disaster

After many months of working night and day, Sam finally decided that going to get things for the restaurant was not enough time off. She wanted a break. She wanted a real break. She decided to go to a museum that was a few hours away by bus. Old artifacts fascinated her. So she locked up the restaurant at a hair before the crack of dawn and took a commuter bus to the city close to her. It was much busier than her city. It had skyscrapers that blocked out the sun.

She started out the day with a buttered bagel and black coffee from a small shop and people-watched while she sat there.

"So many people wearing business suits," she said sotto voce.

Sam felt like a little girl watching the foot traffic pass by. Her mother used to chide her for the way she would just watch people for hours.

"It's not nice to stare, Larou. It makes people uncomfortable!"

"But Mama, how am I supposed to know what people are like if I don't look at them?"

"You look at everything, Larou, not just the person. Look at where they are going, where they have been, let your eyes travel. If you keep your eyes on a person too long, it's like you're drilling a hole in their personal space!"

So Sam had learned to take in everything. It was a skill, and she perfected it, blending in so that she could see the world pass by, and she used it again now. Multiple times she witnessed other people taking a break on the benches scattered around the bank square. A few of them had only sat for minutes before the bank security guard asked them to leave. Three of them were people of color. Sam felt disgust. She had been sitting for almost an hour, and no one had asked her to move. She checked the time on her phone and started her long walk to the museum.

The museum building was a piece of art in itself. Swooping curves reminded her of the Guggenheim. Colored portal windows and crisp clean edges between building and lawn. A wide front entrance was extremely modern and inviting. The museum was sectioned. History, Art, Natural, Scientific, Children's. Sam started with the historical section. Tiny hand-carved sarcophagi caught her attention, then axe heads, whose method of metal work was still a mystery. The art section had a tree made of wrapped wire stems. The wires themselves were amazingly thin. It took thousands upon thousands painstakingly wrapped to make the tree. At the end of the branches were globes that caught the light streaming in from the window. It was very peaceful.

In the science section the lab had a large glass panel that let people see what the scientists were doing. A monitor not only described the process of the current experiment, but also showed a picture via the streaming link from the International Space Station where the same experiment was being done.It was confusing, but fascinating. The nature section was currently populated by the skeletons of creatures ancient and modern such as fish, beavers, birds, and even mice and rats.

Eventually she had exhausted all there was to see, and she decided it was time for a late lunch before the commuter bus took her back home. While she was at lunch she kept her ears open, and she heard a couple talking softly next to her. Their heavy accents told her they weren't native to the country, but being unfamiliar with languages, she couldn't identify where they might be from.

"Did you see all the homeless people over on that street?" the man said. "That's what happens when you don't have social services. Those poor people have no roof over their head when it rains; they can get kicked out of any restaurant or even a public park. What happens when they have to go to the bathroom, and there isn't a public bathroom open? They lock them here at night!"

His wife made a few noncommittal sounds while chewing and swallowing and then replied.

"I can't imagine not even being able to get up to get a cup of tea for myself or knowing if my stuff was safe from being stolen. I'm glad we don't live here."

On the one hand, Sam felt an instinctive urge to defend the country she lived in. "They were doing the best they could!" she wanted to say. On the other hand Sam knew that wasn't true; they were not doing the best that could be done. Many people who had more money blocked the efforts of those with less money, and that was the point. It was all about money. If you didn't have money, it seemed you didn't have any power. Sam wished she could just make it all better. Every last problem. She knew it didn't work like that, but it was a good-fairy wish. On her way back to the bus, she tossed a coin into the Children's Wishing Well and wished for just that. For things to stop being complicated and the problems to stop.

The ride home was long. The bus driver had dimmed the lights for those who wanted to sleep, and Sam was grateful that he had also turned up the heat. She slipped into a half drowse, waking only to take her medication on time with a sip from the bottle of water she took with her. When she got back, she noticed that First Street seemed awfully dark. Every street light was out. She groaned. Brown and blackouts were not common, but they did happen. She hoped it would end soon. She had a whole fridge full of food.

Then she turned the corner. The sight that faced her was like a crowbar to the gut. Every last window in the restaurant had been smashed. The door hung open—literally hung—from one hinge. The large heavy tables, so solid they were unbreakable, had been gouged. The small tables had been smashed beyond repair. Sam listened carefully at the door for any sounds. Nothing. She reached for her phone and dialed the police.

The waiting was agony. She sat across the street while they went through the building to make sure it was safe. One of the officers began to question her. Where had she gone that day? Why had she gone? Did the door have locks? Whom did she interact with? How much did she drink? What drugs did she do? They asked her if she had kept any weapons in the building, and when she shook her head, they questioned her about it again. When they didn't seem to believe her, going so far as to ask whom she had made angry recently, she felt like exploding. Her *life* was in that restaurant, and they were treating her as if she had *asked* for it to be destroyed! As if *she* were the one responsible!

The crushing weight of defeat seized her in the chest. After a minute she realized that the weight didn't seem to be going away. A fine time for a panic attack. Right in front of the police! She was thinking that all the way up until she realized her face had hit the concrete, and this pain was real. It was like a heart attack. She could hardly breathe, each breath taking vast effort and delivering only a minuscule amount of air. She was sure she was going to die, and there was nothing, absolutely nothing she could do about it.

All she wanted to do was breathe! Finally she passed out just as an ambulance screamed toward them.

She didn't wake up for several days, and when she did she was in a VA hospital. She had a breathing tube, and her hands had been secured to the bars of the bed. A nurse was sitting right next to her and saw her eyes flutter open. It took Sam a minute to recognize what the nurse was saying.

"Larou. You're on a breathing machine. I know that you can't feel much. The doctor will be by in a few minutes to check on you, and we'll see if he will let me take out the breathing tube. For now, try to relax. The restraints are only to make sure you don't rip out the breathing tube. I promise I won't leave. Okay?"

Sam managed to blink. She wanted so badly to struggle, but she felt as weak as a newborn kitten. She was grateful to feel air in her lungs again, though. She closed her eyes at the relief of it and felt tears slip from the corners of her eyes. The nurse noticed and dabbed at them gently with a tissue.

"I know it's scary, but you are alive, and we're taking care of you."

Finally Sam slipped into a half doze, letting her eyes close. Then the doctor was there.

"Larou? Larou, I'm Doctor Sajak."

Sam tried to smile and lifted her eyebrows.

"Yes. Like Pat. Now, please hold still; we're going to take your blood pressure, and I want to listen to your heart."

Sam couldn't help it; she shivered in anticipation while the doctor was examining her. He also briefly flashed his light into her eyes.

"Good responses. I think we can take the tube out now."

The nurse began unhooking some of the extraneous equipment and seized hold of the tube.

"Cough please Larou.."

Sam did her best to try to expel the tube from her throat. It felt like she was choking. Then her gag reflex triggered briefly. Then it was gone. She sucked in a breath on her own. Her eyes uncrossed, and she blinked. The nurse set the tube aside and unwrapped the restraints from her wrists so she could rub her eyes. Sam stretched a little and then tried to respond to the nurse's questions, but all that came out was a little squeak when she tried to talk.

"It's ok Larou. It's normal. Your voice will come back. Here, write it down."

Sam took the pad from the nurse.

Please call me Sam, she wrote. Thank you for helping me.

"Oh, you're welcome Sam. I'll let the doctor tell you what to expect next, and I'll get you some water or some juice if you like?"

Sam nodded. The nurse left. The doctor took her place.

"Well, Sam, what happened is that you suffered a case of pulmonary edema. Do you know what that is?"

Sam shook her head.

"It's when your lungs fill up with fluid. You also had a seizure. We managed to get the breathing tube in fast enough after the seizure that you got plenty of oxygen and gave you some medication to relax you. We need to keep you on the medication. We know that you do have some daily medication requirements. The muscle relaxers will not hurt you, and we will make sure you stay on your daily meds. Right now we do not want you to be tense and cough too much. We definitely do not want you having panic attacks until we know what's going on with your lungs. We took a biopsy while you were unconscious, and those tests will be back in a few hours. After that we can decide what else we need to do, okay? Do you have any questions for me?"

Sam wrote, *How long?* then hesitated, took back the pad and added *have I been out?*

"Two days. You've been unconscious for two days."

Sam nodded and leaned back. The nurse came back in and gave her a glass of juice which tasted enormously good. Sam felt ravenous.

She wrote, *Food?"*

"Oh yes, I will get you some food. The cafeteria has some fantastic pasta if you like pasta?"

Sam nodded.

"Okay. Look, here is the emergency button, and that is the remote right there at your fingertips for the television. The backpack you had with you is right there where you can see it; no one will touch it. You have an adult diaper on, because a catheter was contraindicated. If you have to go to the bathroom, I can take it off you and help you to go now. Do you need to go?"

Sam shook her head and motioned toward her gut.

"Yes, you're just hungry. Okay. If you do need to go, please call for someone to help you. Don't get up by yourself the first time. Promise me?"

The nurse's attitude was very firm, and Sam had to promise in writing she wouldn't try to get up by herself. Then she was alone.

A biopsy. What did they expect to find? Did this have anything to do with the panic attacks she had been suffering lately? And what about those extra x-rays and the TB discussion the exit physician had insisted on when she left the military? She had never responded well to the prick test but had never had to do any more than just one x-ray ever to prove she didn't have TB. Could she have TB? No, they would have isolated her, wouldn't they?

Sam realized she was starting to breathe harder, and the monitor that measured her blood pressure began to blip fiercely. Sam forced herself to stop thinking about it. She turned on the television and watched some inane food show until the nurse came in with a tray. On it was a lovely smell of pasta and a rich mushroom cream sauce. The nurse had to convince her to slow down while she ate.

A few hours later she was able to croak again. She allowed the nurses to help her to the bathroom. She needed the help of two of them. Her legs refused to support her, and she swore like the proverbial sailor.

"Weak...ass...piece of...dammit, legs, *work!*"

The nurse left her recovering her breath on the toilet. She took her time, and twenty minutes later allowed the nurses to help her back into bed. She pointed toward her backpack.

"Please? Computer."

"Oh, sure!"

The nurse helped her set up her laptop, plugging it into a nearby socket and putting it on a bedside table. Sam relaxed as she connected to the hospital's Wi-Fi. Then the nurse pulled out the book from her backpack and placed it next to the laptop.

"Just in case you feel like reading something that doesn't involve a screen."

Sam smiled gratefully. The night shift began, and Sam was left to her own devices. She refused to think about the restaurant. She read; she surfed comic strips; she even read the news and weather reports. She noticed that in the window, a few flakes of snow drifted past the window. With effort, she closed her eyes and tried to sleep.

31

Into the Unknown

For two days Sam sat in the hospital trying to relax and not doing a good job of it. She got a headache from trying to relax so much. They gave her some acetaminophen for the headache and asked her so many questions! She asked her own questions, but to her irritation, didn't get much in the way of answers. Finally a bevy of doctors made their way into her room a few days later and shut the door behind them. They each took turns talking about what was wrong with her. She listened carefully, but it wasn't until the doctor who had initially seen her talked that Sam finally got the point.

"Sam. You have lung disease. We don't know how long you have had it, but at this stage it is very bad. It is very likely that it is associated with some damage to your brain. It is a type of pulmonary edema. The damage to your brain may have caused the seizures and the swelling in your lungs. We know you don't smoke, but you have been exposed to several known carcinogens during your military career, and these may have caused the initial damage to your lungs. It wouldn't have been detectable until just a few months ago."

"You said very bad. How bad?"

"The damage to both your brain and your lungs is irreparable."

"Are you saying I'm going to die?"

Instead of giving a cop-out answer, such as, "We're all going to die at some time," the doctor looked at her and nodded.

"Yes, Sam. That is what the evidence is pointing to. We believe the seizures will get worse before your lung problems do, and at some point your brain will no longer be able to function."

Sam tried to take it in. All she could think of at that moment was denial. Her mind threw all kinds of reasons that she couldn't die at her. Wasn't there some list of stages of grief or something? Had she gone through them? Maybe when she wasn't aware of it?

"Sam, I'd like to call a counselor for you. Is that ok?"

Sam took a deep breath, aware that with every breath she was just getting closer to never breathing again. She shook her head. "No. Just leave me alone."

The doctor was reluctant to do so, and a nurse was posted right outside her door. Sam tried to think past the lump in her stomach. Her restaurant was destroyed, and she was going to die. "Unfair" just didn't describe it.

After a week of recovery, Sam took the only course she could imagine. Action. She dug up an attorney, and from her hospital bed, she filed insurance paperwork for the restaurant. Then she went home. She had new medication; she had an inhaler; she had the number of a grief counselor. Her footsteps crunched on the shattered glass. The vandals hadn't left much. The equipment had been too heavy to move, but there was spray paint over every surface. The hydroponics had been torn to shreds. All her food was gone. Her sleeping bag and all personal effects upstairs including the briefcase were gone. Tito found her struggling to pull the large stainless-steel prep table up again and rushed to her aid.

"Sam! Sam! I'm so glad you're back. What happened? Are you okay?"

Sam sat on the prep table, and she felt the prickle in her nose. She wiped at it with a tissue.

"They hate me. The neighborhood hates me, Tito. I don't know why."

"Sam, they don't hate you. This was just some punks who want things, but they don't know how to get them, so they destroy what other people have. Sam, please tell me what happened at the hospital."

Slowly Sam told him, and he listened to it all. His eyes were downcast when she stopped talking. The tears from her eyes soaked the tissue until it fell apart. Tito handed Sam his handkerchief.

"Sam, the neighborhood doesn't hate you. I promise."

Sam babbled about not realizing some people existed while paying attention to others, sure she was talking nonsense. Finally Tito stopped her.

"Sam. I'm going to help you sweep up, and then I'm going to go get a mattress or blankets or something for you to sleep on. I know we can't replace the windows, but I'll sleep down here while you sleep upstairs. You won't have to worry about anybody breaking in, okay? Then tomorrow we'll figure out what to do."

"I already filed an insurance claim..." Sam whispered.

"Then tomorrow we'll see if they got it. Come on now. They didn't take the brooms."

Cleaning up all the glass inside and out helped shore up Sam's feeling of helplessness. The room was bitterly cold, even when Sam got the fireplace going, and in the end they both wound up sleeping next to the fireplace, the wind whistling through the remains of the glass windows.

32

Recovery from the Impossible

It was the insurance representative who caused Sam to take a look at a bigger picture. The man was enormously tall, dressed impeccably, and definitely the darkest man of color she had ever seen. His striking features almost caused Sam's heart to stop again.

"He's not just a black man; he's a black work of art!"

She shook off the feeling after just a few moments of soap-opera-like delusional emotional overload.

"Ms. Olabode?"

"Oh, Sam will do. Are you from Quantified Insurance? I was expecting Suzanne."

"Yeah. A lot of people are clamoring for Suzanne's attention right now. I'm sorry, your business is smaller than all of the others, so I'm afraid we had to send, well, me."

Sam ignored the flip flop in her stomach. This was no time to get funny feelings. She attempted a sardonic but welcoming tone of voice.

"Well, if you're qualified, then you will just have to do. I don't mind, really."

"Oh, yes, I've only been with Quantified specifically for two months, but I'm experienced. Since Suzanne knows how to handle large damage claims, they put her on the big ones."

Sam shook his hand, "I'm sorry, I didn't catch your name."

"Oh, I apologize, my name is Andrew Borenheim. Please call me Andrew."

"Well Andrew—large claims? Is there a rush of large claims right now?"

"Well, I'm not supposed to say, but yes. Actually, I would say your business was probably hit by the same people that have hit several big buildings, the mall, a supermarket, and three coffee shops. That's only our clients. I don't know how many exactly got hit, but I recognize the spray painted markings on your walls and equipment. These guys had it out for someone, and I'll bet you got in the way."

"Have the police caught any of them yet?"

"I don't think so."

"Well, that's a shame."

"Yes. Yes, it is. So I notice that you have cleaned up some of the glass here; did you take pictures before you cleaned up anything?"

"Oh dear...I..."

Tito's voice interrupted them, "Yes, I took them! I took pictures. I just need to run down to the drugstore to get the photos. I used one of those little throwaways. Is that ok?"

"Yes, I don't see why not. Can you tell me what you photographed?"

"If you want, I will go down right now and get them. It's not far."

"I suppose I can do some inspection while you do that."

Sam flashed Tito a grateful smile. "Thank you, Tito. I didn't know you had done that."

"When the police didn't, I figured that we needed some kind of record."

Andrew looked up from his clipboard as Tito left and said, "The police were here?"

"Um, yeah. It's a long story. I haven't been here for a little over a week."

"Which explains the delay in reporting. I see. The police are not known for their exacting attention in this particular part of town, but I *do* have to be exacting. May I see the upstairs?"

"Oh, yes. Please feel free. There's nothing up there. It was all taken."

Andrew wandered around upstairs for a few minutes and then came down,

"They even took your bathtub! That's..."

Sam restrained her first impulse, which was to correct him, and made noncommittal sounds. Andrew continued on his way, and when he inspected the hydroponics area, Sam had to clamp down on the urge to yell at him to get out. It felt like anyone's being back there was sacrilege. When he came out of the area, he stared at her for a moment.

"Say, are you okay?"

"Oh, yes, why do you ask?"

"You look pretty pale, and I just saw you flinch."

"Reaction, I guess. I'm, well, this place means a lot to me. It took me a long time to get it going, and it's going to take a lot of effort to put it back together."

Suddenly a smile touched Andrew's face, "Well, I'm glad to hear you say that. I don't think I've had a single small business owner want the payout option yet."

"Payout option?"

"You did read the policy you purchased, right?"

"Oh! You mean the payout if the business has to close down permanently. Well, yes, I thought about it, but I really need this place. More than that, people have depended on me for a few months now, so I think they might need this place, too. It isn't fancy, but it serves a purpose and fills a need."

"Most small business owners seem to feel that way, and occasionally a big business owner who interacts with their companies or stores on a daily basis seems crushed when something like this happens. They seem to take it as a direct hit to their employees. It can be a pleasant change from those who only view their business systematically in a profit-loss pattern. Well, pleasant to see socially. It is not pleasant for the insurance adjuster who has to go through the lists and lists of claimed losses and decide what fits the claim."

Tito had made his way back and handed the pictures to Andrew.

"These are good. They should do just fine. Here is a copy of my paperwork for you, Sam. I know you have already submitted your financial information, but this tells you how to calculate damages, whom you can call for estimates, and this is all the information I put down from my visit today."

"Thank you. Can you tell me how long it might be?"

Andrew frowned sympathetically. "I'm sorry, Sam, I really can't say how long it will take to process. It could be up to six months before you actually do get paid."

Six months! Sam swallowed hard and nodded. She had trouble finding her voice.

"Okay. Thank you for your time, Andrew."

As he left, Sam sat down to take some deep breaths. Tito sat on the floor across from her.

"How are we going to go six months without windows? Without chairs or anything? I could board up the windows I guess, but where are we going to get enough money to restock with food? I won't be able to pay Elizabeth or Tony. My disability check allows me to live, but it won't cover this."

"You could get a small apartment somewhere and just come back when you get paid. Or you could board up the windows and just live in here until they pay you."

"I can't. I can't sit around. Doing nothing is like dying one day at a time. "

"Maybe you could ask the patrons for help. You could pay them back when you get paid."

Sam put her face in her hands. It was cold, and she had trouble thinking. She was scared and angry, and she still hurt. She had this terrible urge to just lie down and go back to sleep. Tito's hand on her shoulder reminded her that the real world was still there.

"If we clean up outside and start washing the spray paint off, will it make you feel better?"

Sam nodded. They swept the sidewalks and got rid of all the lingering glass from the broken window sills. Sam took the front door off. It was worse than useless, since it wouldn't close at all as twisted as it was. They painstakingly scrubbed and scrubbed at the walls, the floor, the equipment. Sam spent a little of the money she had for the month on strong cleanser, and it worked nicely. After a few days they could only see traces of the graffiti. It was exhausting. Sam fell asleep in front of the fire every night with aching lungs and, more often than not, a burning headache.

It was very, very early in the morning when she saw a shadow moving around outside of one of the empty windows. Sam slipped out of her blankets with ease and crept bent over to the front door, turned the corner, and stared at the shadow. It was much smaller than she was. She heard what sounded like a half-hearted rattle. The shadow fiddled with a can in it's hands. Then Sam knew.

"No windows for you to paint today. Sorry."

"Oh. It's okay," said James. "I was hoping there might be some glass left so I could put a heart on it. I don't want you to leave."

"Well, for the record, I like your graffiti a whole lot better than whatever those punks broke in wrote. They didn't make anything artistic at all. Just a bunch of ugly signs."

"Yeah. I know. I had to lay low when they came through. It's why I don't sign my stuff. So they don't know it's me, you know?"

"Yeah. I get it. Why don't you go on home. Tomorrow come back and I'll give you a sandwich. Maybe we can work something out inside, okay?"

The shadow hesitated, "You'd really let me paint the inside?"

"Yeah. I really would. I think you've got talent and I wouldn't mind displaying it on one of my walls."

"Thanks, Sam."

"You're welcome."

The destruction had affected not just Sam and not just her customers. It would hit workers across the spectrum: retail, construction, realty, hospitality. Even more people packed up and left the city. Why the vandals did what they did was a mystery. It didn't seem to be a protest; it didn't seem to be for any particular reason other than they just wanted to destroy.

The next day, Sam had a chance to pick up a newspaper that headlined interviews with several large business owners who also held no small amount of political influence in the city. She read it out loud while Tito was getting pots out to cook with.

"Head of a major accounting firm, Jeremy McCaffreg, began a storm of controversy today with his announcement that he was helping to reform the city's welfare system. 'No one should be able to take advantage of our city and then destroy it like these hooligans,' he said. While the police have found no evidence to lead to any specific person responsible for these crimes, other business owners have pointed fingers at the city's lower section on First through Seventh Streets. Bank owner Michael Chern was heard to state, 'These people have to start pulling their weight. Their immoral ways have caused destruction to our fair city.'"

Sam put the paper down, feeling a little punched in the gut. Tito slammed a pan down a little more forcefully than strictly necessary.

"These people? *These people?* These people *who?* The poor? The Blacks? The Latinos? Anyone who isn't a white guy making as much money as he does? Just who does he think isn't pulling their weight? Even the homeless walk around picking up more trash than he does!"

Sam couldn't say anything. It appeared as though their whole neighborhood was under fire. The response, of course, made people resentful. There were protests, and backlashes, and police. A few hard-working people Sam knew dropped out of sight, behind bars, swept into the penal system. It felt as if those large business owners really, really wanted this section of the city to die a very ugly death. Sam swallowed her pride and called the patrons who had given so generously before. She hoped they would still see her in the same light.

33

No Way But Up

Three of the patrons agreed to come down to the restaurant with their significant others. The other four had said they would send her money, but they wanted to stay home. She declined the free money; it wasn't what she was after. She and the three patrons stood in the kitchen of the restaurant drinking coffee and eating cheese sandwiches. It was the only thing she could afford to give them. None of the three complained.

"Thank you very much for coming today. I know it took a lot of courage after the vandalism. I am not asking for money this time. What I am asking for is help. I sent each of you a copy of the restrictions the insurance company has given me as well as all the work that needs to be done. Unfortunately these businesses will give me quotes, but they will not do the work unless they are paid first. This is what I would like to do. I will get a quote from the business that you think is best to do the work. If you and the business agree, they will do the work, and you will pay them. Your allotment will come out of the insurance check that will return payment to me. I also need to ask for money for basics, which is to say, food. I have made a list of all the staples I need, and, of course, as soon as I get the money from insurance *or* I make it back from the restaurant, I will repay you. I have contracts written up, but feel free to add to them, and we'll review it together."

One woman looked up from reading her copy, "And may I ask why you don't want to wait until the insurance can pay you?"

Sam took a deep breath, "Well, for one, the people in this community were relying on me for quite a while. If they have to go back to what they were doing before I got here, they may not come back to me at all. The other thing is, I don't know if I have six months to give."

This elicited silence as they all turned to look at her.

"Can you explain that?"

Sam did, in as matter of fact a tone as she could. She knew this increased the patrons' risk. If she died before the insurance payout, they might or might not see their money come back to them.

"The good part is, I have no debt. The entire payment could be apportioned through a probate lawyer. I do not know how the insurance company will deal with the payment, though. They may refuse to pay it at all if I die."

It took a moment for the patrons to respond,

"Well, I know this business. I think I can get them to do the windows and wait for payment from the insurance company. Don, how about you?"

"That door is going to have to be a heavyweight. The wall around it will need to be rebuilt for it. I'll pay for restructuring the wall, but I'd bet if you asked the insurance company to cover an online order of the door, they'd do it. That's security in their pocket right there."

In the end, only two of the three patrons would be owed anything. The person who offered to influence the window company also insisted on doing some small marketing after the restaurant was back up.

"Nothing fancy. A few flyers, some words in the right places, so we can get people back in here. Let them know you are open again. This is not negotiable."

Sam reluctantly agreed. One of the patrons took the conversation in a philosophical direction.

"Most people would have been run out of here by now. Surely the first place that was here left because it got too hard. If you want to stay, then we'll help you stay. It's no hardship on us, and it's the right thing to do."

"Honestly, for me, there's nowhere to go but up," Sam said. "I'm at the bottom. I have nothing left. Not even time."

The hugs she got from the patrons were supportive and warm. The very next day she heard someone pounding on the open door frame even before she'd rolled out of the blankets by the fireplace.

"Hey, yous in here?"

The voice was rough, and the character even rougher. Sam came awake all at once as she almost always did. Still dressed in jeans from the previous day, Sam reluctantly left the fireplace.

"Hey, I'm Sam. How can I help you?"

"I wuz told to git my shiny ass down heah and check yous guys' windows. It looks like doze assholes really did a job on ya."

Sam wondered if the guy was a prankster, or if he really spoke like that.

"I'm sorry, which shop are you from?"

"Al's Glass. We're down the street."

"Oh, yes! I understand now. Yes, they really did a number on this place. Every window will have to be replaced. I'm hoping the frames are still good enough to put the windows into. Can you check that?"

"Oh, no worries, darlin'! I'll check that right now. If you'd be kind enough to sign this here quote ordah, I'll git goin on 'em. Got seven places to do today!"

"May I ask where you're from? You sound familiar."

"Oh! I'm from Brooklyn. Been heah four yeahs now. Ya can still heah it though, can't ya?"

"Oh, yes. A bit."

The guy laughed, a snorting, barking sound. Sam's memory took her back to walking into a bakery with her mother.

"Ah, theah's the little dahlin! Hello, sweethaht! Ya wants a cookie? Look, it's cho-co-late chip!"

There was no way she was going to misbehave with a baker who gave her chocolate chip cookies whenever they walked in the door. She took it and smiled. Her mother sighed in frustration.

"You spoil her!"

"Oh, who else is gonna spoil her if I don'? She's so good in heah!"

"Because you give her cookies!"

"Ahhh, and theah's the trick, Ma!"

She remembered the last hug she ever gave that baker. The day she went to boot camp. The man had tears in his eyes. Sam put on some coffee while the man from Al's measured each window with painstaking care.

The swim instructor, she thought. Sam remembered her, too. The first day she went to the pool dressed in her little pink-flowered, one-piece swimsuit, she dropped her towel, and before her mother could even scream, she had leapt full force into the water. No fear. The instructor had been quick, leaping in after her and lifting her up before she had time to take a lungful of water, though the instructor had told her mother, "This kid's got some great instincts, Ma. She held her breath!"

Sam's mother had not been impressed. If the swim instructor had brought Sam to the edge of the pool, Sam would have gotten one unholy smack on the butt. Wisely, the instructor saw how angry Sam's mother was and decided to start the first lesson then and there.

And everyone had called her mother "Ma." She had no idea why. She hadn't been back in many years, not since her parents had died; it was too painful. These were all people who had known her mother and father. It would only remind her of the loss. The memories were kind to her, though. She liked remembering her early life. The way they would all, as children, torment substitutes with paper balls when the sub's back was turned, playing Hulk Smash at the junkyard. Pretending to take iron bars and pound the already pounded cars then run screaming after their friends. She knew very few of the children here had memories like that. A few of them, maybe, but most didn't walk down the street even with friends, let alone by themselves.

Her father had been the one to teach her to be unafraid. Or at least he taught her how to deal with fear so it wouldn't be so crippling. He also had not questioned her wish to be called by a different name than her given one. His thick brooklyn accent had been comforting.

"Look La -- Sam. I don't care whatcha want to be called. I'll call ya Jesus if'n ya want me to. I loves ya no matter what."

When she was little, he had taught her to deal with bullies directly, although they both knew it was better to have someone at your back. As a scrappy little ten-year-old, she had decided that the direct way was to smack the bully full in the face, in class, in front of everyone. They had immediately called her parents and suspended her. Her father hadn't yelled at her for doing it, but he did drive her down to where the bully lived. Sam and her parents lived in a Brooklyn brownstone that wasn't too shabby, but the boy who had bullied her lived in a true dump. It was a single-story heap of crumbling brick with a tiny yard. It was in a scary area of town where she knew people walked openly with weapons. If you didn't belong on that street, they had no problem killing you for what you had.

"I know ya can't let people walks all over ya, Sam, but ya gots to realize why people do what they do. The boy you punched lives here. I know his parents. They aren't very nice, and they aren't very patient. If you lived in a place like this, with parents who didn't seem to like ya much, you might not be a very happy person, and that might make you a bully just to have some control over somethin'...I know you did what you thought you had to do, and you learned sometimes there's a price for that. You can change the way you do things, because you gots all kinds of stuff that he don't. Now not everyone turns out mean that comes from here, but some people do. Try not to hate 'em for it. Don't let 'em walk on ya, but don't hate 'em."

She had never asked the bully why he singled her out, but she didn't push him around either, though she wished she could. She really did want to humiliate him the way he had done to her, but she knew she'd get in real trouble for that. She wound up just leaving him alone, and he left her alone from then on. The vandals who had hit her restaurant didn't even seem to have a motive, and it made it that much harder for Sam to understand why they did it.

Sam came back to the present as the man was finishing filling out his forms. He gave a pink copy to Sam and kept the rest for himself. She was tempted to try to keep him around for a while. He brought up familiar feelings and memories. She hated to let them go.

34
Eli

Work had begun on the windows. Al's Glass had insisted on repairing some of the old wood around the sills. While they were working, the construction company arrived to rebuild the front entryway. They all insisted that Sam leave, take a break, take a walk, go see something else besides the restaurant. Tito was at the forefront of that conversation. So Sam grabbed her jacket and took a walk.

About a half mile away, she found Eli sitting next to a dumpster, sifting through some bags. Sam took a seat next to him.

"Hiya Eli. I haven't seen you in a while, what's up?"

"Cans are scarce here. Got to keep movin'. Police don't like me lookin' through the trash."

Sam reached over and nudged a filth-smeared can toward him.

"Yeah, they can be downright nasty down here sometimes, can't they?"

Eli nodded slowly.

"You come on back to the restaurant tomorrow, 'kay? Come get a cup of coffee with me."

Eli nodded again, looking up at her and smiling for a moment. Sam smiled back, then got up and moved on. A few times she looked up as kids called out from windows.

"Sam! Sam! Hi, Sam! Your restaurant open yet?"

"No, not yet. You come by tomorrow, though, and you can get some tea!"

Sam came across a woman who was slowly pushing a cart across the street. The woman stopped when she reached the curb and banged the cart slowly into the cement, making no effort to lift it. She appeared confused. The cart was filled with a collection of trash bags. When Sam got close enough she found it didn't smell too good, either. She moved forward to help the woman, but a man suddenly appeared from around the corner and moved toward them. Sam stiffened, but he waved Sam down.

"I take care of her. I take care of her. Here, I'll help her. It's okay."

The woman seemed to recognize the man. Sam stepped back hesitantly, then more confidently as the weathered looking woman patted the man on the arm. He lifted her cart with great care onto the sidewalk. The woman moved the cart forward a few feet to a fence and took out a little container. Sam watched her spill some of the contents onto the ground and make kissing noises. Suddenly four cats leaped out of the crack in the fence and surrounded the woman. She patted and talked to them while they wolfed the food down as fast as they could.

Sam turned to the man.

"What's your name?"

"Oh, I name not important."

Sam gave a start of surprise before replying,

269

"You seek I."

"Message received."

Sam smiled broadly, "You know it!"

"I know it. Used to watch it constantly. Stella knows it too, but she doesn't remember unless she hears the music."

"Music?"

"Yeah, the music. Music moves us all, you know. It's the base part of us. We remember everything with music! But Stella, she's a good girl. She doesn't do drugs, not like me. She remembers the music. I even got a little player with headphones so we can listen to whatever we want. It's cool when I'm out of it."

"You do drugs?"

"Yeah. I'm not proud of it. I do cocaine, weed, heroin. Whatever I can get, really. What else am I s'posed to do? It gets so bad out here. I just don't want nobody to hurt Stella. So I walk along with her most of the day, you know? So nobody can't hit her or rape her."

"You ever try huffing?"

"Like glue?"

"Yes, or paint."

"Once or twice, but it's better if I offer to sell a bit of a bag on the side for a dealer. People don't like me goin' in stores."

Sam patted him on the arm in similar fashion to how the old woman had. When the couple moved on, so did Sam. At this moment Sam started to notice more, just walking instead of purposely going somewhere. She noticed quite a few of the people sleeping on the street in nooks and doorways that she hadn't really seen before.

As she moved beyond the boundaries of her neighborhood, she then noticed the change in the population. The next neighborhood seemed to be where all the people of color lived. Still sparsely populated, but she noticed them. They didn't meet her eyes very often, and she never had anyone call out to her. After about twenty minutes a sloppily dressed man walked up to her in jeans and a torn sweater.

"Hey, you shouldn't be here. Really, lady, you should not. You need to turn around and go home. This place ain't safe."

For some strange reason, Sam felt grateful. She noticed the man's eyes flickering toward the end of the block. The same chain link fencing and cement buildings were everywhere, but something about that particular area unnerved this man. She nodded.

"Ok, thank you."

The man didn't follow her, but she felt his eyes on her until she got back across the line of demarcation. A feeling of frustration washed over her. This was where her window graffiti artist lived. It was a completely separate community. She walked back slowly, the long way, miles out of the way, thinking hard the whole time. She was a person of action. She couldn't be passive about this. She at least had to let that community know she was available. The only way to do that would be to take a huge chance and intrude. Slowly a plan percolated through her brain. No, flyers wouldn't be good enough for this plan.

The next morning she was gratified to see Eli walk through the now-completed doorframe. He touched it and marveled at the new windows, unscratched and crystal clear, double paned for insulating warmth. When Eli tapped them with a horny fingernail, all that came back was a dull plastic-like thud instead of the ring of glass.

"These will be real hard to break, Eli."

Eli took a mug out of his coat, and Sam reached out a hand.

"Now, Eli, you know my rule. You can only use your own mug if you let me wash it, right?"

"There's nothing wrong with that mug."

"I know, but what if some dirt got in it, and you got sick from drinking the dirt along with my coffee?"

"Nobody never got hurt from drinking dirt," he grumbled softly, but he let Sam take the cup anyway. She brought it back filled with hot coffee.

"Sorry, Eli, I don't have any cheese left, but I have a bit of bread. Would you like some?"

Eli nodded eagerly and didn't complain as she handed him the two end slices of bread from the bag she had left. He ate them slowly, a bit at a time, interspersed with coffee.

"Eli, I'm thinking about doing something dumb."

Eli looked up at her, "Dumb? What's that?"

"I'm gonna go feed those people there on Fifth street. Just feed em."

"You're gonna go over there? You're right, that's dumb."

"I don't know any other way to talk to them."

Still chewing, Eli shrugged, "It's true, food talks across barriers, don't it?"

Sam smiled, "What do you think I should make?"

"Well, don't make fried chicken, 'tato salad, and watermelon. They'll kill you before they eat it sure enough."

"It wouldn't keep anyway. How about sandwiches? Cold sandwiches, green salad, juice? Cheese is cheap right now, cheese and crackers, maybe some fruit."

"That soup you do, that'd be nice."

"How am I going to keep soup at the right temperature though Eli?"

"Get one of them lit stands. They get real hot."

"You mean one of those -- um -- what are they called..?"

"Chafing dishes."

"Right, chafing dishes. That might be expensive."

Eli shrugged, "I don't know another dish that you make that's better."

"I thought my bread was better."

"Nope."

"Well, ok then."

In consideration of the potential danger, Sam recruited some of the most trusted people she could find. Men and women who wouldn't flinch. They would help her set up, but then they would retreat, leaving the whole affair to Sam.

Sam's graffiti artist was painstakingly painting her window sills. He was dotting them in what Sam thought made no sense, but he just told her, "Be patient and wait. I know what I'm doing."

So as he worked she talked about her plan and wondered if it might do some good if he dropped a word in his mother's ear about the whole affair. He grinned at her wickedly.

"Now don't do anything drastic. I don't want drastic. I want calm. I just want people in that neighborhood to know I'm open, and they are welcome. I want to show them what kind of food I serve. It's marketing."

"Don't show up with fried chicken."

Sam sighed, "No sir, you can bet I will not. You have an hour left, I need to start cooking."

Eli showed up more frequently as Sam worked. He brought in his own stool and sat watching her.

"Eli, tell me about where you grew up."

"Well, I grew up in a little town in the midwest. It was a mining town. We did charcoal, reg'lar coal, it was a messy place."

"I can imagine."

"It was okay. My parents loved me. I was drafted back in the sixties. Held a gun for almost a year until some sonuvabitch shot me in the groin. They put me in a hospital for a long time while that healed. They said that it clipped an artery and shattered my pelvis. I almost died afore they got me back. The whole time I was in that hospital, I didn't want nothing more than to go back to high school. I just wanted to read and write again."

"You like to read?"

"Yeah. Westerns. I get 'em in the trash now and again. Newspapers more though."

"How did you make it here?"

"I moved out here a few years later. I couldn't get a job in my hometown; my leg wasn't near strong enough after that. I saw there were jobs here, little ones, so I came. There weren't any big buildings here then though. The glass factory was the biggest. Then came the steel mill, the other factories. It was booming business then. Every man wore a suit, every lady had a pretty handbag and matching shoes. Lots of people built houses. I had lots of money. I put my money into lots of things, mostly businesses. Then some years ago, the factories started closing down. Said there weren't enough people buyin' their stuff anymore. The market went all bonkers. All the businesses I had invested in shut down first. A while after that I couldn't get a job to save my life. I hadn't even finished high school, you know? No one wanted me. Little by little I kind of got shoved into this part of town. Anytime they see me in the big part of town, I get harassed. Sometimes four, five times a day a cop is giving me a ticket for something. So I stay down here. Pick out my cans to sell. It's a living."

It was the most Eli had ever said at one time, and Sam stayed quiet until he was done and drinking his coffee again. Even then she didn't know what to say. Bad luck seemed to run around here. Sam seemed to be the one with the good luck. Eli wasn't a bad guy, but nobody was showing up to give him money for a place to live. Just being what he was seemed to be criminal enough.

When Sam was done, she packed it all up, said good night to Eli, and went out in search of the elusive chafing dish. Most of the ones she came across were impossible. $129? It was in a bargain bin that she saw a "Sterno Soup Chafing Set" made with a sturdy stainless steel support for her soup pot. It was forty dollars. She took it and purchased enough fuel for at least an hour. She wondered if she was doing the right thing.

She wondered if she'd survive the experience.

35

It's Just Food

The sturdy front door went in the same day Sam put her plan into motion. The door didn't seem like much but required pneumatics to help people open it. It was that heavy: stainless steel, thick and solid, broken only by a pane of thick glass decorated with two sweeping stainless steel curves. The curves reduced the space available to an intruder even if they did manage to break the thick glass. The installers started just as Sam's volunteers arrived. Tito stayed to oversee the installation.

The volunteers carried the tables and bags of sandwiches, crackers and cheese, tins of salad, and juice. Sam pushed a volunteer's bike with a trailer attached. Inside the trailer was the chafing dish with the hot soup and plates, bowls, and silverware.

Sam had a feeling of trepidation when she passed the point where she had turned back before. There seemed to be a few people around but not many. Sam and the volunteers set up the tables. Sam covered them with long tablecloths, and they set out the food. As they had been instructed, the volunteers removed themselves from the immediate area, but as they did, she noticed movement around the block. Several tall youths turned into a group of teenagers. They all seemed hostile.

"What the hell is this then?"

Sam shrugged and smiled. "I'm from the restaurant on First. I thought I'd come down and let everyone down here know that I'm open by serving some free food."

The boy snorted derisively. Sam thought she saw a movement from one of the volunteers and she held up a warning hand behind her while keeping the rest of her attention on the boys in front of her. The teen got an ugly look on his face.

"We don't need your crap here!"

He stepped forward aggressively and reached a hand out toward the table to flip it over, his intentions quite clear. Sam whipped her own hand out and grabbed his wrist before he could touch the table. A dread silence fell down. She looked him straight in the eyes and spoke loud enough for everyone to hear.

"You can come and destroy this table, but before you do, I want you to know that I will go back to my restaurant, I will get more food, and I will come back. I will set up more tables and I will serve the food. I will do this as many times as it takes to get the job done. None of you, not one, will stop me."

Sam squeezed the boy's wrist a little tighter with every sentence until he looked very uncomfortable. He yanked his arm out of her grasp just as a tall woman walked out of a door.

"What the hell you doin' over here? Mal, you and your friends better just get back home where you belong, boy!"

"She doesn't need to be bringing her charity here! She doesn't belong!"

"It's just food, you little shit. With your own uncle starving on the street you'd begrudge him a damn sandwich?"

Another voice on the other side of the street joined her. Sam noticed Mal had a resentful look on his face, but he did take a step back from Sam. Sam was surprised to hear small voices of children behind her, but she kept her solid stance, her eyes directly on Mal until his eyes finally fell from hers. At that moment she knew she had gained the upper hand and purposely turned her back on him, effectively turning him over to the voices that were coming louder and louder, commanding his attention until he was driven from the area.

The kids who had come out were looking at the table, pointing at everything. Sam got to work, and for an hour she dished soup. Everyone took their own salad and crackers and filled their own cups with juice. They chatted away with each other and asked her about the restaurant. The more reluctant men and women were dragged out by others, and some followed hesitantly behind children, unwilling to leave them alone near the strange and, to them, "white" lady.

"You don't have any cookies today, Sam."

The shy voice belonged to one of the few white teenagers who lived with her mom here in this neighborhood. Sam handed over her ladle to one of the volunteers who offered to serve for a while.

"I'm very sorry, Amy. I haven't gotten paid yet, but I promise, when I open again, there will be cookies."

"If you're not open, why are you bringing food?"

"Would you like the truth?"

"Um, kind of."

"Well, I noticed people like your mom, your dad, and all the rest of the people from this neighborhood never came into my restaurant. I think they may have felt left out. I never actually invited them in like I did the people in my neighborhood. Now the people in my neighborhood are receiving flyers telling them I'm going to open again. But I'll bet your neighborhood didn't receive those flyers."

"No."

"So how were your mom and dad supposed to know that I'm open? How are the people on the streets down here supposed to know they can come and get a cup of coffee and sit in the warm for a while?"

"Do you mean how are the black people supposed to know?"

Sam shrugged, "I mean everyone from your neighborhood, Amy. You aren't black, even though your mom and dad are. Everyone is welcome in my restaurant. Even those little assholes that tried to ruin the whole thing. If they came in to eat, I'd feed them, too."

"They'd just want to wreck the place."

"But if they did, I'd bet you dollars to donuts that they'd be stopped by the people who do eat in there."

"I'd stop 'em. I like your restaurant."

"Thank you, Amy. I'm glad you like it."

There were a lot of people who didn't come down to eat. Some just stared out their windows. Sam couldn't pretend the whole neighborhood loved her for being there, but she did her best to ignore the hate-filled glances cast her way. She was pretty sure that Mal might take any opportunity on the street to really hurt her, but even he wasn't stupid enough to try it where others could catch him at it unless he had some deadly weapons or a whole lot of backup. By the end of serving, there wasn't a scrap of food left. Sam returned home with every plate, every dish, every cup, and every piece of silverware. All the folding tables came back with the volunteers, and she gave the volunteers a huge helping of gratitude for their part and their restraint. She hoped her plan had helped.

Best of all was what she came back to that day. When everything had been put away, Sam went upstairs and found a neatly made twin platform bed with a brand new mattress and bright red wool blanket, a chest of dark-stained drawers, and even a heavy bathtub in the bathroom area already hooked up. She had no idea how it had been done, but she knew Tito had to have been part of it. Sam sat on the edge of the now-comfortable room and cried.

36
Getting On

An indicator that things were still not where she wanted them was the relief Sam felt over having boxes of canned food. She was still at the bottom, but she was working again. The shelves were full. Tito staggered in with a box.

"Oh! Milk, cheese, cauliflower...where did you get cauliflower?"

"Just wait until you see the *other* bags. Don't cry at the last one."

"A *turkey*? Where did you get this? It's so huge, it's like a mutant!"

"It was the last one they had. No one wanted it, and it was in the discount freezer. I don't think you could put that thing in a home oven. It would break the racks!"

"Well we're going to have to use two just to be sure. Maybe we should cut it in half after we thaw it and cook it that way."

"This restaurant is going to smell good for days."

The neighborhood seemed a bit hesitant, the customers slow to return. As food went wanting again, stuck in the freezer for Sam to eat, she fell into a slump. The good thing was that the kids in the neighborhood had returned in full force. Every morning there was another new face asking for a lunch. Dollar by dollar the lunches kept her going. Eventually, adults started coming back, too. Then the late afternoon teenage gang who took advantage of her warm fireplace had a question for her.

"Hey Sam, do you think we could have a dance in here?"

Sam raised an uncertain eyebrow and pulled her head back.

"A dance? What do you mean, a dance?"

There was some uncomfortable shuffling, and one of the tall boys from Fifth Street came forward.

"Shit, just tell her, man! When the assholes shot that kid at our school, the school decided that they didn't want no more dances there. It's too dangerous they said! What a load of bullshit that is. We put money into that dance! We booked a DJ and everything. We just want to have some fun, but if we don't have no place to have it, the DJ is going to take the money, and we won't have nothin'! This place is the safest place we know of."

"Well, guys, I don't really have the space for hundreds of kids. You know that."

The boy hitched his pants up in a defensive gesture and shook his head. "No, man, it's not like that. It's just the committee. The rest of the kids don't want it no more. There's twenty, maybe thirty of us that put it all together."

Sam thought hard for a minute.

"I'll tell you what. If there is an adult here for every five kids, it's okay with me. We won't bother you as long as you don't destroy the place, but I don't want you walking home late at night all alone. Oh, I need to see the permission slips you got signed too. I know there had to be permission slips."

"Yeah, I can git those, no problem."

The boy turned to the others, "See? I told you she was cool. All you had to do was ask!"

Sam turned around before she smiled. The boy swaggered back to his table to the clapping appreciation of his peers. They horsed around instead of doing any schoolwork that day, but Sam refrained from chastising them for that, either. She knew her place, and it wasn't playing mom or dad.

The dance turned out to be a good idea, and the adults who showed up were all perfectly friendly. For the price of some hard labor putting the hydroponics back together, the kids received a buffet for their dance consisting of custom pizzas from scratch, a truly horrifying mixture of sodas they said was absolutely necessary, and an array of desserts, chips, dips, and even classic punch that Sam had made herself from a recipe she found in some odd cookbook. The whole restaurant was darkened and strung up with lights. The noise level was abominable, and a few of the parents brought earplugs. But then there was one song. It was nothing but an extremely heavy beat that smothered the sound of the person who made noises that could have been related to singing or rapping. It was the beat that went through Sam's chest, through her bones, and into her feet. It felt good, almost like a massage. It almost took her breath away. The kids jumped up and down in time to the DJ's hand, almost like a mosh pit. Sam had never felt anything like it. After the song was over Sam was certain the police would show up. For a wonder, they did not.

There was no other song completely like that, though there were a few to which the kids danced similarly. After it was all over, Sam asked the DJ what the song had been.

"Oh, that one! Actually, that's mine. It's a sampling of beats from *Baby Got Back* and some heavy metal, a little acid there at the end. The kids like the hell out of it. I think it makes them feel really free."

"It's pretty good. If you have it online, I'd pay to download it."

"Really? You? I'm kind of surprised."

"Well, I really mean it. If you do put it online, let me know; it's cool."

Sam decided to leave the strings of lights up. The kids had paid for them, and it was almost the holiday season anyway. It would be nice for them to see some of their decorations not go to waste.

The next day she noticed she was significantly busier. Not just that, but the money the customers left seemed greater. Very few one- or two-dollar customers. Five was the average. In the weeks that followed Sam also noticed a change in the population of her customers. Walking in through the door were men and women from Fifth street, from Seventh street, and then she started seeing a few middle-class neighborhood customers, though to be truthful, they were people she had talked to before. She knew many of her own neighborhood customers, but this was mostly an influx of people she had never seen before. Her profit line rose steadily, and she was able to serve far better food and offer choices to those who came in. Giving those kids a chance to be kids was the instigator for a whole new wave of acceptance.

37
Winter

That winter balanced Sam's happiness at being useful and accepted with heartache. One of the kids who showed up for the bus every morning began pounding on the door very early.

"Sam! *Sam*! Please open the door!"

Sam poked her head out the front window. "What is it? It's only six a.m. Are you okay?"

"Sam! Sam, you gotta come down! There's an old man down by the dumpster, and he's callin' your name, but he looks awful bad!"

Sam tore down the steps yanking on a thick sweater and boots. She followed the child, and her heart rose into her throat when she saw Eli, curled up into a ball against the wall. She touched his very pale face, and he opened those startling blue eyes at her. "Eli. It's so cold out. Would you like a cup of coffee? Maybe we should get you inside."

"Thank you kindly, Sam, but it's not really cold out today. I think you just live inside too much...spoiled, you know?"

His voice was very soft. Sam held back tears as she realized Eli wasn't shivering. She turned to one of the children and handed the child her phone.

"Call 911. Tell them we need an ambulance."

Then she turned back to Eli, who was looking at her with a kind of bright wakefulness that made Sam very cold. She tried to joke with him a little while motioning to several of the teenagers to help her lift him up and carry him to the restaurant.

"Well Eli, I won't argue with that; I've been without food very few times, and I never came close to starving."

They sat him in front of the fireplace and started it up.

"You know, Sam, sleeping out here never was easy. Whenever I found a place, I got told to move on. They'd ditch my stuff...burn it even."

"Eli, that's—it's awful."

"Yes 'm it is. It would have been harder if nice people like you didn't offer a sip of something warm in the winter. Too many people just seeing me as competition. I'd a carried a job if I could. What competition could I be? I hear them yelling about how they didn't get their new road 'cause I got my health checked or 'cause the police had to spend money on moving me on. I learned, though. I never did leave nuthin' behind. I took just what I could carry. Ain't got a home. Never will."

"Oh Eli. That's not true. Your home is with us, right here in our hearts. Right here in mine. I don't know what else to say to make you feel better."

"Say that you'll tell them 'bout me after I die. That I was a little boy once, that I worked in a charcoal factory, that I didn't want nobody to suffer just 'cause I lived. I just wanted to be, you know?"

Eli seemed sleepy, and tears streamed down Sam's face. She

wanted to deny that he would ever die, but she knew it wouldn't do any good. She sat next to him, took his face in her hands, and kissed his forehead. Then she just hugged him.

"Yes, Eli, I know. I know."

She was still holding him when the ambulance showed up. Sam watched them lay a sheet over him and place him in the ambulance gently. The tears kept streaming down her face as she watched the ambulance leave.

"I wish I could have done more," she said to Tito later that day.

"Sam, nobody could have done more for that old man than you did. You treated him like he was a human being. You were there for him all the way until the end. He came to you, Sam, because he knew that in those last few moments, you wouldn't turn him away. He wasn't alone, that's what counts."

Sam choked back a sob, "I don't want to be alone either!"

"No, Sam, nobody's gonna let you be alone when you go either. I promise."

Sam spent at least fifteen minutes crying her eyes out while Tito held her. She drank coffee; she drank tea. Then she served customers.

She walked around listlessly all day. The customers eyed her and shot looks at Tito. There wasn't much conversation. It took a few days for Sam to return to a semblance of normal. She didn't seem as energetic after the loss, however. Tito wound up helping more; Elizabeth came back and so did Tony. There were some times when Sam had to just sit. People would come and talk to her. She even learned a few illicit card games. She drank more coffee than she knew was good for her, but she loved it. It was the one thing she could always count on. The warm earthiness of it promised a bit of hope in the cold landscape that was the place she had settled down. She watched a startling array of customers come in, enjoying the food, leaving warm, fed, dry, and comfortable. It gave her even more hope that perhaps this neighborhood was on its way to a path of recovery. It might take a long time, but there were very few that would just vanish without a trace—and certainly not entire neighborhoods anymore. Everyone had a story, and in her restaurant, they were free to tell it.

Epilogue

Dear Sam,

You've been gone six months now. We all miss you more than you could ever know. Tito took over the restaurant. He said he figured no one wanted it more than him. He didn't even know that you left it to him in the will. He's been doing a damn fine job of it. Better food even. He's a master with pasta, makes it fresh every morning.

Everyone who crosses the shade of that doorstep is still welcome. Your little graffiti artist repainted the Lettuce Cup sign and even put "Every Body Is A Person. Every Person Is Welcome" under it.

The insurance company paid up the day you left us. A whopping $75,000, minus all the payments to repair facilities. Tito had $20,000 left. He spent $5000 on a cooking school. He's doing great in it. Then he spent some more on actually making the restaurant a company. I don't know where he learned that, but I think the man who sold you the property had something to do with advising him on it.

There's talk of plans to sell stuff with The Lettuce Cup's logo on it. Everything from painted spoons to chocolate candies. A woman chef from Louis' restaurant came over and gave Tito chocolate-making lessons. She's a tyrant, that one. She verbally abused him up and down after he screwed up three batches of chocolate in a row. But Tito fell in love at first sight and does everything he can to be in her good graces. She was very happy when he paid out to go to that school.

I don't think the Lettuce Cup is going anywhere in a hurry, Sam. I don't think the people will let it. Even if Tito left, there are a slew of others who would step in to take it over. Tito's got so many apprentices and helpers it's a wonder he gets anything done.

And me? I'm going to MIT, Sam! Me! Just a run-down, no-good snot head from back of beyond. I'm going to go design the next generation of cars for the world to drive.

We miss you, Sam, and we're all really glad you came to us.

Sincerely,

James Sutton